I0601328

CLEO BROWNE

Marx

Devil's Rose MC Book Six

First published by Meihana Pinker Ltd 2025

Copyright © 2025 by Cleo Browne

All rights reserved. No part of this publication may be reproduced, stored or transmitted in any form or by any means, electronic, mechanical, photocopying, recording, scanning, or otherwise without written permission from the publisher. It is illegal to copy this book, post it to a website, or distribute it by any other means without permission.

This novel is entirely a work of fiction. The names, characters and incidents portrayed in it are the work of the author's imagination. Any resemblance to actual persons, living or dead, events or localities is entirely coincidental.

Cleo Browne asserts the moral right to be identified as the author of this work.

First edition

ISBN: 978-1-0670576-9-5

This book was professionally typeset on Reedsy.
Find out more at reedsy.com

Contents

Trigger Warning

This book deals with badassery in all its forms.
Please be aware that in order for these characters to be badass,
this book contains content that some readers may find
disturbing,
such as graphic descriptions of violence and torture, and R18
sex scenes.

Hey Readers!

I know you've all been waiting for this one for a while, and up until recently, Marx wasn't saying much. Well, other than to insult Lovely (idiot!).

Anyhoo, I was well on my way to writing another story and then BAM! Marx was all like "Oh hey, it's my turn!" and off he went, telling me all about it.

There are twists and turns AND a character so awful that I just had to name her after my Elizabeth's Phoenix Trust auction winner. I mean, when your book has an awful, nasty female character that needs to see the inside of the Rev Room, what better name than Renae Sullivan? Just jokes, Renae is amazing and generous and gave me fabulous material to work with.

I can only hope her demise is as horrific as she wanted and Marx and Lovely's story is as amazing as you all hoped.

Enjoy.

C

Who the heck is that?

Devil's Rose MC

Marx - Pres

Rhodie - VP and Enforcer + Tuesday Tombs (Chewy) Icer

Rider - SAA

Wire - Secretary/Hacker + Remy Wright

Jovie (Wire and Remy's adopted child)

Tank - Member + Mira (Doll) Campbell

Switch - Medic

Judge - Member

Sniper - Member

Fox - Member

Nitro - Member

Savage - Member (ex Death Rider) + Nat

= Rosie

Dex - Member (Ex Death Rider)

TumTum (Jimmy) - Member

Chef (Takoda) - Member

Tav - Member + Blanche (Pixie)

= Niko, Sage, Cove, Elio, Tess

Niko - Prospect

Tombs Security

August (Gus) Tombs + Ana Tombs
= Jr (Sidney)
Jules Tombs + Violet Davies
= Juno
Tav Tombs + Blanche Landry
= Niko, Sage, Cove, Elio, Tess
Tuesday (Chewy) Tombs + Rhodie
= Laney-May
Sidney (Pops) Tombs + Debs Taylor (Mother of Ana)

Bartashev Bratva

Roman Bartashev + Sasha Bartashev (BFF's of Ana)

Prologue

Marx

Fuck.

I shake my head, trying to get the ringing to stop, but it doesn't clear anything. My eyes feel gritty every time I blink and I can barely hear my brother's shouts over the ringing in my ears. I feel disoriented, expecting the shouts to be in the foreign language that usually comes with these scenes, but no, these are words I understand. I'm not in the middle of a shitty sandbox far from home. I AM home. Fuck.

I take stock of my body. I'm flat on my back and aside from the ringing in my head nothing feels broken or busted. My head lolls to the left and I get my first look at the clubhouse. It's devoid of screams and cries even though I know that there are women and children inside. Rolling over, I get my feet under me, shaking my head again, this time clearing things a little. But not the sound of gun fire, ringing out around me, the shouts of my brothers as they rush to the front gate, guns drawn.

"Pres! Get Lovely and move the fuck outta the way!" Judge barges past me, his large form moving with a speed I've not seen since we served together.

I stare at his retreating back for a moment before his words reach my brain. Lovely. Looking around I pay no mind to the destruction surrounding me, not when my gaze freezes on Lovely lying on the ground, blood staining her pink sweater.

"Shit, shit, shit!" Dropping to my knees, I feel for her pulse with one hand, the other pressing into her chest, blood bubbling from her wound, warming my fingers. My forefinger finds a light flutter of a pulse and I let out a breath of relief, but it's only for a moment. I need to get Lovely to safety, fast.

Lifting her in my arms I turn, ready to take her into Switch's clinic before I stop, eyes on the carnage in front of me. The back half of the clubhouse has been destroyed, the roof caved in. Electrics are sparking off and I need to find my men. My family.

An SUV fishtails, screeching to a stop, blowing up dust into my still gritty eyes before Nat shoves the backdoor open.

"Get her in here!"

Peering into the vehicle, Sage's wide eyes meet mine. She's in the trunk, holding the throw Mama Debs bought for the new couch over Fox's stomach, her hands stained red as Nitro cradles his head in his lap.

"Pres! We need to get them to the hospital, NOW!" Nat shouts in my face.

I gently move Lovely into the backseat, Nat's open arms welcoming her, ready to put pressure on the wound that is bleeding far too much.

"Just put press-"

"I got this." She nods, eyes full of determination.

"Where's-"

"Chewy has the kids and women. The men are stationed around the compound." Blanche says from her place in the driver's seat. She turns her body to meet my gaze. "Give them hell."

I have time enough to nod before Blanche peels out, heading toward the back of the compound, likely taking the back roads to the hospital. Turning my head to the sound of my men fighting I move like death himself. Rage consumes me. Someone came into *my* town. Attacked *my* compound. Hurt *my* family. And they're going to pay with their lives.

Chapter 1

Marx

Her luscious curves jiggle as she helps Jazz herd the kids onto the short bus. She's smiling and joking with them, some of the kids fight to hold her hand as they walk to the bus steps. Of course she lets them, she's Lovely. Shit. I need to apologize. I don't know what the fuck came over me that had me running my mouth like that. No, no I do know. I want that woman more than I can say and a fuck load more than I deserve but she deserves more. Better. Someone not fucking 10 or so years older. Someone gentle and understanding or something. I don't fucking know. The only thing I do know is that she doesn't deserve me speaking to her like she's just some hang around.

She turns in my direction, her smile dimming a little as she walks toward the clubhouse. It's now or never I guess so I carefully step toward her until we're standing just outside the clubhouse, flanked by my brothers rides.

"Lovely I-"

"Marx, it's OK."

"No, Lovely, it's not. I didn't mean to spout that shit," I scrub my hand down my face, looking for the words. *I've led men into war and I'm getting shaky and nervous trying to apologize to a little lady whose dark gaze is locked somewhere behind me, probably watching the school bus leave through the gates.*

"Marx–"

"No I need to get this out –"

"MARX!" her scream shocks me and then I'm moving backwards, stumbling, falling, my head hitting the ground, ringing bursting in my ears along with the shouts and screams and the –

"Pres?" Nitro's voice snaps me out of my thoughts, taking my mind off what happened and bringing it back to the present and the damn hard chair I'm sitting in.

I bolt upright, gripping Nitro and pulling him in for a moment before gently shoving him back. "How is he?" I ask, wanting to know, no, *needing* to know how Fox is doing.

"He's stable. They're going to leave him in an induced coma for a couple of days to let him heal ..." he trails off.

I grip his shoulder, giving it a gentle squeeze. "He's a tough bastard, you know that right?" I search his gaze, until he lets out a breath and nods. "He's got this. Now go look after your man."

He gives me a look, shocked that I could see what hadn't even occurred to him until the moment Fox took two to the gut. Nitro swallows, his Adam's apple bobbing as he tries to find the words.

"I can't lose him, Pres." He blinks moisture from his eyes.

"I know, and you won't. Now get back there and make sure he knows you'll kick his ass if he doesn't wake up soon." He gives me a chin lift before turning to leave the room.

He stops in the doorway, looking at me over his shoulder.

5

"Pres? You do the same for Lovely, yeah?" My eyes dart to the person in the bed behind me, before meeting Nitro's gaze. I give him a single nod, and he leaves, walking through the doors to Lovely's room.

Sitting heavily back down in the chair I let my gaze run over the woman lying before me. Gentle. Kind. Brave. Lovely.

A knock breaks me out of my thoughts once more and I snap to attention again, my men, no, my family need me.

"Come in,"

"Just me," Rhodie says, leading Pops and Mad Dog into the room. He swallows, taking in Lovely's small form on the hospital bed. "How is she?" I just shake my head. Her condition hasn't changed since she came out of surgery. He nods in understanding. "The clubhouse will be a complete rebuild. Turns out fire and liquid nitrogen don't mix."

Fuck. Leaning forward in my chair I scrub my hands down my face. Where the fuck is my MC going to go? I open my mouth to bitch about it, but I'm stopped from saying anything at Pops' raised hand.

"I live in a big fucking farmhouse. I'm surrounded by land, and it's private. The MC can have the house until we're back on our feet," he says earnestly.

I stare at him. This pain in my ass has just offered us sanctuary. Pops, who spends his time pissing us off on purpose, has selflessly offered up his home.

"Well, fuck, don't go soft on me, kid. You got vengeance to reap."

I'm shocked when a laugh bursts out and I let it rumble over me, my shoulders relaxing as one really big fucking problem has now been solved by Sidney Tombs.

"Pops, thank you." My voice breaks at the end but I don't

give a shit.

"You're family, kid. Through better or worse."

Mad Dog grips Pops' shoulder, giving him a squeeze, then they turn to leave. "We'll sort out the MC. You get the rest of your shit in order," Dad calls over his shoulder.

"Anything you need brother, call me. Chewy and the Computas have relocated to the Tombs offices for the time being. They're working around the clock to find anything of use. Roman called, he and Sasha are bringing in Dima to help."

"Good, that's good." My phone vibrates and I pull it from my cut, glancing at the screen. "Landrys will be here by tonight."

"Fuck." Rhodie's eye's drift to Lovely.

Scrubbing my hand down my face I let out a long breath, "I know brother."

"I'll go help Pops and Dad, get the walking wounded settled and hit the streets with Jules. Someone out there must know something."

I give my little brother a nod, stand and then pull him into my arms. "Be safe out there,"

"Always."

He turns to leave, knocking twice on the door jamb, leaving me alone with the woman who has had me in knots since she first set foot in my clubhouse.

"I know I've been an ass, but listen to me, and listen good," I whisper to her. She doesn't move, not even a flutter of her eyelids. It doesn't matter, I have to get this out. "Fuck all that shit I said, you're mine. Hear me, Lovely? You. Are. Mine."

Chewy

They're going to pay. They're all going to pay. I'm not even sure who they are just yet, but no one puts my family in danger.

My gaze flicks from the knives I'm sharpening, to the mess of dark ringlets attached to the little girl lying starfished out on mine and Rhodie's bed. Whoever did this endangered not only the men, women and children who were at the compound, but they also endangered *my* daughter. So screw them, they're going down.

Chapter 2

Marx

The doors fling open, jerking me awake. Switch fills the doorway, all ginger hair and bulk stuffed into a white coat.

"I think she'd probably feel better quicker if you went home and showered," He says, taking a dig at the state I'm in. I've been sitting next to Lovely's bedside for close to 48 hours. I'm not leaving until she wakes up.

"I need the full breakdown. The doctors wouldn't tell me shit because I'm not next of kin for Fox or Lovely and they barely told the Landrys shit either." I growl. It's one thing to keep information from me, but her brothers? It was fucked up none of the staff would tell them exactly what was happening with her. Something to do with her paperwork and the cult they grew up in or some shit.

Switch eyes me then drags a visitor's chair from the corner, until he's sitting next to me, both of us with eyes on Lovely.

"Fox took two to the gut, as you well know. They were

through and through, nicked an artery on the way out. Needed four units of blood and he'll be in an induced coma for another day or so to help with healing. He's fit and reasonably young so he'll be fine. Will be fucking tender for a while though."

I nod at the news, and feel a small amount of tension drain from my body. "Good, that's good. What else you got?"

"Judge, Dex and Rider all have flesh wounds, they'll be fine. Laying low at the farm."

I run a hand down my face, breathing out a sigh of relief. "And Lovely?" my fists clench, and it feels fucking wrong to have this conversation as we stare at her, tube down her throat, IV lines in both arms.

Switch is quiet for a moment, opening and closing his mouth once, twice, "She's going to be OK. Bullet had a clean exit."

I turn my head to stare at him in disbelief, "Why was there so much fucking blood? I've seen fucking wounds like that before Ryan, and ain't none of them have survived."

He rubs his hand down his beard, before turning to me. "The bullet nicked a small artery, hence the bleed. The girls, Blanche and Nat, without them driving like fucking Dom Torretto, neither Lovely or Fox would be alive right now."

Fuck. I owe those women. I owe all of them. Not only did Blanche and Nat save lives with their quick thinking and in Blanche's case her lead foot, but Chewy cleared the clubhouse of the rest of the women and children, getting them to the safety of the farmhouse.

"You can tell me to piss off, but I need to know something," Switch says, still speaking in a tone I'm not used to hearing from him.

I wave my hand, gesturing for him to go ahead.

"Where exactly were you and Lovely standing when this went

down?"

My brows pull down. "We were standing between the parked bikes, outside the clubhouse."

His eyes narrow a little, "I mean, in relation to each other, and the road."

I think back. We were standing face to face, the clubhouse door on my left hand side, the curve of the road running past the clubhouse at my back. "The bend in the road was behind me, and Lovely was standing facing me, and the road, I guess. Why?"

His ginger brows pull down, a frown marring his face, "Where were you when the shots rang out?"

I lean back, thinking. One moment I'm trying to apologize, the next my ears are ringing and I'm on the ground. "Fuck, I, I'm not sure. I was looking at Lovely, and then somehow I was on the ground." I run my hand through my hair, probably making it stand on fucking end from the amount of hair pulling I've been doing. A hand bats away mine, before Switch stands, running his hands through my hair, looking for... something. I'm not sure.

"Shit, that's a big goose egg you got there Pres. Do you remember hitting your head?"

"Not really, but I remember being on the ground and all hell breaking loose." The look on Switch's face unnerves me, "What the fuck is going on?"

Switch sighs heavily. He runs his hand down his face, combing his fingers through his red beard before leaning forward in his chair, elbows resting on his thighs. He stares at Lovely for a beat, before looking down at his hands.

"Switch!" I growl. His unusual silence is really starting to piss me off.

"I'll have to check the footage, but shit, Pres, I think Lovely saved your fucking life." My head flies back as if I've been hit. "Would you say you're at the very least, a foot taller than Lovely?"

"I'd say I'm over a foot taller than her."

He nods, his red hair flopping everywhere. "Let's say the shooter shot straight and true, yeah? If we measure the height at which it hit Lovely compared to where it would hit you, I would bank money that bullet was meant to hit you, from behind, and tear through your abdomen. Best case scenario, at that height, would be colostomy bag for life."

"And the worst case?"

He stares at me, and I know that look. Motherfucker. Lovely took the bullet meant for me. Without Lovely I could have died out there, in the fucking dirt outside my clubhouse. My head hangs and my eyes close as I try to control my rage and guilt. Getting worked up isnt going to do me any fucking favours right now. The door opens and closes, Switch leaving me alone. I close my eyes, thinking of strategies, intel I need, plans I need to make, people I need to mobilize-

"You need to take a break." My eyes open at the sound of Rhodie's voice. He stands in the doorway with the Landrys at his back, cups of coffee in their hands.

"I'm good, brother," my voice comes out in a rasp, thick with fatigue and guilt.

"Like hell you are. You can't lead shit if you're burnt out." He frowns at me, clearly not impressed with how crappy I look. My smell probably offends him too. He had no trouble with smells until Chewy and her damned bloodhound nose turned up. "Go home, take a shower, catch a couple of hours sleep. Vic, Dom and Chris have got this."

I open my mouth to tell him to fuck off, but he raises his hand, "Brother, your men need you. You haven't seen the new digs, you haven't checked in with the wounded brothers. We need to have Church, the Computas have found some shit -"

"No," I growl, standing to my full height, going toe to toe with my brother. "She fucking *saved* me, Rhodes." My anger rushes out of my body, deflating me and I slump into my chair. "She shoved me out of the way and took the bullet meant for me, brother. I'm not walking out of here when she needs me. I want to be here when she wakes up, I *need* to be here when that happens."

He stares at me for a moment, his green eyes boring into mine. Rhodie's eyes are like his mother's, the woman who raised me.

"I know where you're at. I know exactly why you feel the need to be here, at her side, but is that what Lovely would want?"

I scowl at him before looking at her brothers who have remained silent this whole time. "What the fuck is that supposed to mean?"

He takes a seat, letting out a long sigh. My gaze bounces between him, Dom, Chris and Vic.

"Marx, what do you think is the most important thing in Lovely's world?" Vic asks softly, placing his hand on Lovely's.

"Little Bee," I answer immediately. Lovely adores that little girl.

"Do you think Lovely would like knowing that Bee is being bumped from person to person at the moment? That she's unsettled but too little to know what's going on?" Chris says, eyes never moving from his sister.

Closing my eyes I let out a breath I didn't even know I was

13

holding. I shake my head slowly. I know for a damn fact that if Lovely were awake she'd demand her little girl be here with her. She'd want to see with her own eyes that she's OK.

"How about you go home, get a couple of hours rest, wash because you fucking reek, and then bring Bee back to visit her mom?" Rhodie says.

I eye him then the Landrys for a moment. "Guilt trip, huh, fuckers?"

"Whatever works." Dom shrugs. "And I didnt want to say anything, but I can't do another minute in this room with your unwashed ass."

"Everyone is a goddamn comedian," I mutter and I move to stand then head for the door. "Message me as soon as anything happens."

Vic gives me a chin lift then takes my seat and Rhodie moves to my side, waiting for me to leave. I take one look back at Lovely before heading out, Rhodie at my back.

"You claiming her?"

"Yeah."

Rhodie side eyes me, "You got a lot of work to do."

I grunt at him, "Know that brother, but she's fucking worth it."

Pops

I tug my chino's up a little higher and my hands find my hips as I survey the surroundings.

"You did good, Sid," Debs beams up at me as she lifts my arm and snuggles under it. I squeeze her to me, soaking up her warm adoration.

"Needed to be done babe." The last of the mobile homes that could fit on the section between the house and the cabins moves into place, bringing the total number of mobile homes on the property to five.

Thank fuck this property is huge and empty. After my son and his wife were taken I kept the place, not wanting to move the kids. I'm glad we did, now we have enough space for the MC. *Our* MC. Because that's what it is. Now I just have to wait for these bastards to give me a cut. I ain't prospecting so they'll just have to hand it over.

"Well, if it ain't the fearless leader," I mutter, watching Rhodie drive in with Marx in the passenger seat.

A rush of air leaves me as Debs backhands me to the gut. It's her favorite move. "Behave, Sid. He's been with Lovely."

"As he should. He should have locked that woman down well before now, but the kid is way dumber than he looks." She gives me a disapproving look before rushing up to Marx's door.

As soon as he steps out of the SUV she pulls him into her arms, running a hand down his hair before shoving him backwards, jiggling him a little while she barks orders at him. I fucking love when she's in her bossy mode. I can feel myself starting to get a chub and if she keeps going I'll have to drag her away to have my way with her.

"Stop ogling my grandmother," Tav whines, coming to stand next to me, my new little granddaughter nestled into his chest.

I make grabby hands and Tav places his hand protectively over Tess, angling her away so I can't have my fill of baby

15

goodness.

"You're my least favourite grandkid."

"You have a million babies here to love on! Go grab Laney or something."

"I can't. She's napping and Dayz is sharpening her tools. If I wake the kid up I'll get stabbed." I grin.

Tav lets out a sigh and gently hands over Tess. I breathe in her baby scent before snuggling her against my chest.

"So, who we got living in the mobile homes?" Tav lifts his chin to the mobile homes dotted around the yard.

"Oh oh, I can tell you that!" Debs bustles back over now that she's bossed Marx into the house. She nestles back where she belongs, under my arm, and I cuddle her and Tess to me. "You, Blanche and the kids will have one."

"I call dibs on that fancy one far, far away from Gus," Tav says, hand up in the air like a school boy.

"Done!" Debs giggles. "I'm putting Fox and Nitro in the smaller one, Fox will need the quiet to heal. Marx and the couples will get first dibs on the others. The single men and Niko will be bunking down inside until we can sort something out long term." She nods.

Tav brows raise. "You do know this is just temporary, right?"

"We'll see," she grins, and I roll my eyes. If she had her way she'd adopt all these bikers. "Oh, and so you know, Marx is showering, eating, then napping. He'll be calling Church tomorrow."

"Did he decide that or did you?" Tav asks.

"Bit of both?" Debs grins and the twinkle in her eye does something to me.

"Take your kid, I need some alone time with my woman." Debs' laughter rings out and she races away from me. I let her get a head start before I chase her.

I'll always catch her. She's mine. Til my body leaves this mortal coil.

Chapter 3

Marx

I make my way through the farmhouse, stopping here and there to look at the pictures of Chewy and her brothers lining the walls. There's one of them in sports uniforms, another with their arms thrown over each other's shoulders, smiling. Well, the boys are smiling, Chewy is staring down the lens in that unnerving way of hers. My lips tug up at the sight. I move further down the line, finally coming to the hall cupboard where Mama Debs directed me. Opening the door a fresh linen scent hits me, the towels inside are fluffy as hell so I know they're going to feel like heaven after days of sitting in the hospital.

Opening doors until I find the downstairs bathroom, I step inside and rid myself of my clothing as quickly as I can. I never noticed it so much when I was on that hard ass chair in Lovely's room, but now that I'm out in the world the guys were right, I downright reek. Hanging a towel on the rail I notice the pile of clothes left on the vanity. I have no idea how the hell she did it, but Mama Debs has left my own clean clothing for me. Shit, if she wasn't Pops' woman I'd try and set her up with Mad Dog. Speaking of, I need to sit down with him and the rest of my men. I guess that'll have to wait until after I sleep. Mama Debs' orders.

Cranking the water on, I step in immediately, welcoming the cold water on my skin, the blast waking me up a little before it grows warmer. The water beats down on my shoulders and back and I can feel my age. My back cracks like a damned glow stick these days. Grabbing the Old Spice body wash, I can't help the smirk that paints my face knowing I'll smell like Pops.

I can't believe the old man has not only opened his home to us, but from what I could see driving in, has also arranged extra accommodation for the club. I know when he first turned up he was nothing but a pain in the ass, I mean, he still is, but shit, there isn't a man, or a family I'd want at my back more than the Tombs. They should really patch in. Maybe when shit settles down I'll bring it up in Church.

Washing off the suds I face the water, palms to the wall, head angled down so the water rolls down my back, washing away dirt, dust and hospital funk. Closing my eyes I take two long, deep breaths, turn off the water, dry myself and dress in quick succession. Looking at my dirty clothes I contemplate what to do with them. They're stained with Lovely's blood and the sight makes my hands shake and my throat tighten up. She's lying in the hospital, without her little girl because of me and here I am wanting to make her mine. I don't fucking deserve a woman like her. She thinks I keep her at arm's length because I think she's weak. That couldn't be further from the truth. I keep her at arm's length because she scares the fuck out of me. That little woman survived shit that could break a grown

19

man, and yet she's out here, eyes wide open, experiencing everything the world has to offer with little to no judgement. She's kind and loving, mothering everyone she comes into contact with, and yet like a Mama Bear she will throw down with the best of them. Case in point, the pep talk she gave me at Christmas when she basically told me to get my head outta my ass. Lovely is like a fucking phoenix, she walked through fire and came out the other side as pure light.

A knock at the door interrupts my thoughts, "Leave your clothes on the floor, *e tama*, I'll put them in the incinerator when you're done. I have a load to do anyway," Mama Debs' voice calls through the door.

Incinerator? What? I'm frozen in place with confusion and just cannot wrap my head around this new information, even though shit like this is par for the course with these guys.

Someone's fist bangs against the door, "Get out here, Son. Your men are asking for updates,."

Opening the door Mad Dog stares at me mid-knock. "Hey Dad. Did you know these guys have an incinerator?"

His brows hit his hairline before a thoughtful look comes over his face, "Is that so? And how big is this incinerator?"

"Big enough to get rid of the half blown up cow carcass the kids were experimenting with," Mama Debs replies, bustling past.

"Well, remind me never to piss you people off," Mad Dog mumbles as Mama Debs cackles, carrying my dirty washing with her. "Come on, Son," Dad's heavy hand lands on my shoulder and he guides me down the hall to what looks like a living room.

One half of the room is packed with kids' toys and a pretty couch Blanche, Nat and Mira are perched on, kids surrounding them. Little Bee is sitting on the floor at her aunt's feet, her dark hair pulled up into two cute pigtails. She looks up, staring directly at me for a moment before a smile blooms across her face, showing off her little teeth. She leans forward, planting her hands on the floor, using them to balance as she gets her feet under her. She pushes up and then she's running to me. I meet her halfway, swinging her up into my arms. Bee throws her arms around my neck and cuddles in. I'm not sure how I feel, that the first time I've held this little girl is days after her mother risked her life to save me. Something about that really hits home and I hold her to me, trying to swallow down the lump in my throat.

"Looks good on you, brother," Rhodie smirks, passing me to perch himself on the arm of a large leather sofa where the wounded seem to be propped up.

I let out a whistle, calling everyone to attention. "I'm calling Church tomorrow,-" I hold my hand up, stopping any comments from my men that we need to act fast. "At the moment, we're hurting. We have two family members in the hospital and we have injuries. They'll be bringing Fox out of his induced coma tomorrow morning, and Lovely should wake up any time now. Tonight we rest, lay low, enjoy each other and enjoy the home the Tombs' have given us. Tomorrow we plan our hit on the fuckers who did this." I nod once, before looking every person in the room in the eye. I want them to know that we're all on the same page. We're in this together and I have their backs as much as they have mine.

Walking over to my men on the couch, I make sure to check in with each of them. As expected Dex and Judge wave away my concern.

"Pres, this shit is for the birds," Rider whines.

21

He's perched on the couch, but he's not sitting square. Instead he's leaning on an angle, a donut pillow under one side of his ass. I raise my brows at his positioning. Rider huffs, crossing his arms over his chest, glaring at the men in the room.

"Go on Rider, tell Pres what happened," Flack goads from his seat in an armchair nearby.

Rider mumbles something but I can't quite make it out.

"Yeah, Rider," Mira pipes up. "Tell us where you were hit." She grins up at Tank, his arm over her shoulders.

"I was hitintheass," he mumbles.

"What the hell did you say?"

"I said, I was hit in the ASS." Rider's voice grows in volume until he yells the ending.

Bee's head snaps around to look at Rider, she opens her mouth and a loud laugh erupts from her body, shaking her little frame. I can't help myself, hearing her little girl giggles and knowing the brother who is the biggest pain in the ass got shot in the ass, well, I lose it along with everyone else.

"Yeah, yeah, yuck it up, fuckers," Rider grumbles.

"Hold up, isn't this the second time you've been shot in the ass?" Savage asks, and an argument breaks out among the brothers.

Before I can wade in, my phone goes off. Checking the screen, Dom Landry's number flashes. I hesitate, unsure if I want to know. Looking up I'm met with eyes on me. I swipe the screen and bring the phone to my ear.

"Marx? She's waking –"

I don't even wait to hear the rest. I yell to the room that I'll be back, I need to get me and Bee to the hospital. I need to be there to look into her dark eyes when she opens them. I need her to see her little girl and to know that I'm all in. Whatever it takes.

Lovely

Everything feels heavy. Everything. I've been trying to move my fingers and toes and I'm not sure if it's working. There are voices around me but they don't sound like the one that has been keeping me company. Marx. I'm not sure if I dreamed it or if it was really him, but why would he be here? With me?

In my mind I'm stuck in a weird loop of watching the school van leave the compound and then seeing the SUVs with the dark windows speed toward us. The window lowering and the muzzle of a gun pointing directly at Marx. I can't for the life of me remember what he was saying, but it didn't matter. He needed to move. I used all my strength to push him out of the way and then...nothing. I don't know if he was hit. I don't know if anyone was hurt. I don't know anything. I want to open my eyes, to move my lips, to ask questions, to find out what happened, but I can't. My eyelids are stuck closed, my lips feel like they've been glued shut.

I take a deep breath. I can't give up. I focus on my eyelids. They're light, thin pieces of skin, they should be easy to move. I will my eye muscles to lift or raise or something. Frustration tugs low in my stomach, making the muscles in my legs feel tense. *"One more minute, Lovely. Just one more minute,"* I tell myself. I count down sixty seconds in my mind. If I can do

23

something for sixty seconds, I can do it for another and another. I want to snort at my own advice. No one step at a time for me, nope, I like to count down. It's how I escaped Eden's Keep. I was scared out of my mind, but every second that I counted down represented another step away from the prison I lived in.

Twenty-seven seconds and light starts to break through. Excitement and triumph starts to bubble up and I feel as if with that one sliver of light my body is coming back online. My time is up and another sixty seconds starts. I count down once more, again and again until my eyelids become unstuck and I'm blinded by pure, white light. I don't slam my eyes shut. I welcome the light and stare into it. The Keep always taught us that this is what we'd see when we went to Heaven. That we'd be bathed in the light and love of God. I soak it up knowing that I'm not in Heaven, I'm alive, and soon I'll be with Bee and my family.

"Lovely? Can you hear me?"

I blink at the rough voice, my eyes following the sound until I meet two sets of dark eyes. One belonging to Marx, the Pres, and one belonging to my little girl. My eyes screw shut and I try to sob, but there's something in my mouth, causing me to hitch my breath, my chest burning.

"Shit! Dom, get the Doctor!"

Rustling and the sounds of bodies moving swiftly fill the room but I can't concentrate, my chest is heaving and I feel like I'm drowning, both emotionally and physically. I can't take a breath and I need to internally calm myself. *Sixty seconds, Lovely. Count it down.*

Sixty, fifty nine, fifty eight –

"Lovely? It's me, Switch, Dr Hansen. You've been intubated,

24

let me just remove the tube and you'll be able to take a breath, OK?"

I stare up at the large ginger man above me, his kind face and bushy beard so very familiar and yet the soft tone coming out of his mouth feels entirely foreign.

"It's going to feel a little uncomfortable on the way out. Once it hits the back of your throat you'll feel the need to vomit, just breathe through it, OK sweetheart?"

I blink as it's the only way I can communicate with him. He nods once, his hands coming to my face, then gently moving between my lips.

Sixty, fifty nine, fifty-eight, fifty-seven. I can feel it moving inside me, the tube feels as if it's making its way through my chest. It hits the back of my throat and my body heaves. *Twenty-six, twenty-five, twenty-four.* The numbers come out in a rush, just like the tube as it leaves my body on a whoosh of air. Without it blocking my airways I suck in a breath, the cool air dry in my throat. I cough and shooting pain glances through my upper chest. Wincing, Dom moves to help me sit up a little, while Chris brings me a cup with a straw.

I take a small sip, the water soothing my throat. I gulp it down greedily until Switch gently tells me to take it easy. The whole time this is happening I haven't moved my gaze from the imposing man at the foot of my bed. The one that holds my heart in his hands, literally. Bee is snuggled into Marx as if it's an everyday occurrence to be carried around by the President of the Devil's Rose MC.

Vic leans forward, pressing his lips to my temple, then moves back, allowing Chris and Dom to do the same.

"You scared us, little sis," Vic whispers, his eyes looking a little glassy.

25

I move my gaze from Marx to my brothers. "Blanche?" I manage to croak out.

"Tav had to keep her home. The first time she saw you she strapped Tess to her and packed all her gear. She was going hunting," Chris answers.

"Mama Debs put her in charge of protecting Bee and the kids," Dom says with a small smile.

I nod, my neck a little stiff. I get it. Blanche is the epitome of Mama Bear. She murdered our husband, our father and half a cult to protect our families. With the right intel, I'm sure she'd do it again. A rumble fills the room and my brothers move aside, making room for Marx's large body.

"Hey," he whispers, his rough voice rolling over me.

His gaze shifts to my little girl. He whispers something in her ear before leaning down, angling her toward me so I can nuzzle her soft little cheek. Tears slip down my face as I blubber, whispering how much I love her and that I'll be home soon.

"I will be home soon, won't I?" I ask, turning to look at Switch.

"Well," he stretches out the word. "I mean, anyone else I'd tell them they'd be in here at least another week. But as far as I'm concerned, it was through and through, you've had two blood transfusions and you were on a ventilator for two days, however that was more precautionary until you woke up. You're awake now, your stats look good and at home you'll be surrounded by people who are more than willing to help out."

"So does that mean I can go home?" I ask, hope blooming in my chest. I don't want to be away from Bee any longer than I have to be. She's my responsibility.

"Given the circumstances with which you landed here, I think it's best practice that we discharge you into my care. I'll

26

try and spring you outta here first thing tomorrow morning and get you to the farm for safety. Because of the nature of your injury, I'll have hospital transportation arranged. It covers both Rose Grove Hospital and my ass," he says, aiming the last part at Marx. I guess it makes sense. I'd hate to have Switch lose his licence all because I wanted to be driven home in a club SUV.

"Do whatever you need. The safety of our family is top priority," Marx says, adjusting Bee in his arms as he stands to look at Switch and my brothers. "I'm letting you know now, I will be in the cabin with Lovely. I will tend to anything she and Bee may need, and if I can't someone will be assigned to her care."

Wait. What? "Pres, there is no reason to do that, I –"

He raises his big man hand, silencing me. For now. He's lucky I'm not feeling myself because as soon as he made the gesture I could feel my body heat up, fire running through me. In the past when it was done by my husband or father, I would submit. Head down, I'd quietly take their words or fists. But not anymore. I may be soft spoken, but that doesn't mean that I'll put up with garbage from people. I look toward Vic and the smile on his face tells me that I may not have hidden my irritation quite like I thought.

"Lovely, please," Marx implores, "Please let me do this. I owe you my life."

My brows pinch and I know I'm missing pieces to what happened that day. If it was as serious as I think it may have been, then Marx needs to be at the clubhouse, not the little cabin that Bee and I call home.

"What about the MC? The brothers need you at the clubhouse, not with me." Looks dart around the room. Switch looks toward Marx, and my brothers wince slightly at the mention of the clubhouse. "What? What happened?"

"Babe, there is no clubhouse."

Chapter 4

Marx

I'm running on fumes but I don't give a shit. Lovely is awake and talking. And crying. The heartbreak on her face when I had to tell her the clubhouse was no more, almost killed me. Then the tears she shed for the brothers that were injured, even Rider and his wounded ass, almost finished me off. I know she's confused as to why I want to move in to look after her and little Bee, but she'll soon find out.

I lay Bee into her miniature bed in her room and take a look around. I'm not snooping. Oh OK, I'm kinda snooping. Bee's room is decorated with all sorts of bright colors. There are flowers decorating the walls and stuffies of little bumblebees suspended from the ceiling. There is a huge bookcase packed full of books and a little play area where I'm surprised to find an absence of dolls, and in their place there are blocks and trucks and motorcycles.

Leaving Bee's room I head to the living area. I won't violate Lovely's privacy by looking in her room. I can tell enough about her from her living room. She's neat and tidy and there are little tchotchkes strategically placed around the room. There's a mug shaped like a pig with pens sticking out of the top. There is a small row of fat birds sitting on a windowsill, and a crystal hangs above it, in the daytime catching the light and sending prisms of color bouncing off the walls. My lips tip up as I picture Lovely sitting in the window seat, reading a book or perhaps finishing the crochet that I can see sticking out of a yarn basket. She's a woman of simple pleasures, my woman.

I kick my boots off, and flop down on my back onto the large, soft couch, arm across my eyes. My mind is racing, full of thoughts and plans and yet none of them stay in the forefront of my mind long enough before they flit away, replaced with something more pressing, more dangerous or more urgent.

The door opens and I launch myself up, gun at the ready, the once dark room now bathed in light. Blinking away the confusion I'm met with Blanche's pissy look. She has a baby strapped to her chest and the older little kids stare at me like I've lost my mind.

"Whoa, Unca Marx, what happened to you?" Jovie asks, staring at the top of my head.

I scrub a hand over my face, trying to get rid of the drowsiness that still clings to me. I must have passed out as soon as I lay down last night. "Fuck! Little Bee!"

"Bah, don't worry 'bout her," Cove waves a hand at me while Elio stares, "She's lazy and doesn't get up for aaaaaages." Elio nods in agreement.

Glancing at the clock on the wall I note it's only 7.30am.

"They're right. She'll be up in another half hour or so." Blanche bounces the baby in her front pack. "We're here for babysitting and cleaning duty to get the place ready for Lovely to come home. Go grab breakfast and talk to your council. You need to come up with a plan because I'm only going to sit by with my finger up my ass for so long."

I stare at her as she breezes past, knowing that arguing with her is a lost cause. "Got it. Church will be as soon as Switch brings Lovely home. I want everyone there."

Blanche's eyes widen, knowing that women aren't usually allowed into Church. "Well, then, I'll see you in half an hour."

I nod before leaving the house, cataloguing what I'll need to move in. If I fucking own anything after the clubhouse was wrecked.

I make my way to the main house, letting myself in and let out a whistle "Rhodie, Rider, Mad Dog, Tank, Wire and Judge, if you can ride, I want you with me."

My brothers, who had been shooting the shit stand as one, ready to have my back should I need them. I don't say any more, I just walk out to the line of bikes, noting that it's damn lucky our bikes were unscathed. My girl is exactly where she should be. Front of the pack. I throw my leg over, turn the key and hold the starter button until she rumbles beneath me. It's been days since I last rode, and I need the wind therapy before I call Church. My shoulders start to relax as I slowly make my way down the winding drive, waiting for my brothers. Judge pulls in beside me, idling at the top of the drive. He raises a brow and tips his head in the direction of the compound. At my chin lift he turns, leading the pack as Road Captain. We all fall into place behind him, Rhodie and I at his back, then Tank, Wire, Rider and Mad Dog all in formation behind us.

The wind rushes past, blowing out all the bullshit until I feel lighter. The weight of the world melts away and it's just me, the open road and men that I trust with my life. Looking to my left my brother gives me a chin lift, his green eyes holding mine for a moment, as if sending me his strength as we come up on the compound. He's seen the damage, and I'm sure whatever he's told me is not enough to prepare me to see it with my own eyes.

Judge leads the way into the compound drive and we idle while Rider fishes the gate key out of his pocket. His left ass cheek looks padded to hell and I know that as soon as our engines are off he's going to start bitching. I've never met a man with such a low pain tolerance.

He shoves the gates open and we roll in slowly, taking in the damage. It's worse than I thought. I was so full of rage on that day that I don't think I actually took a good look.

The furthest end of the clubhouse sustained the most damage. There's a huge hole that's been blown through the wall facing the road. The roof is caved in and I can only thank the Gods and whoever else is in charge that that part of the clubhouse was mainly storage and not the room we use as a nursery. Unfortunately because the roof at the back had caved, the weight of that has put pressure on the rest of the building, collapsing it enough to make it unsafe to even enter.

I pull into my usual spot, my men following and parking behind me, our engines all shutting off one after the other. I purposely force my gaze past the front door and the ground below it, stained with Lovely's blood.

"Fuck, Pres. This is worse than I remember it being," Judge says in his low rumble.

We sit in silence, taking in the damage. Well, most of us do.

"My ass is killing me," Rider whines before dismounting gingerly.

"I told you we should have taken one of the SUV's," Rhodie

chides him. They've been best friends since childhood, the bulk of that Rhodie has been Rider's keeper. Without Rhodie, Rider would have been punched in the face a lot more often.

"I think we can agree the clubhouse is fucked. So, let's comb the area for anything that may be of help. We all know Chewy is going to ask questions, so the more information we can give her, the easier it'll be on all of us." Mad Dog says with a smile.

Rhodie preens like his Ol Lady is the pick of the bunch. Rider punches him in the arm to bring him down a couple of pegs but with his ass he's too slow to dodge the slap to his right cheek as Rhodie lashes out at him. Rider limps off as fast as he can as Rhodie chases after him.

"How the fuck do you deal with this?" Mad Dog asks, brows pinched.

"We ignore it," Tank answers, slapping my dad on the shoulder and wading into the rubble.

Mad Dog and I decide to take the back left section of the clubhouse, walking in companionable silence. I don't need any words or chatter. I have shit bouncing around in my head. Plans, contingencies, fears, all rolling into one. What if we hit too soon or not soon enough? What if we attack and it causes more casualties? Fuck.

"Wanna talk about it?" Mad Dog asks, eyes on something sticking out of the roof rubble.

"No, thanks. Just trying to come up with a Plan A, then a Plan B right the way through to Plan Z."

"Can I offer a solution?" My dad looks over at me, his eyes almost as dark as mine. In fact, he just looks like an older version of Rhodie and myself. The only difference being Rhodie takes after his mother's fairer coloring.

"Hit me."

"Well, from what I've seen, and learnt since I've been back, the smartest plan would be to let Chewy come up with the plan." His eyes twinkle as he grins at me.

I huff out a laugh, "Yeah, you're probably fucking right, old man."

"No shit, Sherlock."

"Speaking of, I want to run something by you,"

"Hit me," he answers, echoing my words from a moment ago.

"I'm going to call Church. The women will be there."

He runs a hand down his salt and pepper beard. "Of course."

"Even though it's in the club bylaws that women aren't allowed in Church?"

"Marx, you have a woman as the icer. Chewy attends Church, and don't you tell me she's different." He raises his brow, "When shit went down it was the women that jumped into action first. Getting the children and wounded to safety. It'd be a goddamn insult to them to leave them out."

A smile grows over my face, making my dad frown at me. "My thoughts exactly, old man."

A whistle carries on the breeze and I look toward the sound, Rhodie standing over Rider who looks to be bitching about something. We head that way, still scanning the ground for anything that may come in handy.

"Look, Rider's ass saves the day again!" Rhodie says, holding up a shell casing while Rider glares up at him.

"You're a cruel fucker! I was shot three days ago and you're meant to be gentle with me. I'm in pain!" Rider whines.

"What happened to him?" Judge asks, massive arms folded across his chest, staring down at my SAA.

"I was chasing him and he tripped and fell on his ass. And

34

this casing." Rhodie drops it into my outstretched hand and I bring it up to the light to see better. White hot rage burns in the pit of my stomach.

"Find as many of these fuckers as you can. Bring them to me," I bark, storming off to scan the ground for more shell casings.

Within three minutes I have a small handful, the others the same.

"What are we looking for?" Tank asks, emptying his handful into my palm.

I rifle through them all, taking note of the outside of the casing. "Get back to the farm, I'm calling Church."

"Why? What have you found?" Rhodie asks, on high alert now.

"They're carved."

"And?"

"With our names." I meet his green gaze, shock morphing to a hard look.

"Our road names?"

"And the names of our women and children."

Lovely

"You good there, girl?" Switch yells in my face.

A grin pushes my cheeks up and I could blame the pain killers, but it's less that, and more Switch is back to his normal loud

35

self. Don't get me wrong, I love that he keeps us all well and good, but the quiet, measured Dr Hansen is not the man I know and love.

"Well, that grin is a good sign." He beams down at me. "Not long to go now and we can get you all settled on the couch with a blanket and the kiddies around you." He pats my hand and I wrap my fingers around the rough warmth of his.

"Thank you, Switch. For everything."

His gaze softens and his eyes dart away before finding mine again, "Do you know how Marx and I met?"

I shake my head, then twist my body on the gurney a little, until I'm facing Switch a little more.

"It was my last tour. I was taken by insurgents along with my team. Stuck in a shitty cave I worked with what I had to keep my brothers alive. There were gunshot wounds, stabbings, you name it. All we had was water, and whatever I was carrying when we were found."

I grip his hand even tighter, but I'm unsure he even notices I'm here. He's gazing through me. "I couldn't save them. One by one they succumbed to infections or blood loss or they just gave up." He shrugs one large shoulder, runs his hand over his face and sniffs, shaking his head, his clear gaze returning to mine. "Marx found me. Brought me home with him to Rose Grove MC, introduced me to other brothers who had been dealt a shit hand. He and Mad Dog and the old boys who have all passed on, they built us back up from the dirt. I will always owe Marx for giving me my life back. But you, Lovely Landry, I owe you even more. You saved the man that saved me, and that fucking means something. To all of us." He gives me a small smile and I cup his face, running my thumb over his stubble.

"I did what any good person would do, Switch."

He lets out a huff. "You'd be surprised."

We come to a rolling stop and the back doors are pulled open abruptly. "Welcome home!" is yelled by what sounds to be one hundred voices, and its music to my ears. The faces of the people I love are all grinning as I wave from my place on the bed.

"Well, move aside people," Switch booms, stooping a little until he has room to jump down onto the ground outside.

The crowd disperses until the only people who are still standing there are my brothers, my sister, Marx, Bee and the Girl Gang. Switch arranges a wheelchair at the foot of the ambulance and then looks at me, then the chair.

"Fuck sake, move," Marx growls, handing Bee to Nat while he steps up into the back of the ambulance with me, scoops me up bridal style and then jumps back out very gently, so as not to jostle me.

He lowers me gently into the wheelchair, moving to grip the handles, ready to propel me forward.

"Hold your horses, big man," Nat teases Marx, leaning to place Bee onto my lap.

I nuzzle into her dark hair, breathing her toddler smell into my lungs. It's a nicer smell than usual. She smells less like sweaty kids and more like she's been well loved by her aunties. Raising my head I rear back when I see my home.

"Holy cow," I whisper.

"I know right?" Mira laughs and claps as she skips to the side of me as Marx races us toward the farm house. "Pops did all this. The mobile homes are for the couples and families. Although the small one over there is for when Fox and Nitro get back."

My chest aches knowing that Fox is in the hospital. I send

37

out good vibes, hoping it's enough. I stopped praying a long time ago, and though I have faith in a great something beyond us, I just can't bring myself to speak to any one greater being.

Remy rushes ahead, ready to open the door for us as Marx pushes me up a temporary ramp, "Figured it was a necessity, what with Fox and yourself needing a little extra accessibility," Vi says, "Jazz has access to all this cool accessible stuff through her school and when they heard what happened, they wanted to help. The DRMC has been good at donating to the school from time to time," she adds.

I just nod, marvelling at how full of life the farmhouse is. I've visited often, baked in the kitchen with Mama Debs and enjoyed dinners with her and Pops, and it always seemed as if the house was just a landing spot for them. The two of them rattled around in such a large house, so to see it so full of hustle and bustle warms my heart.

"There she is!" Rider yells, limping toward me.

"Ignore the limp, it was a flesh wound to the ass, he's milking it now," Ana whispers.

"Wait, hasn't he been hit in the butt before?" I whisper back. Everyone in the girl gang nods in unison.

"I don't even know how he manages it. It should be statistically impossible to be shot that many times in the ass," Chewy frowns.

"Lemme guess, you've crunched the numbers?" Ana asks drily.

"Yeah. And even the numbers couldn't predict it happening more than once."

"Did you accommodate for the fact that maybe Rider has a big, juicy peach?" Blanche asks with a snort.

All heads snap toward her, including Tav's. "Babe!" he

shouts, offended.

"What? I grew up in a cult! Now I'm out in the world and I'm surrounded by fat booties everywhere."

Everyone in the big living room groans, apart from Rider who's limp is miraculously cured as he minces around, sticking out his butt.

Marx's obnoxiously loud whistle almost blows my eardrums out and I can't help but turn my head and frown up at him.

"Sorry, babe." he says, apologetically.

My brows hit my hairline, and I turn back to face the room, ignoring the smirks coming from my family.

"Everyone here?" Marx says in a slightly less booming voice.

"Everyone except Mama Debs and the kids," Remy says, settling on Wire's knee at the coffee table, their laptops open.

"Roman will come by this evening after Dima arrives. He's alluded to a lead that they're following as we speak," Ana adds.

A few of the brothers shift in their seats. I know that Roman isn't terribly popular, and his brother-in-law is a little on the creepy side, but they've always been there to help out, and as far as I'm concerned, Roman is a lot less evil and conniving than the men I grew up with.

"Let's get this shit started."

Chapter 5

Marx

I stand behind Lovely, hands gripped on the wheelchair handles like a lifeline. When Switch had the nerve to shoulder bump me and tell me to *"Sort your shit out, there are brothers here who would treat Lovely like the diamond she is,"* I almost lost it. The only thing that reined in my temper was that Switch is the only reason Lovely is safe here, and not exposed in the hospital.

"I've got Nitro on video call, so I'm sharing my screen," Chewy says to nobody in particular.

She can share her screen all she wants, I have no real clue what that means. I just need to know what the fuck we're dealing with and how to wipe out the threats.

"Nitro? Can you hear us?" she says, pressing buttons here and there, even pointing the remote at the TV and fucking around with it. "Are you on mute? I think you might be on mute.... Yeah, turn mute off."

"Hello?" Nitro's voice booms over the TV, causing us all to

jump. Well, all of us except Flack, but I'm certain he has to be some level of deaf.

While this whole fucking thing is going on Mad Dog smirks at me from across the room. His gaze flicking to Bee and Lovely, then to me and back again. I slowly raise my middle finger, discreetly, so he gets the picture. I have no idea why people are giving me looks. Lovely is a beautiful woman, and Switch is right, any of the brothers would be lucky to have her. But she's mine. As soon as I figure out how the fuck to woo her or whatever it is you do to get women to like you. I let out a long breath because shit, I have no idea how to date. My whole adult life I've had pussy on tap, first from being a marine and then Pres of an MC. I've put very little effort into getting and keeping a woman. Now I have one that I have actual feelings for and instead of grabbing her with both hands and loving her, I flapped my fucking gums to keep her at arms length and hurt her. Now anything I say will have her laughing in my damn face. Add to that our clubhouse being attacked and I'm really being DP'ed by the dildo of life right now. Unlubed.

"Good, we can hear each other. Let's get this show on the road," Chewy says in such a cheerful voice that it almost makes this feel as if it's an everyday family meeting, and not Church.

Chewy looks toward me, with a nod, and I thump my fist on the wall behind me, bringing Church to order. "As you can see, Church is going to be a little different today. Ladies, it's an honor to have you join us. Without you some of us wouldn't be here today," I stare at Nitro on the screen, he has dark smudges under his eyes and his hair is sticking up on end, then my gaze flicks to the woman sitting in front of me, her dark head bent as she snuggles into Bee. "Thank you. All of you. Your fast thinking saved lives."

41

"Hear, hear!" Mad Dog yells out, the men cheering along, stomping, clapping and generally giving the women the thanks they deserve.

"As for my brothers, both MC, and Tombs," I clear my throat of the emotion lodged there. "There is nobody else I'd want at my back. We stood shoulder to shoulder, defending our home. Some of us came out of there a little worse for the wear," snickers can be heard as Rhodie and Tank rib Rider, "But we're all here, in one piece, and I don't know about you, but I feel like a little payback is on the cards. No one fucks with our family and gets away with it."

My ears ring with the roar that goes out, not just from the MC, but from the Tombs and the Landrys as well.

Tucking my lip, I let out my trademark whistle, calling the room to order once more. "Chewy, tell me you know who the fuck had the balls to attack us?"

"Of course I do. But maybe we want to call Moss in," she answers, her eyes on her screen.

"Ah, babe, why would we do that?" Rhodie asks, his worried gaze flicking to me, then back to his Ol Lady.

"Because it was Sheriff Kelson who attacked us."

You can hear a pin drop, and then the room erupts. There are gasps, yelling, and Violet is letting rip with an impressive amount of Spanish. Although that makes sense. If I found out my brother's boss was a bad guy, I'd be livid as well.

I wait until everyone starts to calm before turning to Chewy. "Explain!"

"We picked him up on the cameras," Wire answers instead, tapping at something on his keyboard and then looking toward the big screen TV.

The grainy images clearly show Kelson and at least two other men aiming automatic weapons at us before an image of one of them with a small rocket launcher appears.

"What in the fuck is going on?" Savage asks under his breath.

"Why is the Sheriff targeting us?" Lovely wonders out loud.

"Let me enlighten you." Chewy says with a straight face. She's in infodump mode. "So, the first thing you need to know is that as soon as the Computas were situated we went intel gathering. We got the pictures of Sheriff Kelson straight off, but the men in the vehicle were a little harder to pin down."

"So we don't know who he's working with?" Dex asks.

"Don't be stupid, of course we do. I said it was harder, not impossible," Chewy rolls her eyes at the ridiculousness that she, Wire and Remy wouldn't be able to work it out. "Once we learned who they were, we split our resources into three. Wire is working the cartel angle, Remy the adoption scam, and myself, I got the Sheriff and well, anything else. I'm cool like that."

There are snickers and Rhodie beams at Chewy like she's the best thing in the world. I guess to him, she is.

"Let me guess, just because shutting down Candice's operation wasn't enough, we've managed to piss off the cartel and the sheriff as well?" Gus asks, running his hand down his face. Any minute now he's going to pull out his Tums.

"They're one and the same."

"There is no way Sheriff Kelson, the old white guy that has been sheriff since I was a kid, is part of the cartel. No fucking way," Tav says, shaking his head.

The Computas share a look and I know they're going to drop a bomb.

"He's not cartel as such, but he is an investor in the adoption scam business."

43

"And when we shut down Candice's business – "

"Yup, we shut down dear old Sheriff Kelson's retirement plan," Chewy finishes.

"How the fuck did he cross paths with them to begin with?" I ask, because none of this shit makes much sense.

"Gambling debts," Sniper rumbles.

Chewy's head snaps in his direction and she grins wide at him, clearly pleased that someone has put some of the pieces together.

"It's how the cartel get you. They can sniff out anyone with a debt, offer to pay it off and then next thing you know you're in their pocket. Desperate to do anything to clear that debt." He frowns at the wall, staring at nothing in particular.

I know the brother has demons, I've always known. I also know that his family has had trouble with the cartel in the past. If this is the road we're heading down, I'm going to have to keep a tight leash on him.

"Huh. So you know cartel stuff," Chewy says, thoughtfully. "What do you know about Tito?"

Sniper schools his face. "I know that he's one cold motherfucker. You thought the Cordoza Cartel was bad, they have nothing on Serpiente." He rumbles. Roman took out the Cordoza Cartel when he found they had been trafficking his drugs inside sex slaves.

Wire stares thoughtfully at Sniper, running a hand down his stubble, "In all the intel we've gathered we have never seen a picture of Serpiente. Do you know what he looks like?"

Sniper nods once, and then rolls his shoulders back. This shit is taking a toll on him. I make a note to catch up with the brother after this. Looking around the room I realize there's a few people I need to catch up with. I was so focussed on Lovely that I slacked on my duty as Pres. After we're done I'll take Lovely home, get her and Bee settled and then track down the people I need to. My role isn't just to bark orders, but to also keep my MC healthy, both physically and mentally.

Wire taps a few keys and Pops' big ass TV is lit up with pictures of 3 Latino men. Judging from Sniper's reaction, they're all as fucking bad as each other.

"Serpiente, Tito Caram, is the greasy looking guy on the left. The right is Carlos Cordoza's ex-brother-in-law. Got out of the cartel life when he married Carlos's sister Magdelena. He could be back in, I'm not sure."

"If he was active in the Cartel, Roman wouldn't have left him alive when he cleaned the Cordoza's out of cartel-aged men," Ana offers.

She's right. Roman may be a cold bastard, but he doesn't go around indiscriminately killing. We've been dealing with his ass for over a year now, I know his MO just like he knows mine. Killing a husband and father who is no longer active in the Cartel doesn't sit right.

Chewy nods her head at the new information. "Noted. What about the last guy?"

She stares at her computer screen before looking back at Sniper. Well, over his shoulder. Her eyes track him as he moves closer to the screen, his posture rigid. I share a look with Savage before returning my gaze to my club brother. The only tell tale sign that the image of the third man is distressing, is Sniper cracking his knuckles one by one.

"Well? Do you know him?" Chewy asks as she taps at her laptop keyboard.

Sniper clears his throat, "Yeah," he whispers. "I know him."

"Oh good, what's his name?" Chewy replies, completely

45

oblivious to how this is affecting the quiet man.

"His name is Joseph Almaraz. He's my brother." With that Sniper stalks out of the room, the only sound is the thump of his footsteps on the porch and then the roar of his sled.

"Where's he going? He could have some good intel for us?" Chewy asks, looking around the room wildly.

"Babe? Sniper has to get his thoughts in order, so maybe ask him later, OK?"

Chewy stares at Rhodie, then at everyone else in the room before throwing her hands up, "Fiiiine. But he's going to answer my questions," she ends on a threat.

"I'm sure he'd be glad to," I add. "What else have you got?" I ask, eager to get things moving so we can formulate a plan.

Wire looks up from his screen, "Serpiente, or Tito Caram, is a contractor. Cartels hire him to do anything from extortion to hired kills, but it's mainly to look after their businesses. In this case, he's been investing cartel money into his Adopt-a-Kid scam."

This jogs my memory a little as to what Chewy told us before Tav and Blanche had their little girl. "Chewy, you said that Tito had more than just Candice Rogers working for him?"

She claps her hands, accidentally flinging her pen at Rhodie. "Yes! So, it turns out that while Candice may have been the largest supplier of children to needy, infertile parents, she wasn't the only one. During her, um, interview, she mentioned at least three others running operations in different states along the I-10 corridor."

"Any idea who these women may be?" Judge asks, brow raised.

"Rem, you're up." Chewy says, never moving her eyes from her computer screen.

We all turn our eyes toward Remy who almost shrinks at the attention. She may be one of the Girl Gang and a badass in her own right, but she's still the shy woman who landed at our clubhouse from the Death Riders MC a year or so ago.

Wire pats her thigh, giving it a quick squeeze in support. She grins at him, pulls her shoulders back, full of confidence. A thought crosses my mind that this is what I want with Lovely, but then it's squashed almost as quickly as it came. Lovely has built herself up from the ground up. Yes, like Remy she may still be a little on the quieter side and not as confident as some of the other women, but she's gone out there and grabbed life by the balls. She put herself through a computing course so she could work at Devil's Big Tow. She deals with people day in, day out and with her quiet strength has managed to call in all outstanding debts to the company. She regularly is around the men and can joke around or mother them. This woman doesn't need me to protect her from the world, she can do that herself. She knows she can.

I look down at her, sitting in the wheelchair in front of me. She must feel my gaze because she turns to me, her dark eyes staring up at me, a soft smile on her face. My cock thickens as I imagine her in this position in a different moment, on her knees, gazing up at me.

Her brows pinch slightly before her brow smooths. "It'll be alright, you know? The DRMC will find out who did this. Don't worry." She reaches a hand over her shoulder and pats mine, still holding the wheelchair handle.

This woman, the one who saved my life by risking hers, is now comforting me. Fucking hell. I do not deserve someone so pure and kind, but dammit, I ain't giving her up.

My head snaps back to attention when Remy clears her

47

throat. "So, from our time in the Rev Room we know Tito told Candice to move the children. The only way to do that, while keeping Tito's operation running, is to move them to one of the other women he has working for him. There are eight states along the I-10 corridor, and we know that Candice had Texas, New Mexico and Arizona on lock. I've found two other states that have businesses with the same model as Candice's, but only one has put out a statement recently looking for couples wanting to complete their families."

"They make it so easy," Mira says, shaking her head in disgust while scribbling in her notepad. Nat rolls her eyes with a smirk and Tank shakes his head at his woman, pressing a kiss to her temple.

Remy taps a few keys and a picture of a dark-haired woman with a friendly, open face fills the screen. "Meet Renae Sullivan. Owner of Bayou Haven Family Services."

"Fucking hell," Rider says, running a hand down his face. "What is up with the names of these places?"

"Again, they make it sooooo easy," Mira mutters.

"So am I right in thinking that this whole thing happened because we saved Laney, shut down Candice, fucked up Serpiente's operation he was heading up for two cartel families and the town Sheriff, and messed with their lucrative kiddy trafficking?" Pops asks.

"Yup."

"Fucking hell, Imma need to stock up on shit."

Lovely

I think it's the pain meds I'm filled up with, but Pops' comment has me snorting and then giggling and then grimacing. I have to stop because laughing hurts my chest but what he said is just so funny. The MC is being targeted by two crime families AND law enforcement and all Pops is worried about is whether he has enough "supplies" to go around. I snort again and another round of giggles breaks out. Bee must also think it's funny because she stares at me for a moment, then throws her head back and lets out the fakest laugh I've ever heard, causing the whole room to break out into chuckles with her.

"Well, I'm glad Bee thinks that this whole situation is laughable," Mad Dog says. "I leave for one year and I come back to absolute chaos. You lot sure know how to spice things up."

The large living room is full of grumbles and chuckles and I'm glad to be home. I know I was knocked out for a lot of my hospital stay, but the times I was awake were so lonely. It was the first real time that I've ever been on my own. Well, kinda. Marx was there on and off, making sure I had everything, and when he wasn't there I knew TumTum and Chef were on the door outside, but since birth I've always been a part of something larger than myself.

The Keep, for all its faults, was a good place to grow up. I had my mom and a slew of aunts that looked after us, brothers and sisters and cousins and friends to play with. As I grew older I made close friends and worked in the laundry rooms with other girls my age. Then when I was sixteen that all came

49

tumbling down. I remember the day as if it was yesterday. Aunt Charity visited me. She brushed my hair and instead of the loose braid us girls wore our hair in, she left it long and wavy down my back. When she told me I looked beautiful, I was taken aback. We were good servants of God, there was no room for vanity in our lifestyle. She cupped my face and told me I'd make my husband a happy man. That was all the warning I was given. Half an hour later I was married to my uncle, my father's brother. A man forty years older than my 16 years, with a cruel streak a mile wide.

Weight lands on my shoulder, making me jerk, pain lancing through my chest. "Shit, are you OK? Sorry, I didn't mean to startle you. Fuck!" Marx's rough voice works its way through my foggy mind, still stuck between memory and present.

"It's OK, I must have been away with the fairies for a moment," I smile at him over my shoulder.

He stares down at me, eyes as black as night, before giving me a nod. "I was, ah, just checking on you."

My brows pinch at Marx's concern, but I guess it's par for the course. He's a good Pres, always worried about his people. In some ways he's similar to my father, always worried about his flock. Although that is where the similarities end.

"I'm good." I nod once and turn back to focus on Chewy and whatever her plan for us may be.

I marvel at how she can command a room. She's front and center, working through all the threads of information to come up with a plan. What she says goes, that's how high in esteem the MC holds her. But she's not the only one. Each and every Ol Lady here brings skills. Nat, Blanche and Ana all bring sass and the ability to speak their minds and go to war for their men if needed. Chewy and Remy beaver away in the background, feeding us with intel and all the things we need to keep ourselves safe. Mira and Vi, while new at this Ol Lady thing, have the ability to bring out the best in their men, while helping keep a rein on the Girl Gang. I used to think that I would never fit in, but since our little fun in the Rev Room I've learned that perhaps I straddle the space between the women. I'm brave and ballsy in my own way, and like Mama Debs, Vi and Mira I like to nurture and care for those around me. I'm not quite the woman who left the Keep all those months ago, scared to enter the wide world around me. I'm out here holding on with both hands to make my life, and the life of my daughter so much richer, and I have all these people to thank for that.

"So, what's the plan?" Nitro asks, over the big screen where his face is showing in a little square in the corner.

It's quiet except for the rasping coming from behind me. I know without looking that Marx is running his big, tattooed hand down his beard, tugging on it while he thinks. There was a time where all I could think about was what those hands would feel like on me. Would they be rough to the touch? Would they be gentle hands or would they grip and massage me firmly? I could never decide. Although the one thing I knew deep in my soul, was that those hands would never hurt me. Not when his words could do that on their own.

I swallow the lump in my throat, remembering what he said, that I was just his MC brother's sister-in-law. It hurt at the time, but thinking deeper I get it. He is a man with the weight of the world on his shoulders, and to him I'll always be the woman who needed saving. Even though I'm stronger than he'll ever know, I also know that I'm quite naive when it comes to men. My attraction to Marx is just a silly school girl crush. An attraction to a man so completely opposite to

51

my husband, so handsome and caring and gruff, instead of the slick, smarminess of Royal. His words popped the bubble and I see that at this moment, at this time, Marx is not the man for me, and that's OK. I believe that love, the right love, will find me when it's ready, and when it does I'll grab on with both hands. I smile to myself as I nuzzle my face into Little Bee's hair as she rests on me, her legs straddling mine, her arms hanging loosely at her sides as she rests against my chest, her body plastered against me. Her little breaths puff out of her plump lips and I feel dampness where I'm sure she is drooling on me.

"These men came into my town, and tried to wipe out my MC, my *family*." Marx pauses, as if weighing his words. "I can't make the decision alone. Whatever we decide, we decide as a collective, as this affects all of us. Some of you have Ol Ladies, children, babies–" Marx rests his hand gently on Bee's back, stroking her gently before pulling back to stand. "We need to make the decision based on this, and not just revenge. I say we think about it for the rest of the day. I'll be coming to talk to each and every one of you. I want your thoughts, fears, anything that you think is important. We'll then make a decision after dinner." The tension that had been hanging in the room lessens as everyone nods at Marx. Nat and Savage have their heads together, as do Gus and Ana, whispering to each other. The couples with children all look thoughtful, but so do the single brothers. Everyone wants to make the right decision for our family, and I couldn't be more proud to be a part of this. "Roman and his crew will be arriving in an hour or so. Rhodie, I want you with me to rep the MC, Gus, you'll rep the Tombs and Vic, if you could rep the Landrys."

The men all nod in agreement. "I'll be there, I may not be MC, but you're still my Pres," Gus answers seriously, Vic nodding in agreement.

"Good. OK, Church dismissed, I'm going to get Lovely settled and then I'll be doing my rounds. Stick together, watch each other's backs," he looks toward where Chewy and Pops are having a conversation, "and don't do dumb shit."

With that he twirls my chair around until we're pointing in the direction of the doorway, where he pushes me at a fast clip out of the room and away from Pops' complaining.

Chapter 6

Marx

"Um, you know that I could probably get one of my brothers to get me home, you don't have to do this," Lovely's soft voice washes over me as I stride out of the house, down the ramp and make a beeline to her cabin.

I dodge a few kids' bikes that are lying on the path, and make a note to have a word with Mama Debs and the kids. With Lovely in a wheelchair, and probably Fox when he comes home, it'll be best to keep the path clear.

"No. I'm looking after you," I grumble down at her.

"Pres, stop." Her voice is firm and I do as she says.

She twists to look up at me over her shoulder, and I know it must pull something because she winces slightly before covering it up. Not wanting to be an asshole I move to stand in front of her, and then feel like more of an asshole as I loom, so I squat down, face to face with the woman who has had me in knots for longer than I care to admit.

"I appreciate everything you have done and are doing to

make sure I'm OK, and I am OK. But you have a whole group of people relying on you and your decisions."

"Lovely, I–"

"No, Pres." Her eyes search mine for a moment. They still have that kind look in them, but where she used to look at me with stars in her eyes, that look has faded. She gives me a tight smile. "You're the leader, it's up to you to lead, not play house with me and Bee." She pulls her shoulders back, straightening a little. "I'd really appreciate it if you could maybe get me into my house, and then we'll be fine from there. Vi said she'd hang out at mine and keep an ear out for Bee while I nap." Her smile turns genuine, and I know that I won't win this battle.

I keep my mouth shut, and nod jerkily, moving to stand behind her, I grip the wheelchair handles and push her to her cabin. Vi must see us from her window because she comes rushing out of the cabin next to Lovely's and meets us on the porch. Damn woman butting in. I don't even know when they arranged all this, I was with Lovely the whole time. I should have known that winning over Lovely wasn't going to be as easy as I hoped. These women are sneaky.

"I can take over from here Marx," Vi says, smiling up at me. She doesn't even wait for my reply, just hip bumps me out of the way, grabs the handles and shoves Lovely and Bee through the front door. "Byeeeeee!" she calls over her shoulder, a huge smile on her face, as if she knows she's ruined my plans.

Shit. Looks like I'll be doing the rounds of my brothers sooner rather than later. I tip my head back, and take in a deep breath, exhaling before rolling my shoulders.

"So, what's the plan?"

I don't even need to look to see who's standing next to me. I can smell the Old Spice emanating from him, not to mention he jabbed me with his boney elbow to gain my attention.

"Pops, were you even listening in Church?"

"Yes. The end of Church concluded with there not being a plan. But I'm not talking about Church, I'm talking 'bout Lovely."

I glance at him from the corner of my eye to find him full frontal, glaring at me. I could feed him up on some bullshit, but Pops is a wily old bastard with the ability to make my life a living hell, so I may as well tell him.

"Somehow get her to forgive me."

His bushy brows pinch in as he nods thoughtfully. He even adds in a chin stroke, like a wise, old man. "It's a shit plan, but pop off if that's what you want to do."

He turns on his heel and starts to walk off. What the hell? No. Reaching out I grab his forearm, stopping him in his tracks.

"I'd advise you to take your big mitt off me, kid. I may be old but I bet I can break at least two of your fingers before I go down."

My hand pings back as quickly as it shot out and I can't believe I just manhandled a senior citizen. "Shit, sorry. Fuck, she's got me all tied up in knots and it's my fault for flapping my gums and saying some shit I didn't mean."

"Well, I'm glad you can admit you were a grade A douche canoe," Pops nods. "When Lovely told us girls at Mommies Group I had to swear not to go down to the clubhouse to kick your ass."

My brows fly up at his words, "Mommies group? Why are you at mommies group?"

He steps into my much larger body, poking me in the gut with his bony finger, "Because I raised those kids that you like to go to for advice, so I'm their fucking Mommy, you got

56

that?" He shakes his head in disgust. "Jesus kid, you just gotta open that trap sometimes and rub people the wrong way, huh? Now, do you want to come up with a shitty plan to woo Lovely yourself, or do you want a spectacular plan, with my help?"

My eyes narrow as I take in his offer. "Will there be explosions?"

"Does Lovely look like the type of woman who likes explosions?"

Does she? I don't know. I would lean toward her not really liking them, but what if she does but I just don't know that about her? Actually, in the scheme of things, I don't really fucking know *anything* about her.

"If you have to think that long about it, then you don't know the girl. Tell you what, spend a little time talking to her, and then when you know what she likes, come find me."

"You're really willing to help me with this?" I ask, raising a brow.

Pops takes a deep breath, then lets it all out. "Look, I see that girl as a granddaughter to me. And the MC is my family. For me, family comes first. If that means I have to help you, a huge ass with no fucking filter when it comes to women, then so be it." I nod, taking in his words. "But we do it *my* way. In this realm I'm the Pres. The Love Pres, if you will. Got it?"

I glare at him and he glares right back. I mean shit, if Pops was pissed at my treatment of Lovely, then the rest of the women will be too, and they're a force to be reckoned with. If I want to have a real shot at making Lovely mine, then I'll need allies. And help. If I do this on my own I'll probably fuck it up even worse, so I decide to make a deal with the devil.

"OK. I'm in"

"You're in, what?"

"I'm in...to woo Lovely?"

"No, you need to say 'I'm in, Love Pres'," Pops says with an entirely straight face.

"No. Hell no. Fuck no."

He shrugs and starts to turn, "Ah well, mustn't want it enough then,"

I close my eyes, letting out a breath. "I'm in, Love Pres," I say through clenched teeth.

Pops spins around faster than a man of his age should be able to, and thumps me on the shoulder, before gripping it fucking hard and shaking me slightly, "Good shit, kid, let Operation Dumbass Woos An Angel commence." He beams at me, then using the grip he has on my shoulder he turns us toward the farmhouse, forcing me to follow. "The first step is to check in with your men. You have a house full of testosterone and people wanting revenge. We need guidance, oh great one, and also, women don't like men who can't get their shit together and lead an all out war on two cartels. Just saying."

I let him lead me through the front door, because he's right. I need to pull myself together and get this shit sorted. I can't wish to have a life with Lovely and Bee if I can't keep the club safe. I need to get my head in the game and take care of this cartel shit. Once that's done I can claim Lovely. I hope she's ready for me.

Lovely

"Right, to bed with you young lady, and Bee," Vi giggles, and then grins at me.

"You know, I'm sure we'll be fi-"

"Nope. I'm on Lovely and Bee watch this afternoon. Besides, Jules is having daddy-daughter time. They do it every Wednesday afternoon, and because we're kinda all stuck here for safety reasons, me coming here lets them keep their routine." She smiles softly, and I love how much she loves Jules and Juno.

I have a soft spot in my heart for those two. I guess because I live next door I've seen all the ups and downs he's had becoming a dad. It makes me feel all gooey inside knowing he has found the woman for him. Vi is the absolute best mom to Juno and she understands both Juno's and Jules' quirks. She even shares the grumpiest pictures of them on the Girl Gang messenger group and it always makes me giggle.

"If you're sure?" I don't want to be a burden. In the Keep if you were a burden you were sent away. I never knew where to, but they didn't want people who couldn't pull their weight.

I shake off the thought like I do every time the Keep invades my mind. I'm not there. Actually, the Keep is no longer there either, thanks to my siblings and the MC. I've not visited the old site since the boys took over, but I know they're using the place for good now instead of evil.

"I'm super sure. Besides, I need to be here to run interference. Marx is up to something, and there's no way I'm letting him say shitty stuff to my friend. *El idiota*."

I give her a look. "Be nice. He's the Pres. And it was just

a crush I had. I mean, I get it, he's the *Pres.* He has all of us looking for guidance and he's running businesses and keeping us all safe. It's a huge job. He doesn't need me mooning over him. Besides, it's not like he's the only man in the world."

"Exactly!" Vi says, pointing at me. "He's probably the first hot guy you saw when you left that cult place. There are plenty more fish in the sea."

I nod, a grin tugging at my lips. "Plenty more pebbles on the beach,"

"Plenty more links in the chain," Vi snorts.

"Tons of hotdogs at the barbecue," I chortle as Vi bursts into giggles.

Bee starts to wriggle in my lap, obviously hearing the party of two and wanting to join in, but it's her nap time so I quietly shush her and bounce her in my lap, gently settling her.

"Here, let me take Bee and put her to bed, then I'll be in to help get you out of the chair, OK?" Vi gently shifts Bee's weight from me to her, and I can hear her whispering in Spanish to my little girl as she settles her in her room.

I'm not too sure how I'm going to maneuver myself into my room, but I'll give it a go. If the Keep taught me anything, it's to be hardy. I grip the rims of my wheels and try to propel myself forward, but it tugs something fierce in my shoulder, causing white hot pain to glance through me. *Fifty-nine, fifty-eight, fifty-seven...*

"Whoa, whoa, whoa, what the heck are you doing crazy lady? Sheesh," Vi slaps my hands off the wheels and then shoves me in the direction of my bedroom. I really hope she's better at steering a stroller than she is a wheelchair. The woman is not only a speed demon, but is also terrible at judging little things like furniture and doorways.

She moves me into my bedroom, flicks on the brakes and moves to flip up my foot rests, guiding my feet to the floor. She readies herself to help me stand, but instead of awkwardly standing behind me, she moves to my side, slips one arm under my arm, twines her forearm through mine until our hands are clasped tightly. With a nod I push myself to stand, Vi offering not only stability, but taking some of my weight. With a flick of her foot the wheelchair brakes are off and she kicks it out of the way, so she can move with me until we've turned half a circle, and my butt rests on the edge of the bed.

"Down you go," she says cheerily, guiding me down until I'm lying against no less than six pillows.

"Thanks Vi. How did you know how to do all that?" I ask on a yawn, my eyelids growing heavy.

She gives me a sad smile. "Jazz has Rheumatoid Arthritis. I know she doesn't look it, but it's something that plagues her. She has flares where things get bad, her mobility is affected, and then other times she's fine. She's in a good space at the moment, but there have been times that haven't been easy for her."

I grip Vi's hand and give it a squeeze. "She's lucky to have you,"

"I'm lucky to have her. And you crazy girl gang biatches." She tucks a throw blanket around me, beams and then puts on a stern face. "Now go to sleep."

I huff out a breath and weakly wave at her as she quietly leaves the room. Vi and I may be new in terms of my friendships with the Ol Ladies, but as with everyone in the MC I've grown to love her dearly. I love everyone dearly, and now it's time to love myself a little more. I've been given a pretty big second chance to live a full life, even more so than I have been doing.

61

So, starting from tomorrow I'm going to do things that bring me joy. Drawing, reading, time with family, and maybe, if I'm really lucky, I may even start dating. A smile plays on my lips and my eyelids grow heavy. Watch out world, Lovely Landry is coming.

Chapter 7

Marx

After catching up with some of the brothers I head for the back porch, thinking about all the roads that led us to this place. I knew each time we patched in a brother, they were loyal to a fault. All the single brothers I've spoken with this afternoon have all echoed the same sentiment. They want revenge, but they won't make a move until the brothers with Ol Ladies and families decide what they want to do. At the end of the day the safety of the DRMC is paramount, whether we want revenge or not.

I make my way to a large swing seat that overlooks the backyard, the mobile homes all parked neatly in a row.

"Mind if I take a seat, sweetheart?" I quietly ask, Sage's dark eyes staring at me from the other end of the porch swing.

"Yeah, of course, Uncle Marx." She tucks her feet beneath her, leaving me space to settle my bulk into the soft cushions.

I raise a brow and she gives me a small smile. Pushing off with one foot, I let the sway soothe the thoughts bouncing around in my mind. I'm sure it's doing the same for Sage as well.

"I just want to say thank you, Sage, for what you did for Fox. I know it was scary, but you did the right thing."

Her bottom lip trembles and a lone tear runs down her cheek as she nods, quickly swiping at it. "I've been doing classes at the community college, you know? I want to be a nurse, to help people, but -" she blows out a breath, "that was a lot scarier than I thought it would be." She finishes in a small voice.

"Hey, hey, look at me, Sage. What happened that day is not something that would or should ever happen to you. That day, shit, it was more like being in combat." I run a hand down my face, ignoring where my mind went that day. I can still feel the cold sweat down my back when my mind took me back to deployment. "Your life, Sagey-girl, your future, will be within the walls of whatever hospital you wish it to be. Although if you wanted, I know damn well that after seeing you with my own eyes, you could handle being out in the field, working on the wounded. Shit, what are you? 19 years old?" she nods at me, eyes wide, "At 19 you handled shit a lot better than well-trained, fully grown men. Whatever you wish to do, sweetheart, you'll fucking do it and do it well."

She stares up at me, eyes identical to her aunt's, then she launches at me, arms around my bulk as she bursts into tears. I pat her back and wait it out.

"Thank you, Uncle Marx."

"Anytime, sweetheart, anytime."

A rustling sound catches my attention, and Blanche stands leaning against the corner of the porch, a sheen to her eyes. It's not often I catch that woman looking so emotional, so I must have done something right. She mouths the words "thank you" at me and I give her a simple nod. It's my role as Pres to look after everyone in the club.

Blanche makes her way to the swing pulling Sage from me and taking my place on the seat.

I move to leave them in peace but Blanche stops me with a hand on my wrist. "You're a good Pres, Marx. Whatever you decide, I'll stand by your decision."

I tip my chin as she releases my wrist and I can't help but rub my chest. Having Blanche at my back means a lot. I've seen the woman in action. If people think Chewy is scary, she has nothing on Blanche's pure unadulterated rage. I stood by her as she brought down a cult full of men, the same that Lovely escaped from. I know for a fact if I were to command it, she would lead the DRMC women in an all out assault. Scrap that, Chewy and Remy would lead them from behind their screens, Blanche would lead the rest on the ground. I freeze in place, realizing that without knowing it the DRMC women work as one, much like a special ops team. Fucking hell, our enemies won't know what hit them if we let the women loose.

Shaking my head I follow the veranda around the house, stepping over Chomper, who is sunning himself on the back porch. Laney is sitting next to him wearing denim overalls and rain boots on the wrong feet, with Mad Dog on the steps below her.

"Should we be worried about how much my granddaughter loves that gator?" he asks me, eyes never moving from the pair.

"If Rhodie married a waitress in town, then yeah, we should be worried. Instead he has Chewy as his Ol Lady so I think this is normal."

Mad Dog lets out a snort, bending a little to ruffle Laney's hair. She looks up at him and gives him a huge smile. I watch the old man melt and I wonder what he would be like with Bee and the rest of my kids, when I have them. I'm pretty sure mine won't be obsessed with alligators. Hopefully.

"What's the consensus so far?"

"The single brothers want to wait to hear what the brothers with families say. But the ones I've spoken to are all in favor of clapping back."

"And the women?" Mad Dog raises a brow, in the exact same way I know Rhodie and myself do.

"The women want blood. Their babies were put at risk. Chewy has some ideas for payback, Blanche, Nat and Vi want to storm their homes and Mira is in it for the storyline. Remy and Ana are happy to go along with what the others are proposing." I give my father a look and we both chuckle.

"Best thing that ever happened to us was when the women joined." Mad Dog shakes his head, a smile on his face.

"Kinda like the old days, huh?"

He grins at me before turning as the sound of crunching gravel gains our attention. A slick, black saloon car makes its way down the drive toward the house. I stand to my full height, arms crossed over my chest as Rhodie and Gus make their way to the bottom of the steps, each of them flanking Mad Dog as he stands.

The car slows to a stop, the engine dying before Sasha exits the drivers side. The large blonde makes his way to the back passenger side, eyes scanning our surroundings, as if determining whether it's safe or not.

"Don't you ever get sick of opening his door for him?" Rhodie smarts, a smirk on his face.

"Do you ever get sick of making sure Chewy is safe and

sound?"

Rhodie lets out a huff, "Touché Sasha."

Sasha steps back from the open door, allowing Roman to emerge.

"My friends, it's good to see you all in one piece. I'm sure you all remember Dima?" I nod at the other large blonde man. His piercing blue eyes cut straight to me, before looking past me at the house. I stand my ground, not taking my eyes off him until Roman interrupts. "Let's chat, shall we?" he says in such a jovial manner that it irritates me.

I grunt in response then turn to the door. Everyone knows this meeting is happening so they've all made themselves scarce. Vic Landry waits just inside the dining room for us, greeting Dima in a much friendlier manner than I did. I guess they're used to seeing all sorts of weird shit in Louisiana.

"So, what do you know?"

Pops

"Are you sure this is a good idea?" Ana asks, looking sceptical.

I don't bother to answer. Of course it's a good idea. They're all in my dining room learning important shit, and I don't know about everyone else, but I'm a nosy fucker.

"You know that Marx will just tell us what happens next anyway," Nat says in a bored tone.

"If he doesn't then I'll just get it out of Gus and then tell you all," Ana shrugs.

"Yeah because we can't rely on Chewy," Mira adds.

"Wait, why can't you rely on me?" Dayz asks, affronted that Mira would even suggest she was unreliable.

"You-" Mira jabs a finger in her direction, "are an unreliable witness. You can be in the same room as the men and still have no idea about any of the juicy stuff."

Dayz's brows pinch. "Why would I? I'm there to dazzle them with my superior brain, not listen to gossip." She taps some buttons on her phone, then gives me a thumbs up.

"Do you think you could go any faster, Pops? You're a lot heavier than you look," Remy grunts.

I should have grabbed the ladder, but with all the excitement around here getting everyone settled, the ladder is trapped in the back shed with a trailer in the way. "Sorry ladies, a little longer."

"Ow, he's on my boob!" Nat whisper yells, and I can hear the other women snorting.

"Those boobs are huge, surely they can cushion an old man for a little bit longer," Mira teases.

I finish securing the camera to the upper window frame, angled just right to get the picture and sound feedback from inside the dining room.

"You people own a security company, surely you have some fancy gadget that can do all this, not an old man on a pyramid of women," Ana says through clenched teeth.

"Nope," Dayz answers, tapping more damn buttons. "We're in, ladies and man. You can let Pops down now."

"What are you doing?"

I spin from my place at the top of the pyramid at the same time Ana and Nat do, causing us to wobble wildly.

"Someone grab him!"

Mira lunges from her spot next to Dayz, using her height to wrap her arms around my waist, holding me off the ground. Gasps sound out along with a shrieking belly laugh I recognize.

"You better not tell any-"

"Oh I won't have to tell anyone, I'll show them." Rider wanders off, staring at the phone in his hand before he bursts into giggles.

"We're getting that back, right?" Mira asks, but because she's still holding me like a wayward toddler, she breathes the words into my ear, creeping me the hell out. "Oh sorry, let me just put you right...there." She dumps me unceremoniously on the ground.

I take a good look around, checking if there are other brothers lurking out there, and thankfully I see nothing. But you can never assume shit when the DRMC is around. Dusting myself off I notice Lovely and Vi staring at us.

"So, are you gonna tell us what this was all about?" Vi asks, circling her finger in the air at us.

"Pops just put a bug at the top of the window frame so he can spy on Marx's meeting," Chewy says, matter of factly.

Lovely's brows make out with her hairline, close enough they're touching. She's still in her wheelchair, Vi pushing her.

"Um, does Marx know you're doing that?"

"Nope, and I'm not gonna tell him either," I answer, packing up the random bits and pieces surrounding us. I don't want to let on that we're spying.

I head toward Dayz's cabin, that's where we'll set up to watch Marx and the others. Debs is arranging popcorn and snacks as we speak. Obviously Lovely and Vi are just as intrigued as we are, because they follow behind. By the time we've made it

69

to Dayz's we've picked up a few other hangers-on. Rider has joined, as has Tank who came to give his woman a kiss and decided to stay. Mad Dog, Flack, Dex and Savage have turned up, and even though Sniper stormed out earlier this morning, he's now back and perched on the arm of my favorite chair. I should kick him off, but the kid is having a rough time.

We all squish in as best we can, Dayz dropping the projector so everyone will be able to see better. Vi parks Lovely up next to my chair, and I pat her hand in reassurance. I know that she respects Marx, even though she should just kick him to the curb, but anyway, she respects him and I know that this will be rubbing her the wrong way. She'll get used to it though. We're all on some level a bunch of rebels, so she'll come around. Besides, it's not really spying. If we wanted to do that we would have used the really high tech stuff. This is just us playing around. Yeah.

"OK, *koutou*, you all, I have three different flavors of popcorn and the brownie will be out of the oven soon." Debs says, bringing me my own plate of goodies. "I'm outta here to keep an eye on the babies. And to not get my arse kicked once Marx finds out what you lot did."

"Technically, it was only Pops, Nat and Ana," Chewy help-fully points out.

"Yeah, and I almost lost a titty for my troubles," Nat grumbles.

The bickering goes on a little longer, until Marx's voice booms through the speakers.

"Whoops, sorry guys," Remy apologizes, frantically hitting the volume button.

The whole room settles down, except for quiet bickering about fat asses taking up too much space on the couch and so on.

"*So, Roman, what do you know?*" Marx asks, leaning back in the spot I usually sit in. Cheeky fucker.

Roman wanders around the room, running a finger along the top of Marx's chair, before moving around the table, doing much of the same.

"God, that guy is such a dick," Rider says under his breath. "Oof, what was that for?" he asks when Ana claps him on the back of the head.

"That's my bestie you're talking about. He's just misunderstood," she harrumphs.

"*I know that you have pissed off the two Cordoza allies.*"

"*I believe it was you who pissed them off when you killed all the men in their family.*"

Roman grins at the statement, before schooling his features once more.

"*Besides, Cordoza didn't have any allies.*"

"*Ah, but he did. Two of his sisters married low level drug runners. The next thing you know those drug runners are lords and running their own cartels.*"

Marx doesn't give anything away. The kid is cool as a cucumber and I have to admit, he's good at this shit. He leans back in his chair, the only tell is a flicker of his eyes at Rhodie. "*In that case I haven't pissed off two cartels. **You've** pissed off two cartels with a familial grudge and they're taking it out on us.*"

"*I do believe it was your little Icer that pissed them all off when she shut down their lucrative operation.*"

Marx's eyes narrow as he stares Roman down. "*Are you trying to say we're in this together?*"

Roman bobs his head this way and that. He unbuttons his suit jacket, flicks the back and takes a seat. Right in front of

71

the goddamn camera, blocking our view of Marx .We can still see Vic, but it's Marx's reactions we want.

"Oh fucks sake! Get him to move his head, I can't see anything now!" Rider whines.

"How the hell are we going to do that, dumbass? Call Marx and get him to ask Roman to scooch to the right a little?" Flack growls.

With Roman's head in the way we can't read any of Marx's body language, or cues, to see if what Roman says is affecting him. Yeah, we can hear a little of what they're saying, but without watching their faces, it's just a game of outfoxing each other with the information sharing. Or lack thereof.

"Chewy! Zoom into Vic's face. He's never had a poker face, it might work in our favor," Blanche says.

"On it," Dayz frowns then zooms in on Vic.

Blanche is right, the kid has no poker face. I don't even know what Roman is saying, given he's facing away from the camera and Dayz must have given us the cheap, nasty surveillance equipment, but judging by Vic's face it's not good.

"Is it me, or does he look like he's going throw up?" Dex asks.

"Nah, that's just his face," Blanche comments, then snorts.

"Well, this is a waste of time. Nat, pass me that tray of brownies, would ya?" Savage asks, taking them from her outstretched hand and making a start on devouring them.

I shrug and decide to join him. It was a good plan, until Roman's fat head got in the way. We'll just have to wait to see what Marx says. If that doesn't work out, I'll just have to get on Gus's nerves until he caves. Either way, it'll be fun.

Chapter 8

Lovely

"Well hey there sleepy head," Marx smiles down at me and I'm not sure whether to be alarmed or not. I mean, I've seen him smile before, rarely, but this smile, it's full of teeth and I just never expected him to have so many. Or them to be so perfectly straight and white. I stare up at him while he beams down at me and I have no idea what to say or do. I can't even blame the pain meds because I'm sure they've worn off. Judging by the pain in my chest, they have.

I swallow a couple of times. "Um, hello."

My eyes dart around the room, looking for, I don't know what. He must notice because he turns toward the door before spinning back to look at me, "Oh, Vi has Bee in the farmhouse playroom with the other kids." He grins down at me. "Bee was full of energy when she woke up so we thought that would tire her out, playing with the big little kids."

What is happening? My brows pull down low and I grasp the throw blanket to my chest. Marx's eyes clock the movement and he frowns back at me.

"Um, would you like help getting up and maybe going to the bathroom?" He raises his bushy brow and I relax a little. This is more like the man I know. All gruff and growly.

I wriggle around in bed, trying to move myself up a little, to a more seated position without using my arms. My gunshot wound is in the upper left side of my chest, not far off my collar bone, so any real arm movement on that side sends sharp pains through me. Digging my heels into the soft mattress, I use my legs to shove my way up the bed until I get stuck on the pillow mountain Vi made for me.

"Whoa, shit, what are you doing! Stop wriggling!" Marx's large hands wrap around my waist as he gently lifts me to sitting. My wriggling has caused my shirt to ride up, the heat of Marx's hands sending a shiver through me. But it's all a silly crush. I need to get myself together and stop mooning over the wrong man.

Once I'm balanced on the side of the bed, my legs dangling over the side, Marx slowly removes his hands.

"Let me just get this chair and we'll wheel you into the bathroom."

There is no way I'm wheeling in there with Marx pushing me. For one it's tiny, and, secondly, he's been so overly helpful that he'd probably want to help situate me on the throne, and I'm not having that.

"I'd like to see if I could stand, maybe?" I ask him. He gives me a dubious look, one brow pinching in to a half frown almost. "Maybe ask Switch? I'm sure he'll be happy to help me."

"NO!" Marx growls. He stares wide-eyed at me, before softening his voice. "No, no, it's OK. I can help." He mutters something under his breath but I can't quite hear it.

74

I side eye him. He's been acting all screwy since I was in the hospital. Maybe he feels guilty because I took that bullet for him? That wasn't actually my plan, my plan was to get him out of the way. I would have done it for any of my family. Well, this family. Not my previous one. I know that makes me a bad person, but I have very little love for the people I left behind at the Keep. The ones I loved, they all got out and are helping people find new lives, better lives.

"So, ah, how do we want to do this?" Marx shuffles a little on his feet, shocking me by seeming nervous.

Looks like it's up to me to decide the best way. "Well, how about you hold your hands out," he holds his hands out palm down, tattoos on full display, "facing up." I grip them and turn them over, the heat from his hands surprising me.

I take a deep breath, shuffle my bottom closer to the edge of the bed so I can place my feet on the floor, then placing my hands into Marx's I use my leg strength to stand, Marx's hands keeping me steady. Once I'm upright a sway a little and Marx grips me tighter until I find my footing.

"There, I'm up," I whisper to myself, a little tug pulling at my lips.

I've lived through a lot of pain, and this is completely bearable compared to some of my past lessons.

"You good?" Marx bends his knees a little and dips his head so he can see my face.

"So good." I smile up at him and then shuffle forward a little.

It's not bad, so I take a bigger step. Then another. Then another, Marx stepping back with each one of my forward steps. Before I know it I'm outside the bathroom and I feel like doing a little dance. Joy spreads through my body and I know that today is just the first day of many joyful days. If life thought I had a hold of it before, it's gonna freak out at what I have in store for it now.

Marx helps me into the bathroom, and I let go of his hands, placing mine on the cool tile of the vanity.

"Thank you, I should be fine from here," I smile at Marx.

He dips his chin before backing out of the small room, closing the door gently behind him. I manage to do my business, redress and wash my hands all by myself, and once again I can feel my inner Lovely doing a dance. I don't really know how to dance, but I'm going to add it to my list of New Life things I want to do. Right under dating. I snort to myself and then choke on my spit when a loud knock almost beats my door down.

"Shit, sorry!" Marx calls through the door, "I just spoke to Switch, he said it would be OK for you to shower, if you wanted."

I gasp and then feel giddy at the prospect. My long, dark hair feels greasy and gross, as does my whole body. I'm sure I stink of disinfectant and hospital.

"I'd love that!"

"Ah, just one thing. I may have to help you." The words hang in the air and I'm not sure whether to cry or not. I really want that damn shower, but can I stand to be naked in front of the guy I had a crush on?

I grip the vanity as I look down my body and think 'damn it all the heck'. I know it was a crush that was going nowhere, and when I look at him now he's just my Pres, and maybe a friend I can rely on this one time.

"Yes, I'd love that. The shower, not you helping me." I cringe at my reflection, and mime banging my head on the wall.

"OK, I'm coming in."

Marx enters the small space and instantly the room is swallowed up by his bulk. He looks as awkward as I feel, which leaves me feeling a little bit better about the whole thing.

"So, ah, I think I'll just need you to help me with my shirt and bra, and then, ah, I'll be OK with the rest," I stammer out. "I have no idea why I'm being so weird, I've been naked in front of people before." Marx's eyes shoot to mine, and now I have verbal diarrhea and can't stop. "I mean, not strangers, couples. Couples, I knew" His face turns thunderous. "My husband used to run sex education for married couples in the Keep and he would, um, he would do live, um, what's the word? Lessons?"

Marx's jaw ticks. "He would use you to demonstrate sex? In front of people?"

"Couples," I whisper. I have no idea why the hell I shared that. Could the drugs have addled my brain?

He says nothing, just turns the water on. We wait in silence for it to heat up before he turns to me and grips the hem of my shirt. He gently tugs it, letting me tuck my good arm in through the arm hole before he moves it over my head, then lets it fall from my bad arm. His warm hands land on my shoulders as he gently turns me to face the shower, unfastening my bra with lightning speed, then pushing it forward, letting it fall from me onto the floor.

"I can do the rest, thank you," I say, my voice thick with emotion. Mortified that I shared one of my secrets, and raw, so raw at the memory.

A grunt sounds out before I hear the door click shut. I drop my pants and panties then step into the small shower stall. I manage to wash my body with one hand, trying to avoid my dressings. It's difficult, but I'm sure Switch will be able to patch them up if I get them too wet. I decide to go for broke and try washing my hair too, but it's a big job and halfway through I can feel myself starting to flag. I'm puffing a little, and my good arm aches.

"Lovely, are you alright?"

"Yeah, um, just trying to rinse my hair,"

I'm certain I hear a grumble from the other side of the door, and then I hear it on the other side of the stall. A squeak escapes me and I feel myself going down, down, down, down until large hands grip me.

"Shit, fuck, I just can't stop fucking up," Marx curses. "Sorry," he says to me. "Sorry, I gave you a fright. Um, why don't you turn around and I'll rinse out your hair? Um, no need to feel shy, I've seen all this before. Nothing special, same stuff, different woman, you know?"

I freeze and Marx sucks a breath in, "Fuck! I'm sorry I didn't mean-"

"It's fine!" I rush to say. My cheeks heat and my lower lip starts to tremble.

It's nothing, he's seen it all before, I'm not special. I repeat the words over and over until I've blinked away the tears threatening to fall. If there was ever a reason to move on and find myself a good man, it's being told by the one you used to have feelings for that they've been with so many women that what I've got is nothing special. The same shit, so to speak. Gah, I don't even know why it affected me. I've had worse insults thrown at me. Weak. Barren. Frigid. Disgusting. Good for nothing.

"Is this OK?" Marx's murmur breaks me out of my spiralling thoughts.

"Yes, that's fine."

"Good. It's, um, I think it's done. Let's get you dried and dressed. We have dinner and then Church."

I nod and follow his lead. He wraps me in a huge, fluffy towel and, with mechanical motions, he has me dry without sparing me a passing glance. I guess that's better than being ogled by someone who doesn't like you like that.

He helps me dress in a soft gown, then my fluffy robe because, " You'll be in bed after Church, no use getting changed again," then back in the wheelchair.

I'm emotionally exhausted after that shower and yet I feel better than I have in days. Now all I have to do is get better so I can move on with my plans for my life.

Marx

What the actual fuck is wrong with me? Why do I keep saying horrible shit to Lovely? I must have some type of brain damage because there is no way, *no way* I just blurted out that I've seen it all before and it's nothing special. Because that's the exact opposite of what I think. She's breathtakingly beautiful, and I'm a pig for admiring her. When I stepped into the bathroom and saw her dark hair plastered to her back, water sluicing down her curves, I almost swallowed my tongue. That was after I'd left the bathroom to beat the hell out of the mattress on the bed when she revealed that she'd been used as a sex toy by her husband. Perhaps that's what had me blurting shit

79

out? Not only was her husband a filthy animal, using her in public for his own sick desires, but here I was ogling her like a teenage boy with the Sears catalogue. Clearly my dumb brain thought the best way to make her feel comfortable was to say some fucked up shit.

I growl at myself and take a deep breath. I need to pull myself together. Roman as per usual decided to piss me off and offer some level of help, but there's always something needed in return. I'll have to run that by my men and women. Joy for me. At least Sniper seems to be doing marginally better after the conversation we had.

"You alright, brother?"

Sniper looks at me, his dark eyes giving away nothing. "Not really, Pres. How the fuck do I choose between my patch, and my blood brother?"

"Why do you need to?"

He gives me a bored look, before gazing out to the backyard. This is the second time today I've found myself on this swing seat, and I have to say it probably won't be the last time I'll sit here, thinking.

"There's no way he can walk away from this."

I run a hand down my beard, "Is he the reason you dislike cartels?"

He shakes his head, eyes never moving from the horizon. "I hate them because the Cordozas kidnapped my baby sister when I was away on tour. Refused to give her back even when we paid the ransom. They got her hooked on drugs, then charged my family for the cost of them. The debt was so huge there was no way my family could cover it. Not even with my salary." He lets out a deep breath. "I came home for leave, found my mother and younger siblings living in poverty, all the money I had sent went to the Cordozas to pay a debt that wasn't ours. I decided to fight for her, bring her home, get her the help she'd need to heal." He swallows, voice thick with grief. "The day I found her she was in a Cordoza whore house, four guys were running a train on her dead body. She vomited at some stage and aspirated."

"Fuck, brother, I didn't know, I'm so sorry."

He turns his gaze to mine. "She was 14."

I reach out and grip his shoulder. It's all I can do, to pass my strength on to him. "What would you like to do?"

"I want to burn them all to the ground, but most of all, I want Joseph. I get to put him down. No one else."

"Adam, that's your brother–"

"No brother of mine would join the men who killed our sister. I know who my real brothers are, and they are all here in this house."

"Marx?" Lovely's voice cuts through and I give her a tight smile. I'm pretty sure I've smiled more today at Lovely than I ever have in my life.

"Let's roll out," I say lamely. I can only hope the Love Pres has some advice for me because this version of me is not only messing shit up, but he's also pretty fucking dweeby.

We head out, joining the rest of the Tombs family as we all walk the path to the main house. I'd rather get Church over and done with, but I told them we'd make a decision after dinner, and Mama Debs has been cooking up a storm, so the least we can do is enjoy her food and each other's company first. It isn't going to be as easy as I had hoped, but if we don't get this shit under control they'll just keep coming for us.

"Bout time you lot arrived, I'm starving," Pops grumbles from the head of the table.

Looking around, Pops is at one end, Mad Dog at the other, and somehow, it feels so fitting. We all fall in line, squishing around the large, wooden table. A table that is as scarred and as battered as some of the people around it.

"I know that we have heavy thoughts on our minds, but for tonight, let's just enjoy each other's company. Eat, drink, laugh and then we'll get to the heavy shit, *ne?*" Mama Debs says, each of us huffing out a laugh,

"Here, here!" I yell, thumping the table a little. The brothers join in stomping their feet and we all get into the food, passing dishes, ribbing each other, the meal a welcome stress relief to the shit we're dealing with.

I help Lovely by cutting up her food, and at some stage Bee ends up on my lap and she eats from my plate and Lovely's. Lovely's eyes have been wide the whole time, and I'm sure my change in behaviour has to have her head spinning. I really need to sit down with her and lay out my intentions, but I want to do that when we're in a more settled time. Not when I'm juggling revenge. I want her to be my full priority, and until that point comes I'll just have to show her how I feel with these little gestures. And maybe keeping my mouth shut.

"Pops! There's some police mens coming up the drive!" Cove yells from her seat at the kids table near the window.

Chair legs scrape the floor as we all stand in unison, cutlery clattering, the women herding the kids further into the middle of the house.

"Don't worry, there's a panic room in the basement," Lovely murmurs, reading my thoughts exactly.

I lean down, place Bee in her lap and stare at her as Mira wheels her away. "TumTum, Chef and Flack, you follow the women and children, keep them safe."

"Yes, Pres." My men do as I ask, the rest of us head out to welcome our guests.

I lead the way, VP and SAA following behind along with

Chewy, Pops and Gus, then the rest of my men, the Landrys bringing up the rear. All together there are close to twenty of us, so I know the Sheriff must be shitting his pants right about now.

"Sheriff," I nod as his eyes narrow, taking in the backup I've brought with me.

"John. Just checking in to see how you're getting on. I've had calls that your compound has been abandoned."

"Not abandoned, just undergoing renovation." My grin has him taking a step back.

"Really, huh." He runs a hand nervously down his face, glancing at Moss who is leaning on the front of his cruiser, a smirk on his face. "I must have heard wrong."

"Perhaps," I shrug.

Silence hangs in the air while Sheriff Kelson sweats it out. I'm not sure what his play is, whether he's come to see whether I took the bullet aimed at me or not. As law enforcement he should have known that I wasn't hospitalized as all gunshot wounds are reported immediately. Goes to show how shitty a Sheriff he really is. He chances a glance behind me, his eyes stopping on each one of my men, probably doing a head count or some shit.

"I heard you had a man at the hospital, terrible business with a gun, perhaps? I was out of town at the time, so I'm only going through reports as we speak." He clears his throat.

"Yeah, like you said, terrible business." I don't give him anything else. Fuck him.

If he's here on some type of recon mission, then he can do his own work. Clearly the hit he led did nothing except paint a target on his fat, pasty back.

"Well, I'll leave you all to it. What is this? Family dinner or

83

something?"

"Or something."

"Right." He hesitates for a moment, then waddles his ass back to his vehicle, slamming the door behind him. He stares at me through the windscreen with pure hate in his eyes before peeling out, kicking up dust, three other cruisers following behind.

"Well, that was anticlimactic," Moss says, watching his boss and colleagues leave like a bat outta hell.

"Wanna join us for dinner?"

A smile tugs at his lips, "Who am I to say no to a Mama Debs special?"

We turn back to the house and I know that we need to sort this shit out, ASAP. But first, we got dessert to finish.

Chapter 9

Lovely

"So, I guess we just...wait?" Vi whispers as we all sit together in the panic room that Pops has.

I have to admit, taking it in, that he's done a good job of it. At the Keep the panic room was basically a tornado shelter. Here, it's furnished with plush fabrics, there's a large screen TV and a selection of DVDs and video games. There's a kitchenette area as well as a fully stocked bathroom. Chewy even showed us all the back rooms (yes, Pops has back rooms to his panic room) where he keeps shelves of food and toiletry goods all laid out like a grocery store.

"Grown ups are always complaining," Cove says in her overly loud voice, rolling her eyes at Elio and Jovie. They're on the floor playing some type of board game. Bee, Laney, Juno, Nat's daughter Rosie and Ana's son Jr are all around the sameish age, so they're toddling around messing up the big kids' game.

"Grown ups have a lot of things to worry about," Mira says.

"Like what? Making moony eyes at each other?"

"Ugh, gross! My mom and dad do that ALL the time," Jovie says in disgust.

"So do mine! But maybe less since Tess was born," Cove replies.

"I'm way too tired for all that," Blanche says, addressing the adults. Well, us Girl Gang because Chef, TumTum and Flack are busy comparing their guns and knives.

"Hear, hear!" Ana says, leaning over to high five her.

"Wait, your kid is like, old." Chewy says, wide eyed.

"Yeah but he still doesn't sleep through the night." Ana replies, smiling down at Jr as he toddles toward her.

"You need a proper routine for him. Feeding, educational, physical activity and then a good bedtime routine. Laney is a good sleeper because of all those things," Chewy says with a nod.

Some of the girl gang roll their eyes, but I just smile at Chewy. One of the ways she likes to care for people is to give them strict routines and statistics.

"Ladies, we have the go ahead to head up now. Marx is calling Church," Chef calls out.

"But my browni-"

"Church with dessert," TumTum adds, looking just as relieved at the prospect as Mira.

The men do some type of complicated code on the touch screen pad thing attached to the wall before the door slides open, revealing the basement. It looks like every other basement, slightly neglected with all sorts of forgotten items neatly stacked on shelves.

"May I have this honor?" TumTum asks as he bends toward me. I give him a grin and a nod and he slides his arm around my back, the other beneath my knees and lifts me into his arms.

We slowly climb the stairs, my arms holding around his neck in the hopes I can keep my full weight off him. I'm short like my sister, and all Landry women are built sturdy. Since I had Bee I've also filled out a little, making me nowhere near as light as a feather. Flack opens the door at the top of the stairs and TumTum carries me through to the main living room, where we're met with a low growl.

"What the fuck do you think you're doing?"

"Just helping Lovely up the stairs, Prez." TumTum gently places me in my chair that Flack has just parked up next to us.

"You don't touch her." Marx jabs a finger at poor TumTum who looks equally confused and like he's going to soil his pants.

"He was helping me. I don't suppose you'd want me to walk up the flight of stairs, would you?" I ask in my calm voice. No need to raise it. I've done that before out of anger and well, let's just say I learned my lesson.

"He had his hands all over you!" Marx whirls around, glaring at me.

"You are being ridiculous and we have bigger things to worry about than who has their hands on me." I offer back with a serene face even though I want to get my angry, no, livid face on. Who does he think he is? TumTum was only helping.

Marx takes a deep breath and appears to shrink as he lets it out slowly. I know he's under a lot of pressure, but geez, the man needs to get a grip. What and who helps me is of no concern to him. He runs a hand down his beard and nods, stepping back from TumTum. I reach out and grip TumTum's hand before thanking him. He gives me a tight smile and pushes me next to Mira who is sitting at the end of one of the couches.

"That was hot! Did you see him get all 'me man! Don't touch

man's woman, argh'," she rifles around in her top, retrieving her ever present notepad and pencil.

"Why is Mira making wookie sounds?" Chewy frowns. She doesn't even wait for an answer, walking past and taking a seat on Rhodie's lap.

Everyone finds places to sit or stand, the room filling up with bodies. My brothers are along the back wall, the Tombs dotted between MC members and Moss is sitting near his sister and Jules. As per usual Mama Debs and Sage have the kids occupied somewhere. There are so many of them that at some stage it won't be practical for Mama Debs to watch over all of them. I wonder if the club has thought about a daycare or something?

I'm pulled out of my thoughts by Marx thumping twice on the wall, gaining our attention.

"Thank you for being here. We have some things to discuss and some decisions to make." He looks at each and every one of us, before clearing his throat. "We all know that Serpiente is out there and I'm sure we can all guess, with the cartel's approval, he is coming for us. We fucked up their business, so they're going to retaliate. First step was obviously sending the sheriff to do their dirty work. The hit failed, and now Kelson is scrambling. Moss, do you have any insights?"

Moss shakes his head. "I've known he was off for a while. Just a weird vibe. Normally if you came to me and said he's the guy who attacked your compound, I'd have thought you'd all been high or something. But Chewy showed me the security footage, and that along with his unpredictable moods and stress breakdowns, I can't ignore the signs." He tips his head side to side. "In the run up to our little visit just then, he'd spent at least an hour in a heated phone call. On a cell that isn't department issue. As soon as he hung up he left the office like a bat outta hell calling me to back him up."

"Does he know you have a connection to the MC?" Savage asks in his rough voice.

"In fairness, I have a connection to the Tombs. Who happen to have a connection with the MC. It's tenuous at best. I mean, do we even really know each other?" Moss smirks.

Marx huffs out a laugh, as do the rest of us. "So, if we were to ask you to-"

"At this point I'm a senior law enforcement officer with concerns over how my superior is behaving. I believe there is a safety issue around his behavior and I have already reported it. I'd imagine he'll be stood down once my evidence is presented." Marx's brow raises. "Once stood down there will no longer be protection from the force at his beck and call. Be a pity if something were to happen to him."

Chewy grins and claps her hands, sharing a look with Pops. I hope the sheriff has a come to Jesus moment, because if he doesn't he'll be having a Come to Tombs moment, and that seems a lot more painful.

"OK, well that seems like one of our problems is going to be taken care of very soon," Mad Dog grins.

"So, that leaves the cartels," Wire says. "The sheriff is in business with the La Sombre Roja and Cartel de Silencio cartels. La Sombre Roja has contacts in Louisiana, while the other has links here in Texas. They were both small time while the Cordoza family were in power, but when Roman cleaned them out, the other two rose up, splitting the business between them. Up until recently they worked well, split the drug trade evenly and entered into the kiddy market, snatching kids while on vacation with their parents, and then sending them back this way. That's where Candice and this other woman, Renae, come in. Serpiente acted as the middleman, investing cartel money and making sure the women were there to collect the kids."

"And we fucked that up," Rhodie adds.

I grip the armrests of my chair, knowing that men like the cartel and the sheriff don't give up easily. They've had a taste of power and they hate when it's taken from them. It all started with Vi protecting Juno and getting the baby farm operation shut down, then Chewy found Laney and messed it up again. They'll be scrambling, trying to keep power over their businesses, the grip tightening. If we thought they were cruel before, they'll be even worse now. We've kicked the hornet's nest and it's going to get a lot worse.

"So, the attack on the clubhouse with the sheriff and those upper level cartel members, was that a warning?" Rider asks, jiggling his knee up and down. He's usually pretty hyper, but he's looking like a coiled spring, ready to pop off at any moment.

Marx shares a look with Switch, then he stares at me. He swallows, his Adam's apple bobbing. "It was a hit."

The room erupts with "what the fucks?" and it takes a lot of thumping by Marx to settle everyone down. My fingers find their way to the left side of my chest. It still aches, but I'd rather that than Marx to have been killed. I know Rhodie is the VP and will step up, but I just can't imagine the MC ever being the same.

"So, they were trying to take you out?" Flack frowns.

Rhodie steps forward and dumps a handful of spent shell casings on the table. "It was a hit on all of us."

I stay where I am as the men all move forward as one, looking at the casings. "What the fuck!? They have our names carved into them!" Dex yells, throwing one down in disgust.

Blanche explodes out of her seat, baby Tess's body bobbing in the baby sling as she storms to the table. She rifles through the pile, picking one up and then freezing in place. "They have my kids on there! Tav, what the fuck?!" Any shock she is feeling is pushed out by her absolute pure rage. "They die. I don't give a shit how we do it and how many we have to kill, they target my babies, they die." I admire Blanche in her fury. She's like the valkyries I saw in the Thor movie. She's tougher than me. A lot tougher. Physically and mentally.

Marx takes measured steps toward me before dropping to his haunches. He grasps my hand in his, gently turning it over. His fist hovers over my open palm and he drops a casing into it.

"I may be a fucking idiot sometimes, but I promise you, I'll keep her safe." He holds my gaze before standing and moving back to his place at the front of the room.

The cool metal feels as if it's burning my skin, I don't want to look but I know I have to. I can feel the metal is rough from where the name is carved. Turning it over in my fingers, there, in jagged writing is the word "Bee". White hot fury burns through me in a way I've never felt before. My hands are shaking and it's not from fear, it's from the rage pumping through my veins. I don't care what happens to me or my body. I gave up fearing death a long time ago, but the thought that my baby, the little girl that *saved* me, that led me here to this life, a better life for both of us, the thought that she might be taken from me violently by men who are more preoccupied by their own greed than by their humanity, that burns me to my soul. No one will take my baby from me. No man or God. I will see to that myself.

"They will die," I say, louder than I thought as silence

blankets the room.

"Lovel–"

"No! You know where I came from, you all know where I escaped." I look around the room, at my family all gathered here, all of them in danger. "I will not be a victim to cruel men ever again, and neither will my daughter. They need to die. All of them," I say quietly, steadily, with a passion I've never felt before.

Marx's eyes flash with something I can't put my finger on before they fill with heat, and I know that he knows what I say isn't an empty threat. At this moment my body may still be a little weak and battered, but I feel a strength in my soul. At this moment I feel like Blanche, like a valkyrie, and I vow to protect my baby and my family.

They will not win.

Marx

I tear my gaze away from Lovely and the fire that is burning inside her to address my club. "So, we're in agreement?"

"Burn them to the ground," Ana growls, cuddling Jr in her lap.

Cheering breaks out and my shoulders relax a little. I didn't realize how much tension I was holding until this moment. I knew the consensus sounded like they'd all be down to exact revenge, but having women and children in our care means we have to think about their wellbeing too. Luckily for me, our women are more bloodthirsty than we give them credit for.

"You're gonna have a problem on your hands," Mad Dog murmurs as he sidles up next to me.

"You mean other than the two fucking cartels and one sheriff on our ass?" I throw back.

He snorts, looking around the room, his eyes hovering on the women huddled in a group. "You can control your men, we all know that. Your biggest problem, besides the shit coming down on you, is that those women," he tips his head in their direction, "they want blood, and they'll do anything to get it." He slaps me on the shoulder and throws his head back, laughing so hard his body shakes.

I really want to tell him to fuck off, but he's right. I don't appreciate his fucking mirth at my dilemma, so I slap my hand on his shoulder, and whisper in his ear, "In that case, I need a man I can trust. You're on the women and Pops."

My dad's shocked gaze meets mine and the look on his face is priceless. I slap him once more and shove him in the direction of the group of misfits that I can already see are coming up with a plan. Knowing I need to nip that in the bud, I thump the wall again. Everyone settles down instantly. We need to get rid of our little problem as quickly as possible. If this shit drags on too long the women are liable to go rogue.

"Chewy! Give me the first idea that comes to mind on how to get us out of the shit," I bark in her direction. She nods once, then I see her fingers tapping in the way they do when she's thinking.

Everyone waits quietly to see what she comes up with. I may be the Pres, but as my father pointed out earlier, Chewy is the best we have at information, strategy and planning shit. I mean, sometimes it may not be a well defined plan, but they're always diabolical and it'll get us to our particular goal, which is wiping out the threat before it wipes us out.

She slowly moves her gaze around the room, her lips moving, every now and then her head bobbing side to side. She stares at Moss for a moment, before leaning over to Rhodie and murmuring something. They nod to each other and then she closes her eyes, fingers tapping faster and faster.

Her eyes fly open suddenly. "We'll need to split up. Fight them on three different fronts." She holds her hand up, stopping anyone from saying anything. "I know that we see our power as a collective, but that won't work this time. We have people gunning for us from Texas and Louisiana. A coordinated hit on the same day, same time will be the best way to take them out. We hit one, they get word to the other and it becomes a shit storm."

Savage nods in agreement. "It's really the only way to stop them coming for us. Hit them when they're meeting with their contacts stateside."

"Ana, I'll need Roman's help," Chewy states, typing madly on her laptop.

"Yeah, Roman has asked a favor." I say, ignoring the groans from everyone around me. Fuck, I don't want to do anything for Roman, but he's helped us out twice in recent times, so we really owe him. Besides, it's in his best interests. He was pissed when he found out his best friend was at the compound when it was hit. He may come across as a cold bastard, hell, anyone in a position of power does, it's part of our persona, but I know he cares deeply for the people he calls family, and in this case, that's Ana and her family.

"What the hell does he want now?" Flack grumbles.

"He wants any product the cartels have," I answer. Eyebrows raise before Rider chuckles.

"He's going to take over their drug business, huh? Fucking typical. As soon as we clean someone out, Roman comes swaggering in, waving his big Russian dick around."

"Keep my man's dick out of your mouth, thank you," Sasha says in his accented voice.

"How in the fuck did you get here so fast? Wait, why are you here?" Rider says, ignoring the dick in the mouth comment.

"We were at a little cafe not far from here when Chewy messaged," Roman answers with a smirk. "And I do love to wave my big Russian dick around."

"Thanks for coming," Chewy addresses Roman without looking at him. "What do you have for me?"

"I have the information, but this a, how do you say, symbiotic relationship, no?" Roman takes a seat in a recliner that Sniper vacated, choosing to move further near the back of the room.

Chewy stares at him blankly for a moment. "I've forwarded the chemical breakdown of the drugs both Cartel de Silencio and La Sombre Roja are dealing. In theory it won't take much tweaking of their current stock to match yours."

I shake my head. If we were one percenters then I'd definitely be doing what Roman has planned. Take over two cartels' drug stock, tweak them to his recipe and then sell them on with fuck all outlay. He's a criminal mastermind, and that's without the rest of the shady shit I know he gets up to. I glance at him, his crisp suit and slicked back dark hair at odds with his fair skin. Eyes so dark as to almost look black, the dude gives creepy vampire vibes and you can't tell me otherwise.

"Ah, Chewy, have I told you how much I enjoy working with

you?" He grins at her and it makes him look even more like fucking Dracula. "You have two weeks to plan whatever it is you have planned. Both cartels like to deliver on the first of the month."

"How dumb are these people?" Mira bursts out. "The first of the month? That's just begging to be killed. Don't they know you have to change up their movements, be all unpredictable so people like us-" she waves her arms around, "- don't murder them? This exact thing happened in a book I wrote, where the dumb guys weren't cartel, they were Bratva - sorry, Roman-" snickers break out around the room while Roman looks mildly offended, "The Bratva always do their drug drop on the same day, at the same time, from the same spot. My MC figured it out and then lay in wait. But they were even *dumber* than that because not only did they have their drugs with them, but also the scientist guy who was working for them to keep his daughter safe. Obviously the Pres from the MC fell in love with the daughter who it turns out is hot WITH a brain and they had some really amazing sex scenes in the back of the drug truck on the way to the compound." Mira only stops talking because she runs out of breath.

We all stare at her, and I wonder if there's more or if she's done.

"Can I just say that the premise sounds fabulous, but the Bratva would never be that stupid," Roman says, throwing Mira an odd look.

Mira shrugs and cuddles into Tank who looks at her like she invented boobs or something.

"Vodka, Vows and Very Bad Decisions!" Nat yells, pointing at Mira who yells back and they stare at each other flapping their hands. "I *knew* I knew that storyline!" They cackle and

I'm unsure whether I should stop them or not. The noise starts to calm a little and then Nat spins toward me. "Sorry, Pres, as you were."

I nod at Nat, before addressing my club. "Looks like we hit them in two weeks. Computas I want you to pull as much intel as you can in the meantime."

"Aye aye Captain!" Chewy salutes.

"That leaves us with the sheriff," Gus points out.

"Give it two days, max," Moss says. "I've already gotten an email from my superiors asking for me to step up in the interim." He looks around the room. "My little sister was in that clubhouse when you were attacked. Believe me, I won't stand in the way of whatever you have planned."

I step forward, holding out my hand. Moss has always been a good guy, but I never knew how good it'd be to have law enforcement on my side until now. "Thank you,"

"Just bring him to justice. Whatever that looks like," he says.

"Will do, brother." Dropping his hand I move back to the spot I was standing in. I don't know why, but it just feels right for me to be here, in this spot. "We have two weeks and in that time anything could go down. The threat level is fucking high so we need to decide if we shut down the businesses and lock down, or if we keep them open and double up on security. Make it look like we're unaffected." I look around the room, everyone putting thought into it.

It's a fucking hard decision. The few businesses we own we work ourselves, but there are others, like the gym Dex runs and Remy works part-time, that have civilians employed, and there's no way in hell I want innocent lives threatened because of us.

"I know I'm new to how the MC businesses run, but do we

have extra money or something that will cover the non-club employees? I'd hate for us to shut down and our employees struggle," Lovely says in her soft voice.

I try to hide my smile. It wasn't that long ago Lovely was ready to kill. Now she's worried about the welfare of our non-club employees and their families. I really am a greedy bastard for wanting such a woman. Speaking of, I need to corner TumTum later and apologize. When I saw Lovely in his arms, my cool, calm, collected self that I was praised for in the military flew right out the window and I was ready to give the brother a beat down. I really need to get my shit in order but hell, the woman is fucking perfect and I know I have a long road to get a chance with her.

"Yeah, we can cover the wages for a good few weeks, Lovely, no need to worry," Wire smiles at her.

"In light of the situation, I move that we lock down until we can get rid of the current problem." I look around the room, and everyone's hands go up in agreement.

"Can I ask one question?" Pops asks. He's been rifling through the shell casings on the table, standing them up. If I didn't know any better I would say he wasn't paying any attention to what we've been talking about, but I do know better and Sid Tombs sees and hears everything.

"Yeah, go ahead Pops."

"I know who Kaia is, but who the fuck are Annie-Bella and Jackson?"

"Kaia? Are you sure?" Judge says, pushing Dex out of the way to get to Pops, snatching the casing up into his giant hand. The brother pales, and he grips the back of Pops' chair, "Shit," he whispers, "We need to bring her in to lock down. She's going to fucking kill me."

Chewy claps her hands and Mira laughs loudly, "I can't wait to see this go down."

Chapter 10

Lovely

We stand outside the diner, all lined up ready to go inside. After Judge explained in detail who Kaia was to him, it was decided that we would bring her in for lockdown. Us women had already heard the whole story from Kaia's point of view, and I wasn't surprised to find out that back in the day Judge was exactly as dumb as she said he was.

"So, how do we want to play this?" Chewy asks, looking blankly through the window.

"We don't play it any way, Chewy. Remember, we all decided Judge would handle this on his own? We're just here to support both of them," I say, trying to gently remind her that we're here for moral support.

"Yeah, we'll need to go in and smooth it over because as soon as Judge walks in there and says 'Hey, remember the time that we boned and then I went and got a BJ from the head cheerleader when you had important shit to tell me? Well, it turns out, that somehow got you on the radar of two cartels and now your life is in danger so I need you to accompany me on my big, roaring motorcycle that will do all sorts of things to your private parts and I'll bring you to live with me at a farmhouse with the other 435 members of my family because my last home got exploded." Mira says in a deep voice. I really envy how many words she can use in any one sentence.

Chewy rolls her eyes and then nudges Pops who nudges Nat who nudges Ana who nudges Remy who nudges Vi who nudges Mira who nudges me. I turn to do the same to Blanche but I'm met with her palm in my face.

"I've got eyes, I can see him coming." She stares me down then rolls her eyes. "Go on then, just this one time."

I beam at how generous my big sister is and I nudge her, tipping my head in Judge's direction with a smile. He nods at us and is about to get the door when a kid on a skateboard rolls up to him, jumping off, kicking it and catching it in his hand.

"Watch out old man," the kid says, snickering at the look on Judge's face. The face that could probably make grown men pee their pants.

"Uh oh, this isn't going to go well. Look at his face! He looks like he's going to murder someone. We better get in there quick, because he can't approach Kaia with that face," Remy says, rushing after Judge through the door.

The rest of us share a look and then all bolt for the door. I'm already gaining my strength back, and I'm feeling pretty good. Last night after Church I passed out in my bed and woke up 16 hours later, fully refreshed. I reduced my pain medication too. I've had worse pain in my life and managed to make it through. Royal was not a gentle man. I've had all manner of broken bones and injuries. I have half a spleen from a particularly bad beating because he was annoyed I got my monthly cycle. Every month that I wasn't pregnant he would beat me, not even fathoming that the reason we weren't getting pregnant was because he was 67 years old. Each time I got my monthly I felt blessed, until I had to take my punishment. Almost eight years into our marriage and I found out I was pregnant with Bee. I was terrified and excited and nauseous. Looking back I'm glad that I took all those beatings. If I had fallen pregnant early on in our marriage I would never have had the strength to leave.

"Come on Lovely, we're missing the show!" Blanche hisses.

We push through the door and come to a stop. Chewy looks left, then right and then decides that it's better for us to all sit at the counter, seeing as that's where Judge is standing with an odd look on his face. We all take a seat and I turn at the sound of motorcycle pipes outside. There was a time where the sound of the pipes would frighten me, now they make me feel safe. I grin at Mad Dog as he walks into the diner and his eyes land on us all perched up at the counter.

"Hey Mad Dog, come to offer moral support?" I ask as he takes the seat next to mine.

"Nah," he chuckles. "Was in the neighborhood." He gazes around the diner, sizing everyone up, "And I'm on protection detail. I know Judge is with you, and Chewy and Blanche are dangerous in their own right, but you can never have too much back up. Right?"

I smile and pat his rough hand. "Especially with Marx about to put us on lockdown."

"Especially with that," he agrees. "But he knows you women well enough to know that none of you would listen if he put his foot down and said you had to stay home."

A grin stretches my lips. That's pretty much what happened this morning as I got ready to come out with the Girl Gang. I have no idea why Marx has been hanging around my house helping out. I mean it's not unwelcome, as I still struggle with things. I can't pick up Bee or anything and getting dressed is a pain, but Blanche helped with that this morning while Marx looked grumpy on the couch. He tried to forbid me from joining the Girl Gang, and I let him know exactly what I thought of that. I'm grabbing life by the balls and I definitely don't have time or space in my new life to be bossed around by a man. Actually, no, that's not quite right. I'm happy to be bossed around by my Pres when it comes to club things. I may not be an Ol Lady, or a club member, but I still feel in my bones that the DRMC is my family and that I'm a valued member of said family. I'm just not happy with being bossed around in my own home by a man that is not mine.

"Ah dude, wanna stop staring at my sister like that?" All our heads snap toward the kid from before, who is standing behind the counter of the diner, staring Judge down. He looks to be around sixteen or so, but big for his age. He's half covering a girl around his age, a small brunette with a cherubic face.

"Sorry, I was looking for Kaia,"

Both kids share a look. "What do you want her for?" The boy asks, his eyes narrowed.

Judge's cheeks color and he runs a hand over his bald head before gripping the back of his neck. "I, ah, just want to have a word with her, if thats OK?"

The kids share another look before the boy flicks his head toward where we're sitting. The girl nods and then walks toward us. I quickly turn around to make it look like I've not been staring and eavesdropping.

103

"Hello ladies and men!" She greets us cheerily, a big grin on her face. "Welcome to The Diner, what can I get y'all?"

"Well, aren't you the sweetest thing?" Pops says. "I ain't never seen you round these parts, are you a new hire?"

Her cheeks pinken a little and she shakes her head, "Naw, my momma owns this place. Jax and I are helping out after school," She tips her head to the boy that's glowering at Judge.

"Huh, is that so?" Pops says, running a hand down his chin, eyes narrowed.

"Ah shit," Mad Dog mumbles beside me. "This just got real messy."

At that moment a dish clatters to the ground as Chewy yells out "Timber!" We turn to see Judge on his ass on the floor, covered in waffles and sauce, Kaia looking mortified.

"Mom! What the hell happened?" The boy yells, rushing to his mother, the little brunette waitress at his side.

Mira turns wide eyes our way. "MOM" she mouths and we all turn to watch the scene playing out in front of us. Now that Kaia, the boy and the girl are all standing around Judge we can see it clear as day. Those kids are tiny versions of the very, very large man sitting on the floor.

"Ah hell, kid. Let's get you cleaned up and sort this shit out, huh?" Mad Dog says, gripping Judge under the arm.

He's such a good man, and a good father, I can see how Marx and Rhodie have turned out the way they have.

"Ah dammit, I wanted to watch him grovel to that little lady with syrup dripping down his bald noggin," Pops grumbles and I snort because I can see exactly why Chewy and her brothers have turned out the way they have.

Kaia and her kids clean up the mess Judge left behind, and watching them you can feel their closeness. The boy acts as a protector to his mom and sister and the daughter fusses over the both of them. They're a sweet family that would make a great addition to the club, *if* Judge can get them to listen to him.

"Sorry about that ladies and gent, what can I get you?" the girl asks, back behind the counter in work mode.

"Oh oh, can I get a banana shake? And popcorn if you have it?" Mira asks excitedly.

"Um, sorry, we don't serve popcorn," the girl says, her brows pinched.

"That'll do. Anyone else?" Mira asks.

We all nod and order different flavored shakes, waiting for Judge to return. I'm sure Mad Dog is in there counseling the big man, so I take this moment to move toward Kaia, who is busy making sure the floor isn't sticky.

"Um, hi," I start. "You probably don't remember me but I've been in here a few times with the DRMC mommies group." I give her a smile.

Kaia blows a dark curl out of her face and gives me a tired smile. "Of course I remember you. Lovely, right?"

I'm shocked to find she remembers me. I don't think I'm overly memorable. I'm very plain with hair and eyes too dark for my pale complexion. "Yup, that's me. Um, Judge, if he ever comes out of the bathroom, is going to ask you to accompany him, us, to the farmhouse we are all staying at. I'm not sure if you heard, but the clubhouse was attacked. We're all fine, but the clubhouse is not." Her eyes are wide and she darts them to the bathroom door, then back to me.

"Why would I need to go with him?" she asks, suspicion lacing her voice.

"We have reason to believe that the person who did it knows

about your connection to Judge."

"Leo. His name is Leo. Well it was when we were young," she mutters. "Besides, we have no connection to each other at all."

I raise my brows, then direct my look to the two teens behind the counter. "Really?" I ask, my gaze swinging back to Kaia's.

She leans closer to me, "Are you telling me there's a threat to *my* babies and Leo is the reason? Because if that's the case I will cut his balls off with a rusty spoon. It's bad enough what he did, but endangering *my* babies with his life choices? Oh hell no!" She hisses, her small body puffing up until she looks a few inches taller.

The door to the bathroom opens and she glares in that direction, stomping over to a man over a foot taller than she is.

"Ladies, *and* Pops, let's give them a little space, OK?" Mad Dog says, trying to usher us out.

"Hey! We haven't had our milkshakes!" Mira whines.

"I ordered them to go. I figured if Mad Dog didn't ruin our fun, Marx would have." Vi says, nodding at the older waitress that comes out with a tray of shakes for us in to-go cups.

"Fiiiiine," Ana says, picking up each shake, checking the flavors on the side until she finds her one. "But I'm going to nominate Chewy to get the details outta Judge later. I'm invested in this now.

Chewy nods once, her straw in her mouth and she gulps down her shake, staring at me in much the same way toddlers do when they drink. Finally she pulls her mouth off the straw with a loud "aaaahhhhhhhhh."

"You're so weird sometimes," Nat says, shaking her head.

"I'm the future buddy. One day there will be a whole world of neurodiverse people around, making the world a better place."

"Come on world peace, let's get home before our men come drag our asses outta here," Blanche says.

We all file through the door as a dark-haired man about to enter holds it open for us. I'm not sure what it is about him but I get a weird feeling in my stomach, a clenching replaced by a flutter. My steps hesitate so I turn to look over my shoulder, and I know I'm not the only one who feels it. Chewy has her eyes narrowed and Nat and Vi are on high alert. Mad Dog stands over the man as he exits. By the time I turn to look forward, Pops is by my side.

"Keep walking girl, and if anything feels off, you run, got it?" I nod, as do the women who overheard his instruction.

We move to walk past the alley that leads to the back of the diner, our SUV just on the other side of it when Pops gets tugged into the alley. A click pierces the air and I freeze in horror, Pops with a gun to his head.

Three more men come out of the shadows of the alley and suddenly the creepy guy from the diner is behind us, a gun in his hand. There are five of them and ten of us. Mad Dog already has his gun trained on the guy at our backs, and we all stand stock still, staring from each other to the men sent here to do us harm.

"Ugh, so predictable," Mira sighs, sucking on her straw, making an awful noise.

"And boring," Chewy adds before she hurls her milkshake at the man with the gun trained on Pops.

It hits Pops' shoulder, exploding all over him, and more importantly, all over the glasses of the man behind him rendering him blind. Everyone freezes and then a flurry of milkshake is flying through the air, covering whoever the heck these dudes are. One of them yells out, red spreading over his jeans where a knife is protruding from his thigh.

"Where the hell did that knife come from!?" Vi yells, pepper spraying the man closest to her.

"From my butt!" Chewy yells with glee, turning to show us the back of her leggings. Inside the waistband at the back she has half a dozen knives nestled back there.

"Jesus Christ," Mad Dog growls, before he coldcocks the guy in front of him who was momentarily distracted by Chewy's butt knives.

"You should see my pussy knives," She spins and thrusts her pelvis forward. Very clearly the outline of a small dagger can be seen in the front of her leggings.

I stare wide-eyed and then decide I need to get in on this. I have a small switchblade my brother Chris gave me before I left the farm. It's not much, but I know how to wield a knife as well as I can wield a gun. The Keep was paranoid we'd be attacked at any moment, so men, women and children were all taught to defend themselves. I imagine when you brainwash someone enough you think they'll never turn those skills on you. Until Blanche turned up.

"*Oh, entonces sois unas chicas duras*," one of them sneers.

"Yeah, we are tough ladies. Come get it, *pendejo*," Vi hisses back.

Looking around I almost laugh at the sight. One guy is on the ground thanks to Mad Dog, there are four covered in shakes of various flavors, and every member of the girl gang, including Pops, is holding a weapon. From my quick glance I saw knives, pepper spray, a small handgun and even knuckle dusters.

"In the words of the great Shania Twain, let's go girls!"

Marx

"So, what are we meeting about?" I ask, eyeing the Landry brothers sitting across the dining table from me.

They share a look, before Vic clears his throat. "We like what you've got going here and we want to set up something similar in Louisiana."

I stare them down. I've never once thought to set up a chapter anywhere other than here. Devil's Rose MC is part of Rose Grove. Always has been, and I thought it always would be.

"We've discussed it between us, and we know you'd never open a chapter without us patching in so Dom and Chris will prospect first, and I'll run shit back home. If, or once they're in, they'll go home and I'll prospect," Vic continues.

I run a hand down my face. It's a good idea. A fucking good idea. Each of these men have shown their mettle, and time after time have driven the hours to help us out, no questions asked. I mean, it would be better if they stopped fucking bringing gators with them, but thats more a quirk of personality than anything else. I stare them down, one by one, and not one of them flinches. I can't help but think how loyal these men must be. Their sister took a bullet for me and not once in the hospital did they give me the beat down I knew I deserved.

"You're willing to patch in even though your sisters have been put in danger because of the DRMC?"

Chris waves a hand at me, "Our sisters were in danger in the loving christian environment we grew up in. They're in danger every time they cross the damn road. Besides, even if we didn't like the lifestyle you live they wouldn't give a shit either way."

"They're not as helpless as you think, man." Dom continues. "I know you look at Lovely like this fragile baby deer or some shit, but that one, she's the one you have to worry about, not Blanche."

Vic nods his agreement, "Blanche has an explosive temper and has always bucked the rules. We knew that she was going to be the one to bring about the downfall of the Keep. But Lovely, she lasted longer in there than any of us did. She's seen some shit and probably done some shit that would have any other person spiralling. Instead, she has a way about her that galvanizes people together."

I can feel my brow raising. "And you think that somehow makes her more dangerous than Blanche?"

"Fuck yeah. Lovely brings out the best in people, she bands them together, makes them feel a part of something. You must have seen it?"

He's right. I have seen it. Fuck, Mad Dog was here for five minutes and saw it. Lovely's manner, the way she treats people has them eating out of the palm of her hand. Not in a manipulative way, never that. It's just that Lovely *sees* them. Their hopes, fears, dreams. She listens, she helps, she nurtures, she has their backs. And in turn, they have hers.

Vic snorts, "Now he gets it."

Dom holds my gaze. "Men like you lead. Women like Lovely have people going to war for the greater good. Imagine what you could do together."

I open my mouth to answer but the vibrating of my phone on the table interrupts me. The screen flashes with Mad Dog's name and the letters SOS. Fuck! He's on girl gang watch.

"Shit. Something's going down."

"We're in," Vic nods and then follows me through the house

and out the door.

Their SUV doors slam moments before the roar of my bike downs out any other sound. The women are in town, *my* woman is in town, and they need us. I crank the throttle and get lower, hoping that aerodynamics or some shit gets me there faster. I'm pushing my sled to her limits almost, but there's an urgency rushing through my blood, pumping me to go faster, faster, faster.

I pull up at the alley Mad Dog said they were at, only turning when a loud rumble breaks through my panic. The Landrys and my brothers are all at my back. I'll thank them later, for now I need to get my eyes on my woman.

Pulling my piece I walk along the alley wall, back to it so as not to draw any gunfire. Although there isn't any of that. But there is a distinct sound, sort of similar to a wet dishcloth hitting the floor.

"I think you should give him a smiley face," Mira's voice drifts down the alley.

"What the fuck?" Tank whispers, coming to stand beside me.

Soon I'm flanked by the Ol Men, staring at the scene near the back of the alley.

Mad Dog is leaning against a trash can, arms folded, long legs stretched out and crossed at the ankle. Pops is hovering over Lovely and Chewy and the body of some greasy looking guy.

"No! Do a cock and balls!" Vi cackles, the other women joining her.

"Oh, good idea!" Lovely's voice rings out. She sounds light, like she's been having fun all afternoon.

I storm up to my father, wanting to know what the fuck is

going on. "What the hell Mad Dog?" I wave at the women, all oohing and aahing over whatever is happening to that guy's chest.

"We were jumped by Spanish speaking dudes, so I'm guessing they work for the sheriff or the cartels. Anyway, there were five of the fuckers. I know I'm a tough old bastard but even I can't take out five fit, young guys alone."

"Still doesn't explain what the hell is going on now." I cross my arms, mirroring him.

"Well, after they got covered in milkshakes there was, how can I put this, a flurry of activity. Shakes were flying, knives were being used. One guy got pepper sprayed, Pops actually roundhouse kicked someone and Remy attacked another while wearing knuckle dusters." I stare at him in disbelief. "Her gym sessions with Dex are paying off."

Shaking my head I move closer to the huddled group. "Care to tell me what the fuck is going on?"

They spin around to look at me, Lovely shooting upright from her crouched position next to Chewy, eyes wide as saucers.

"Oh, hey Marx," Chewy says casually, still messing around with the guy on the ground, not even looking at me.

They all stand quietly. DRMC has been lucky enough to be graced with not only strong willed women, but beautiful women. At this moment our beautiful women are covered in what appears to be milkshake, blood, and something else I'm not even going to guess. Taking in Lovely's appearance I notice her flushed cheeks, dishevelled hair and blood on her hands.

A growl rips out of me, "What the fuck happened?" I rasp, "Are you OK? Fuck, Lovely, it wasn't that long ago you were in hospital!" I grip her upper arms gently, itching to touch her, to know she's alright.

"Marx," her voice cuts through my spiralling emotions. "Marx, I'm fine. None of the blood belongs to me."

Processing what she's said my gaze moves to her hand, where she's clutching a small switchblade, blood dripping from the end. Following the blood droplets I clock the man on the ground, getting a proper look at him. His shirt is ripped open, his torso covered in wounds. Not stab wounds, no, it looks as though someone has drawn on him. Turning, I look at the women. Sizing each one up, I know exactly who will tell me what I want to know.

"Mira, what the fuck happened here?"

She takes a deep breath, "We were leaving the cafe to give Judge some privacy, oh hey, did you know he's the proud father of some teenagers? Yeah, we didn't see that coming either," she snorts. I raise my brow and she gets all serious. "OK, well, we left the diner and before we know it Pops has been yanked into the alley with a gun to his head! Mad Dog was trailing behind and he managed to get behind the guy behind us. Then three more guys come out of the shadows, real bad guy like. Chewy was all like 'oh hell no!' and threw her *very* full shake at Pops and the guy that was holding him hostage. It exploded everywhere and then like a chain reaction we were all throwing milkshakes. Then one of the bad guys got stabbed in the leg and everyone was like 'where the hell did that come from?' and Chewy was all like 'my butt knives! You should see my pussy knives!'" My brows shoot up past my hairline. "And then Chewy thrusts at us and we all laugh and then Mad Dog hit that guy over there with the hand part of his gun and *then* Vi pepper sprays some guy and Remy breaks some dude's face with those bad butt knuckle dusters and Nat and Blanche do some stabbing

113

and Pops had wrestled one of them on the ground and had them eating trash! Actual trash!" Mira finally takes a breath and I guess I should thank her for getting me up to speed. "Oh yeah!," OK, she's not finished yet. "By the way, two of the guys were on the screen Chewy showed us the other day." She leans into me, holding her hand up next to her mouth, as if she's going to tell me a juicy secret, "One of them is-"

"What the fuck!? Joseph, you piece of shit!" Sniper growls.

"-his brother," Mira finishes off, unhelpfully.

Sniper kicks his brother in the gut before getting in a few more hits. The guy is out for the count so I'm appreciative when Rider pulls Sniper off him.

"Yeah, so this guy is the Cordoza brother-in-law, that guy is Sniper's brother and the rest are just lackies" Chewy says, finally standing. "Your turn, Lovely."

Lovely nods and then kneels down, looking over the man, "You did a good job on the ball hair, Chewy."

She pulls a pen from her purse, snapping it in half, letting the ink flow into the dick shaped wound. Actually, calling it dick shaped is probably an insult. I've never seen a more artistic dick drawing before. The shaft is thick and veined, the mushroom head in perfect proportion - what the fuck am I talking about?

"Look, babe! Lovely showed me how to draw the best dick pic ever!" Chewy boasts.

My eyes flick between Lovely's bent head, and the dick on this guy's chest. I stare as she rubs the ink in, effectively tattooing the guy.

"There! All done."

Holy shit. Holy fucking shit. Lovely, my sweet, innocent, Lovely, just helped carve up a man and tattoo a magnificent dick.

"So, are we going to bag and tag these guys or what?" Chewy asks, hands on hips.

I'm at a loss for words so I just raise a hand in the air and circle it.

"It's going to be so much fun watching you discover all the facets of Lovely's character," Mad Dog says, bumping my shoulder with his. "Probably almost as fun as watching the women and Pops, huh?"

Chapter 11

Lovely

A s soon as we get back to the farmhouse the men split up. Pops gets into his side by side ATV and takes off to the back of the farm, two of the DRMC SUV's following behind. We all know that he's headed to his and Chewy's "office" as they call it. They had an impressive set up in the Rev Room, so it'll be interesting to see what this setup is like. I can imagine it's probably more insane than the one at the DRMC.

We're all sticky and covered in milkshake and bodily fluids, so the consensus within the girl gang is that everyone is heading off to get cleaned up. I'm exhausted after our little fun today so I decide that I'll do the same then have a lie down. Checking the time I realize that it's almost time for Bee's nap, so if I clean up fast I'll be able to join my little girl in the nursery Mama Debs has set up. I'm sure the other kids won't mind me crashing with them for an hour or so.

Taking the path toward my cabin I pause, watching the

big man who just found out he has a whole family out there. Moving closer I stand beside him, staring at one of the vacant trailers.

"How you getting on, big guy?" I murmur. Judge is one of the quieter brothers. Well, when he wants to be. For the most part he's measured and thoughtful. I can't imagine what today was like for him.

He lets out a long, deep sigh. "I'm not sure, Lovely. For years I just thought we lost touch. I mean, what I did was shitty, but that woman was my best friend. One day she was there, the next, poof, she was gone. Packed up, moved out of town. Then all of a sudden she's back, with two kids in tow and she never told me." His shoulders slump and I can tell how much this is eating him up. "Did I really hurt her so bad that she would rather parent twins on her own than tell me?"

I let out a breath and move a little closer to Judge. He's never struck me as a touchy feely person, so I don't want to hug him or do anything to make him uncomfortable. Instead, I stand close enough to feel his body heat, and I hope he can feel mine, to know I'm offering comfort without the pressure of touching him.

"You were both young, Judge. I'm sure there's more to the story than you think. The best thing to do would be to talk to her. I know you were best friends once, but you're different people than you were at 18. Talk to her, get to know each other again, and open up." He nods quietly. "Did she agree to come to the farm?"

"Yeah. But she's pissed about it."

"Well, I would be too," I chuckle.

"But yeah, she said to give her an hour to pack up, and she'll be here."

"Is that why you're standing outside an empty trailer?"

He turns to look down at me, a smile playing on his lips. "That's funny."

I pull back a little, to look up at him, a frown on my face. I feel like I'm missing something. "What's funny?"

"You can read the whole situation with me and what I've got going on. Offer advice. Hell, you even figured out why I was standing here, and yet you can't figure out Marx's feelings for you."

I scoff, before side eyeing Judge. "Marx doesn't feel anything for me. Perhaps gratitude for making sure he wasn't hurt that day, but that's about the extent of it."

Judge's lips tip up even further. "if you say so."

I frown deeper at him until he lets out a laugh. He seems in a much better frame of mind so I decide my job here is done.

Heading into my cabin I beeline for the shower. In a matter of minutes I'm washed, dried, clothed and on my way to the nursery. Stepping inside I find the whole Girl Gang lying on the bean bags or on the beds snuggled up with their babies. Little Bee is starfished out on a bed, her dark hair a bird's nest around her face, fists clenched shut. I gaze at her for a moment then climb in next to her, maneuvering her body so that we're cuddled into each other.

"Job well done today, ladies," Chewy whispers, not wanting to wake Laney or Chomper who are both asleep in their respective beds.

"Yeah, I thought it was pretty successful myself," Blanche agrees from the rocking chair. She has Tess in her arms, gently rubbing circles on her tiny back. Cove, Jovie and Elio will be out on the farm somewhere. They seem to spend their time here living like wild children. I'm not sure if my sister has noticed,

118

but the childhood her younger kids are living is a lot like ours was in Eden's Keep.

"When do you think we get to do it again?" Vi asks. Like me, she is cuddled into a toddler bed with Juno.

"Well, considering we didn't even plan this one, it kinda just fell into our laps, I have no idea."

"Yeah, that's true," she agrees with a snort.

"Ladies, I think the question we should be asking ourselves is who to target next?" Pops offers. He's lying in a recliner, eyes closed but ears wide open. "Think about it. We have three enemies. All of them bad bastards to differing degrees. We'll leave Serpiente to the boys. But that means we still have five men sitting in my office who know things. We also have the sheriff."

"Dibs on not doing the sheriff. Moss would *never* let me hear the end of it. I'd have to put up with the jokes and the jibs about killing his boss. No thank you," Vi says, holding her hand up high in the air.

"We also can't get rid of that Joseph guy, Sniper called dibs on him along with Marx. There'll be nothing left of him once they've finished," Chewy says.

"It's kind of heartbreaking that Sniper is happy to deal with his brother. And by deal, I mean kill," Mira adds in case we didn't quite get it.

"I don't know. I can understand that," Blanche says, quietly.

Rolling my head to the side, I take in Blanche. She's gazing down at Tess, but she has a faraway look on her face. She killed a lot of people that day at the Keep, including some of our brothers and our father. I always wondered how she could take a life so easily, but I'm starting to wonder if it's not as easy as she makes it out to be.

119

"OK. We can't get rid of Joseph or the sheriff. So that leaves four other guys," Remy says.

"And that Renae woman," I murmur.

"Huh?" I'm sure all eyes are turned in my direction, but I can't see them as I bury my face in Bee's dark hair, trying to think of a plan. Clearly I'm no Chewy.

"No, wait, she's right," Chewy says.

Rustling has me looking over my shoulder, Chewy has Chomper in her arms and she's pacing, thinking and stroking him like that Dr Evil guy in an old film Tav made me watch. He's been giving me movie suggestions from the past almost 40 years, in the hopes that I'll be able to catch up or something. If I'm honest, some of them were depressing. That scene in the Never Ending Story where the horse died? I cried like a baby and then asked Elio way too many questions about quicksand.

"Renae Sullivan is the cartel's contact that got the kids we couldn't save. We got rid of Candice, there's no real reason we can't get rid of Renae." Chewy comes to a stop in the middle of the room, looking over us, one by one.

"Well, even if we wanted to, Renae Sullivan isn't even in this state and we're officially on lockdown from 4pm today," Nat points out.

"Who says we have to get to her immediately? We can be patient and wait this out." I sit up so I can see everyone. "The most immediate threats are the cartels and the sheriff. If what Moss says is true then the sheriff will be unprotected soon and he'll be taken care of. The five men the cartel sent to get rid of us are trussed up in Pops' office and they'll be dealt with soon enough. With the immediate threats gone, lockdown should ease up." It all makes sense in my mind, but whether it's a good idea or not is another story.

Chewy's lips turn up, and then a huge, predatory grin stretches her pretty face. "I like the way you think."

"Wait, hold up, I just want to know where this Lovely has been hiding?" Ana says, waving her hand around in my direction.

"Yeah! What happened to sweet, innocent, caring Lovely?" Nat teases.

I roll my eyes. "See! She even rolls her eyes now!" Mira laughs.

"Ladies, she's my sister. Of *course* she's a badass," Blanche teases, before a serious look comes over her face. "Lovely may look like a little lamb, but under that pretty face and sweet voice is a fucking wolf. Mark my words. Those bastards threatened our family and our babies. Lovely ain't gonna let that lie." My big sister nods at me and I can feel my chest filling with pride.

"Um, knock knock?" a voice calls from the other side of the door.

Before one of our lazy butts can get up to open it, Mama Debs throws the door open, herding in Kaia with the two teenagers from the diner following behind. "Come on *whānau*, family, they're not going to bite." She steps in behind them then wraps her arm over Kaia's shoulder. "*Kotiro*, I'm sure you all know Kaia, and these are her babies." The boy snorts but then covers it with a cough. I try not to laugh, but he'll soon see that no matter your age, everyone is Mama Debs' baby. "Jackson and Annie-Bella."

We all wave, and I move to sit on the side of the bed. No one likes greeting people from bed. It's weird.

"Ooohhh, come closer, we need alllll the goss," Mira says, clapping her hands and no doubt overwhelming the poor woman.

"Ae, good idea!" Mama Debs shoves Kaia in our direction, "I'm going to take the kids to find Sage and Niko. They don't want to hang out with the mums and the babies." Debs bustles off as fast as she arrived and we all stare at the back of her.

"OK ladies, I need the full breakdown of what the hell is going on," Kaia says, a frown on her face.

She'll fit in perfectly.

Marx

Standing outside Lovely's cabin I decide I should probably knock on the door rather than force my way in to "look after her". That's been my excuse as to why I've been in her home sleeping on her couch since she left the hospital, but I doubt that excuse is going to fly now. She's healing up well, still a little tired, but she's moving around. She also joined the Girl Gang in a street fight today, so I probably shouldn't piss her off.

Before I can raise my hand to knock, the door opens, Lovely staring at me. "Is everything OK?"

She's wearing an oversized DRMC shirt with tiny sleep shorts and my brain short circuits because I realize I have never seen her legs before. I don't know what I was expecting, but it wasn't this. Usually she's wearing very modest, slightly loose fitting clothing. I mean this stuff isn't fitted by any stretch of the imagination. It's just there is skin on show and now I feel like a Victorian man blowing his load over an exposed ankle or

122

some shit.

"Marx? Are you OK? Do you need something?"

Flicking my gaze from Lovely's shapely calves and thick thighs I see the concern of her face and tell my dick to pull himself together. "Ah, yeah, I was wondering if I could crash here tonight." I clear my throat, to get some of the huskiness out.

Her brows pinch together a little, before realization dawns on her face, "Of course! Judge, Kaia and the twins needed your trailer. Um, I mean, you've slept on the couch the past few nights, if you don't mind hanging out with me and Bee then I guess it's fine. You're my Pres so I'd be glad to share my space." She smiles at me but I can still see a hint of wariness in her eyes.

What I said to her and how I've pushed her away really fucked her up. Which makes me feel like a fucking monster, given that I know a snippet of what she went through with her husband. He treated her like shit and then so did I. As much as I'd love to grab her and kiss the hell out of her, I know that I need to earn that right. Firstly, I need to get her to see me as maybe more than just the Pres of the DRMC.

"Is that all I am? The Pres?"

She swallows and gazes over my shoulder, as if getting her thoughts in order. "Well, I mean, I guess we're friends, too. I really appreciated all you did for me at the hospital and helping me with Bee." She smiles, but I can still see she's unsure.

It's in my nature to push, but not tonight. Tonight I accept that we're friends, which is more than I deserve. Tonight two friends will eat and talk and get to know each other better. Then once I have an idea of what she likes, I'll let Pops help me formulate a plan to woo her, properly like she deserves.

"Friends. I'd like that," I say, with a smile.

She beams at me and then opens the door wider. "Come on in, you already know where everything is. I was about to sit down and watch The Princess Bride."

"Ah, cool. Sounds great," I say, kicking off my boots in the entryway and following Lovely to the couch where she has snacks set up on the table and Bee playing on a rug on the floor.

"Have you seen it? Tav suggested it's one I should watch. He's given me a huge list of movies I had to see to catch up with the rest of the world. I thought it might be a nice, easy watch after the excitement of today."

Lovely sits at one end of the L shaped couch, at the part where she can put her feet up. She pulls a throw rug over her legs, covering those beauties from me. "Oh shoot, you're bigger than me, do you want to sit on this side?"

I huff a laugh. "Lovely, it's fine. I'm all good here," I reply, slumping down a little into the cushions.

She smiles and is about to press play when I interrupt her. "Are you alright? You know, after what happened today?"

She tips her head to the side, studying me with her dark eyes. "Yeah, of course. It was fun," she grins.

"Yeah, I'm sure. You weren't scared or worried or anything?"

"Marx, you may not know this, but I'm skilled with a knife. I can shoot a gun too. Eden's Keep leaders were paranoid we'd be raided one day. I'm guessing by the government or something. Anyway, from the time we could walk we were taught self defence and how to use knives and a gun in case we had to defend the Keep."

"I know it was a shit place, but that's a handy skill to have," I say, impressed. I never once thought Lovely would be capable of shooting or knife work. I'm starting to see that my expectations of what Lovely is capable of is shockingly low. I'm such a douche.

"Don't give them too much credit. They also taught us women that if it looked like we were losing, we'd take the children and the elderly, barricade ourselves in the hall and drink the 'calming' tincture that Royal Landry created."

"Jonestown style?" I ask, shocked to my core that Eden's Keep would go that far.

"I don't know what that is," Lovely says, her confused face is fucking adorable. Jesus man pull it together, you've led men into battle!

"Jonestown was a religious cult led by Jim Jones, I'm guessing similar to yours. Anyway, Jim Jones became more and more paranoid, some members were accused of murder and everything spiralled out of control. They believed the government would come to get them, so they decided to round everyone up and have them drink Kool Aid. It had been laced with cyanide."

Lovely runs a hand over her cheek, wiping away tears. "Ugh, evil men hiding their true selves under the guise of God and his teachings. That's why I like it here. Every man here knows what it is to be good, and just. Do you kill people? Sometimes, but it's to protect the innocent. Those men could never." She drops her hand to her lap, her fists clenching. It's then I notice the ink on her wrist. Leaning over, I gently take her hand, turning it over for a better glimpse. A tiny bumblebee marks the pale skin. I run my thick finger over the ink, trying to ignore the shiver that runs over her. I know I should stop touching her, I lost that right when I said that shit, but I want to memorize the smoothness of her skin for one second longer.

"Didn't know you got inked."

Her lips tip up. "It seemed appropriate. She's my little Bee."

I nod, leaning back into my place on the other side of the couch. Before I can ask anything else she starts the film. I settle back and watch the screen while taking sneak peeks at Lovely. I don't ever remember seeing this movie, but it's not as shitty as I thought it was going to be. It definitely has Tav written all over it. One of the first things I learned about the man was how much he loved watching films in his down time. Weird shit from before we were born almost. Not that it matters because watching Lovely watch the movie is entertaining enough. There's joy, sadness, anger. Every emotion you can think of crosses her face throughout the film. One part there she snuggles Bee into her lap and hides behind her so she can't see the scary parts. I know I have a shitstorm coming my way, and every time I think of the fuckers tied up in Pops' office my blood boils, but this here, with Lovely and Bee somehow pushes that to the back of my mind. It's so fucking domestic and instead of breaking out in hives I want to grab on with both hands.

The credits roll and I glance over to see Bee asleep on her mom, plastered to a sleeping Lovely's chest. Her little mouth is wide open and she's already in her PJs so I very gently slip my hands under her light weight, trying hard not to grope or bump Lovely's healing chest in the process. Once I've extricated Bee, which is similar to extricating an explosive, I carry the little girl to her room. Her night light and the machine in the corner that plays soothing sounds is already on. Pulling back the covers I slowly transfer Bee into her bed, her mop of hair resting against the pretty pink pillow on her miniature bed. Pulling the covers up over her I make sure to tuck her in a little. Don't want her kicking them off in the night. I know that being cold wakes them up; well, that's what Rhodie said. Now his kid sleeps in a big sack thing.

I slowly sneak out of Bee's room, trying hard not to make too much noise and startle her or her mom. Lovely is still on the couch, completely dead to the world and for some reason that makes me feel good. She has the tendency to work too hard, to help too much, and I want her to rest and heal as much as she can. Moving down the hall I let myself into her room. Stepping inside I'm hit with Lovely's scent. Most women smell like flowers and shit, but not Lovely. She's somehow a mix of lemony sunshine and fresh laundry. It's the only way I can explain it. It's fresh and comforting all at the same time. Rolling my eyes at my thoughts I make my way to the bed and fold down the floral quilt, ready for her. I fluff up her pillow too, because why the hell not?

I turn to make my way back to the living room to get Lovely, and a notepad on the desk catches my eye. I know I shouldn't snoop but clearly my feet don't get the memo as with two long strides I'm at her modest desk staring down at myself. Flipping the page I'm met with a pencil drawing of Flack. I flip through pages, one by one, every page has an absolute masterpiece on it. Chewy in full Rev Room glory, the funny grin she gets on her face frozen in time and captured perfectly. Mad Dog leaning against the bar of the clubhouse, smiling at someone just out of view. I turn back to the first page I saw, the one where she captured my likeness. Never in my life have I seen myself portrayed this way. I'm frowning, lips turned down and yet there is determination, grit in my gaze. There's a hardness about me, almost a cruelty that I've never noticed or seen before. Running a hand down my face I curse myself. I've spent a wonderful evening with a wonderful woman, a woman

127

I want to make mine, but I'm a fucking monster. This portrait shows in great detail exactly what Lovely sees when she looks at me.

"That's from the day TumTum was shot. You were so mad, raging at the world and how to get revenge."

I clear my throat, "It was the day I said some shit you didn't deserve too. Actually, I say a lot of shit you don't deserve. I can see why you see me like this. A cruel, hard fucker." I run a finger down the picture once more. No matter the subject, her work is breathtaking.

"That's not true." Her soft voice reaches my ears. "I see you in lots of different ways. Do you say mean stuff sometimes? Yeah, you do." Somehow hearing from her sweet lips the shit I said affects her makes me wince. "But I know those moments are moments where you have the world on your shoulders, pressing down on you. You're not a cruel man, Marx. Trust me, I know cruel men. You're just a man trying to keep his family safe who sometimes says shitty things." My head snaps up at the curse word coming from Lovely's lips, an impish grin on her face. "Turn the page."

"Huh?" I grunt, unsure why she wants me to see Flack's picture.

"Not that way, the other way." She rolls her eyes at me.

I flip to the next page in the book, unaware that there were more. I blink once, then twice. Staring back at me is another version of me. This one is softer, kinder. The type of man I wish I was more often. This one has a slight quirk to his lips, as if about to smile. There's a lightness there that I don't recognize.

"Is this the version of me I should be? All happy and shit?" I ask, not able to tear my eyes away.

"Nope. That's the version of you I've seen the past two days.

Briefly." she adds. "That's how you look when you're helping with Bee. She really is good at making your heart feel happy, huh?" She moves slightly closer, beaming up at me. "She saved me, Marx. She saves me every day. I can put up with anything as long as I know I have her with me and I'm keeping her safe."

"I'll keep you both safe." I vow, my throat tight with emotion. For how Lovely sees all the facets of me. For the guilt I feel for the way I treated her. For her shitty past and the battles she faces every day. For the things we've lost.

"And I'll do the same for you, Marx." She beams at me before a giant yawn takes over her face.

"OK, that's enough heart to heart stuff, let's get you into bed." She laughs but does exactly what I say, climbing into her side of the bed, lying on her side, hands tucked under her cheek.

"Marx?"

"Hmm?" I grunt, moving toward the door.

"Can you do me a favor?" I nod once, knowing I'd do anything this woman asked of me. "Please check on Sniper? I know he put on a show earlier today, but he's more sensitive than we think. Hurting his brother is going to take a toll on him. I just don't think he should be dealing with this on his own. Promise me you'll check on him?"

Even if she hadn't asked, that's exactly where I planned on heading. My MC brother is hurting, and I need to make it right. The fact Lovely could see it too and wants Sniper to be comforted makes me want to blurt out the words that have been filling my chest since the day I thought I lost her. Instead, I look into her deep brown eyes and I say exactly what I think she wants to hear.

129

"As you wish."

Pops

"Why are you being creepy?"

"I'm not being creepy."

"Ah, yes you are. Come on, Sid, stop spying on them!" I swiftly push my hips back, effectively dodging Debs' backhand to the gut. Instead she winds up and slaps me on my protruding ass.

"Oh, do that again,"

She rolls her eyes and snorts, then slaps me again. "Why did I agree to marry you again?"

"Because I'm romantic, thoughtful, have a decent sized dick with good recovery and I have a very skilled tongue."

"Sid!"

I snort and then go back to standing at the window with my binoculars.

"Can't you just leave them be? They'll sort this out in their own time." Debs says from somewhere behind me, most likely getting things ready for tomorrow's breakfast.

"Look, if I thought the kid could pull this off himself I'd leave him to it. But it turns out Marx is way dumber than he looks."

"That's my kid you're talking about."

I jump at the sound of Mad Dog's voice over my shoulder.

"Holy shit! How the hell does a bastard as big as you move so silently? It's fucking dangerous. It'll give me a heart attack

130

one day," I bitch.

No one gives a shit. Debs chuckles and Mad Dog ignores me, moving to steal a muffin off the cooling tray. My woman swats him away before he can get his mitts on them and I can't help but give him a shit eating grin. She let me have one.

"How are they doing over there?"

"Not you too!" Debs exclaims, throwing her hands in the air.

"Yeah, me too. I don't want to think I made dumb kids -"

"Debatable," I mumble

"But shit, Marx just can't stop saying dumb shit. That little lady is perfect for him and the MC as the Pres' Ol Lady, but he fucked it all up and now he has to do the hard yards to win her over. So, how's he doing?"

"Well, they watched The Princess Bride. Lovely and Bee fell asleep, your boy put Bee to bed and then seemed to be snooping around Lovely's room, so we should have a word to him about other people's privacy." Debs' brows fly to her hairline but I ignore the look she gives me. "Then they had a conversation and I know he must have seen her drawings. She's fucking talented, that one. Anyway, he's just tucked her into bed and now he seems to be heading toward my office."

"Good. That sounds like he didn't fuck things up at least."

"Nope. I think he might be learning."

"Well, I mean, I am his father. I've been known to woo women in my time."

"Oh please, this is all because of my guidance as The Love Pres." We glare at each other and I know I should quit while I'm ahead. The last thing I need is Vi to bring her sister's kids here to do another pose off. I need to never see that Rodney fucker for as long as I live.

"And what kind of advice is The Love Pres actually handing out, hmm?" Debs asks, leaning against the counter, arms folded.

"That he needs to find out what she likes. Namely, whether she's an explosions kinda gal. Once we know that, we can move on to phase two of 'Dumbass Woos An Angel."

"That actually sounds like pretty solid advice," Mad Dog says, agreeing with me. We share a mutually respectful look, then nod at each other.

Debs throws her hands in the air. "Leave the kids alone. They'll make it in their own time."

"No, I'm with Sid, they definitely won't. They need outside intervention. I'm old as dirt and need to see my boys happy and thriving. I could go at any time."

"I damn well knew you were diabetic." I point in his direction.

"I'm not fucking diabetic!"

"You're not as old as me and you're talking like you're going to die at any minute. You're also a big bastard, so ergo, diabetes. Or heart disease. Stroke."

"I'm a big bastard because I workout you little shit!"

"Enough!" Our heads snap to Debs who has her angry eyes on and a spatula in her hand. "Out! I have no time to listen to old men arguing. Get out! Shoo, scram, get outta here, piss off!"

I look at Mad Dog and we both high tail it out of the kitchen, chased out by a little woman with a dish towel over her shoulder.

"She's magnificent."

"Hell yeah she is. I'm a lucky fucker." And a horny fucker. Debs all wild like that always gets my motor revving.

I'll leave her to cool off for a moment, and then I'll kiss her and make it all better. Yeah, The Love Pres with another winning plan.

Chapter 12

Lovely

I blow out a frustrated breath and angrily erase the last hour's worth of work I've done. For some reason I cannot get Jovie's hair right and it's irritating me. Or maybe the irritation comes from knowing that it's been two days since we brought our guests to Pops' office and still nothing has happened with them. I'm sure it's all part of Marx's plan, but it irks me knowing the men responsible for our predicament are here, on the farm and we've not taken care of them yet. Well, that I know of. I know deep down I shouldn't want to be there, in the room, but I feel like I need to be there. I need to see that they'll not live to see another day where they hurt people or ruin lives with their greed.

"Shit, what did that notebook ever do to you?"

My head snaps up at the rough sound of Mad Dog's voice. He's standing at the bottom of my steps, one foot up on the porch, leant forward, his forearms resting on his knee. Glancing down at my work I see that I've erased so hard that my paper is thinning.

"Blast! Sorry, I just couldn't get the hair right."

Mad Dog steps up next to me, gesturing to the seat beside me. Tav, for some reason, is very talented at decorating, and the cabin is a beautiful home filled with cozy furniture. The swing seat on the porch is one of my favorite places to relax. From here I can see the farmhouse and everyone else's cabins and no trailers, and I can hear when Bee wakes from her nap.

"Of course, take a seat." I scooch over slightly to make space for Mad Dog.

He and his sons are large men. Tall and wide, they need more space than my short plump body. He reaches out, a questioning look on his face as he gestures to my notepad. I'm usually a little shy with my drawings. Royal said they were a waste of time, and me wanting praise showed I was an immodest woman, begging for attention. I got two broken ribs from that lecture. I shake off the thought and think back to Marx's face when he saw my sketches. He was impressed and that one look boosted my confidence more than any of Royal's words could have ever done. I hand the pad to Mad Dog, and sit back, swinging my legs, watching Judge and Kaia get to know each other again.

A low whistle breaks me out of my people watching.

"Shit girl, this is, fuck, it's amazing." His dark eyes find mine and I see no lie in his words. "You're damn wasted working at Devil's Big Tow. You should be making and selling your art. Fucking something that nurtures your creative soul."

"I love working at DBT. The boys are so nice and I'm helping them. They took a chance on me and I'm grateful," I say, shrugging.

"I dunno girl. This work is too good for it not to be seen." We sit quietly for a moment. Mad Dog flipping through my book. The look on his face is worth more to me than any money I could ever think to make from my pictures. "Lovely, do you know what my job was in the MC?"

"You were the Pres," I reply, brows pinched because that sounds like a trick question.

He huffs out a laugh, "Well, yeah I was. But back in the day when we first started, we didn't have as many or as successful businesses under our belt. We owned a shit bar that made hardly any money because we drank it all, and a tattoo parlor." I'm confused, but wait patiently. "I used to run the ink shop. For a long fucking time until we got the towing business and the garages up and running. I retired from the shop because that shit is hard on your body. Sure everyone thinks you just sit on your ass all day, but you're twisted up like a pretzel trying to reach places, anyway, shit, I've gone off track."

I let out a giggle, and I'm intrigued as to how two large, rough grumpy men managed to come from this sweet man.

"They get it from their momma," he says with a grin.

"I'm so sorry! Holy moley I can't believe I said that out loud!" I press my cool hands to my flaming cheeks, wanting to crawl into the cabin and slam the door behind me.

"You did, but it's fine. No one has called me sweet before." He bumps my shoulder with his larger one. "Anyway girl, I was thinking, what would you say to still working in a DRMC business, but one where you can share your gift with the world?"

"DRMC doesn't have any businesses that would let me draw all day, Mad Dog." I give him a look.

"Not yet. But I'm happy to reopen the ink shop if you want to learn to tattoo." He smiles gently at me and my stomach flips.

I'd not thought about drawing for years. It was beaten out of me, the joy of creating, but in this life, my new improved life, it's something that I've been loving. The quiet moments, trying to get the snub of a nose just right, the look in someone's eye, capturing the emotion. My soul is being fed in a way I never thought it would ever again, but in order to embrace it completely, I'm going to have to share something that has always shamed me.

"I already know how to tattoo. Kinda." I say the words but they come out as a whisper.

"What?" Mad Dog asks, turning to face me, looking a little shocked.

I rub the little bee on my wrist, the one I did myself to remind me that everything I've done, and continue to do, is for Bee. Even if that means confessing to something that has always made me feel like a monster.

Clearing my throat, I repeat myself, trying to sound strong but even to my ears I can hear the waver in my voice. "I already know how to tattoo." I rush ahead to get the rest of the story out before I clam up and bury it. "I've always loved to draw but at the Keep having hobbies or talents was frowned upon. If you excelled at something you'd be accused of doing it to garner attention, and there is nothing more unattractive than a woman begging for attention." My father's cruel jibes ring in my ears, no daughter of his will draw attention to herself like a two bit whore. "When I was around 13 or 14 there was an influx of women into the Keep. I'm not sure where they came from, but none of them looked happy to be there. Some of them tried running away, escaping. Begging other Keep women for help and no one would. They were married off quickly to the leaders and the higher ups in the council, but because of the sheer number of them, probably 30 or so, the men kept getting their wives mixed up."

"Jesus fucking christ," Mad Dog growls, running a hand down his face.

"My father came to me," I continue on, rubbing the little bee tattoo for strength, "asking me to draw a crest for each man's family. I was over the moon. My father had actually given me consent to draw, to produce something for the families of the Keep. I worked day and night on them, making sure I had them just right. Then one evening I was given a tattoo gun. It was rudimental at best. I was told in no uncertain terms that my job was to brand the women with who they belonged to. The first few were awful. I didn't want to do it, the women fought until their husbands and other council members held them down. I cried with them." I choke out the last words, the pain of that night crashing down on me like a wave.

"Oh Lovely girl, come here." Mad Dog moves me closer to him, his heavy arm over my shoulder's grounds me as I let my tears soak into his plaid shirt.

"The first tattoos were awful. I didn't know what I was doing and they got infected. One woman died when her husband refused to get her any help. She died because of me!" I sob.

"No, no, girl. She died because of those greedy fuckers. Not you, never you. You were a little girl, Lovely, you had no power over your actions. Shhhhh, it's OK, I got you." Mad Dog soothes, the gentle timbre of his voice patching up the hurt in my heart.

I bawl for only God knows how long, until I can't cry anymore. I know what Mad Dog says is true, that I was too young to fight back, however I've carried that guilt with me for years. Sitting there, under my skin, knowing those women were walking around carrying brands from the men they hated.

"After that first lot of tattoos my father gave me a book on tattooing. I worked on dead pig skin until I could get it right and not make anyone sick."

"How long were you tattooing in the Keep, Lovely?"

"Until I left. Eleven years." I sniff, wiping my face with the sleeve of my sweater. He hums, the rumble through his chest soothing me.

"Do you know what I think? I think you have a real chance of using your talent to change lives, Lovely. Do you know how many women, survivors of abuse, get tattoos to remind them of their strength? So many want to have it marked on their skin that they survived, that they came out the other side, and those women I would regretfully turn away because they don't want a man to mark them again. They want a woman, a fellow survivor. Someone like you, sweetheart. You can use the gift you have to bring light into people's lives. Maybe that will help color over the darkness you were forced to live in. Think about it, yeah?" His words burrow their way into my chest and my stomach flutters.

Can I turn my shame into something else, something healing? I feel him press a kiss to the top of my head, him murmuring to someone, and then I'm being lifted, gathered into strong arms that carry me into my little home. Marx's dark gaze stares down at me, boring into my soul, giving me strength I know I have somewhere inside me, it's just been exhausted from my confession. He sits on the couch, me in his lap, his arms holding me tight, grounding me to him.

"You're a fucking revelation, Lovely Landry. I can only wish I was as strong as you."

And with that, he presses his lips to mine.

Marx

Every fibre of my being tells me I don't deserve to steal this kiss, but fuck it. I'm an asshole and I'm taking what I want. What I need to ground me before I burn down the fucking world. The need to kill someone, with my bare hands rushes over me and it's only Lovely's sweet mouth pressed against mine that has the murderous urge subsiding.

Pulling back to stare at her, her blotchy pink face, red nose, puffy eyes, and she's never looked more beautiful. Her lead smudged fingers rest lightly against her lips, where mine were just a moment ago.

"Marx?" she whispers, eyes flicking between mine, looking for answers.

"I've been a fucking asshole to you, Lovely, but no more." She bared her soul to my father, within my earshot, and now it's my turn to bare mine. "You scare the living shit out of me." She rears back, confused, and I don't blame her. Shit, hopefully I can get through this without messing up. "You are stronger than anyone, fucking *anyone* I've ever met. I know you have a past, one so shitty it led you to flee in the middle of the night with a newborn. You have every right to hole up in here, and shun the world but you don't. You grab life by the balls and make it your bitch. You treat everyone with kindness and love when you have every right to scream and shout how life isn't fair. You weren't broken by the Keep, Lovely. But you were almost broken by my words and for that I am so fucking sorry. You scare me with your strength and your light and because of the feelings you stir within me, because I know, I fucking *know* that if you chose to love me, I wouldn't deserve it. Ever."

"Marx," she whispers and I have to get this out.

"I'm not fucking worthy, Lovely, but I'm willing to try."

She stares at me for so long that my ass starts to tighten. I can feel myself tensing up and I know that she's going to turn me away. She has every right to. She's probably in love with that loud mouth motherfucker Switch, he's given her more time and care than I could ever hope to.

"I, um, I'm not sure that I'll be able to, um," she takes a deep breath and blows it out, "My husband was horrible, and I don't have very good memories or reactions to touch, in, um, that way, so I'm not sure that I'll be able to-"

I place a finger over her lips, silencing her. "I don't give a shit if we never share anything more than the kiss we just shared. I'm willing to stand by your side, as long as you're willing to stand by mine."

A tentative smile grows on her face, tugging up her lips in the sweet smile I've come to love. "Maybe we could take it slow?"

"Oh, it'll be slow. I've got a lot of work to make shit up to you."

"Like dueling a six fingered man?" The little imp grins cheekily at me. Fuck, she really did love that film.

"Find me a six fingered man and I'll kick his ass."

Her giggle is music to my ears. "So, did you come here to eavesdrop about my greatest shame and then kiss me?" she asks. She's trying to lighten the mood but I can still see the remnants of shadows in her eyes.

"Shit, no, actually I was on my way here to tell you and Mad Dog that we'll be making a move on our guests this evening. I know that the Girl Gang are the reason they're here in the first place so I had to let you all in on it." She raises her brow at me. "OK, and you'd all find a way in even if we didn't tell you." she smirks and nods.

"I'm guessing Mama Debs is in charge of the nursery tonight then?"

"Yeah, Kaia is helping her. She's new to the club and Judge doesn't want her to see what we do to people who cross us."

She nods, "That's a good call. Don't want to give her any ideas on how to hurt Judge just yet." she laughs and then climbs off my knee.

I miss her closeness immediately, as she steps away from me. She pauses, spins back to look at me, then drops a kiss on my cheek and takes off like her ass is on fire. I don't give a shit, I watch her ample rear jiggle as it runs away down the hall.

A loud bang at the door jolts me out of my ogling, pissing me off as I know that I'll have to leave the bubble I'm in and deal with some shit. Letting out a sigh I stand, getting to the door in three strides and throwing it open before Niko has a chance to knock again.

"What's up, Prospect?"

"Sorry Pres, Mad Dog said to give you two some privacy but this couldn't wait," Niko says, eyes darting.

"Well, spit it out."

He shuffles from foot to foot, tips his head back and curses, "It's probably best if you see what it is. And promise me, you won't yell."

"What the fuck is going on, Niko?"

142

He says nothing, instead turning on his heel and skipping down the steps, striding toward Pops' ATV. I've got another three of the things being delivered. It's a long walk to the office and sometimes the brothers are lazy as fuck. I blow out a breath, call out to Lovely that I have to leave. Her sweet voice drifts down the hall telling me she'll see me later. Figuring that I won't have a chance to steal another kiss, I follow Niko, gently shutting the door behind me.

"This better be important," I grumble getting into the passenger seat.

It feels wrong, but Niko was already in the driver's seat and hell, the kid knows the property like the back of his hand. We weave in and out of a few trees, and head for a corner that I've never been before. Actually, I haven't been on half the land, spending my time between the farmhouse, Lovely's cabin, and Pops' office. I could care less about the rest of the property.

Niko slows to a crawl, squinting into the trees before stopping and shutting off the motor. He doesn't say a word, instead assumes I'll follow him. We walk to a hedge and my mouth drops when Niko knocks against it, a wooden sound filling the air.

"What the fuck?"

"Password!" Cove yells, although her usual volume is muffled slightly.

"Cove, it's me, open up."

"No can do without a password."

"It's me!"

"We don't know who 'me' is. Password or no entrance!"

"Fuck's sake," Niko mumbles under his breath. "Niko is a loser who wet the bed until he was eight."

"Password accepted!"

143

An awful metal on metal scraping sounds out and the door pushes outward toward us, Cove and Jovie standing inside, arms crossed and frowns on their faces.

"You can't bring guests!" Jovie says, jabbing a finger at Niko.

"He's not a guest, he's the Pres, and if you want to join DRMC one day, like you're planning, you have to listen to him."

"Chewy doesn't listen to him," Cove argues.

Niko moves to open his mouth but I cut him off. "Cove, Jovie, what's going on here?"

Cove rolls her eyes but gestures that we follow her deeper into the most impressive kids clubhouse I've ever seen. Firstly, it's about the size of the DRMC common room. Secondly, it has electricity. There's a TV playing cartoons on one wall, the kids have their tablets charging on a table in the corner and there even looks to be a small bathroom and kitchenette. All hidden from the outside by hedging and trees.

"What the actual fuck?" explodes out of me in a splutter.

Turning wide eyes at Niko he smiles apologetically, because there, in the middle of the room, tied to a chair with a minions pillowcase over his head, looks to be Sheriff Kelson.

"Is that-?"

"Yup." Niko walks over, snatching the case from Kelson's head. The older man is wide-eyed and gagged.

Elio walks toward him, a beaker of some blue shit in his hand. The seven year old comes to a stop standing toe to toe with the old sheriff. A grin slowly spreads across Elio's face, showing his two missing front teeth. It's fucking unnerving, and I'm not the only one who thinks so as Kelson flinches in his chair.

"What the fuck?" I murmur under my breath. I don't know whether to yell or laugh my ass off.

The reason we hadn't taken care of our guests was because

we were missing Kelson and Chewy wanted the whole set. She's not wrong, having all five of them and interrogating them where they can see the pain and suffering of each other makes our job easier. The only problem being that after getting word on Wednesday Kelson had been stood down, he fell off the radar. Remy had no sightings of the man and she and the Computas have been scouring the internet to find traces of him. Somehow the MC kids found him first.

I turn to stare at Niko and he's as lost as I am. I know I'm the Pres, but fuck if I know how to deal with this. I'm gonna need a moment. Then it hits me.

"Got a plan, Pres?" Niko asks as he places the pillowcase back over Kelson's head.

"Yeah. I'm gonna call their moms."

Chapter 13

Lovely

I roll my lips between my teeth and bite down a little. I can't laugh. If I laugh I know it'll set off everyone else.

"What were you kids thinking?" Remy says, her voice steady but I can tell she's a bundle of nerves.

So far Blanche hasn't said anything, preferring to give Elio and Cove perhaps the angriest eyes I've ever seen. None of the kids seem to be worried. In fact, Cove has already argued their case. Twice.

"Sheriff Kelson is a bad man. If you saw him around the farm you needed to tell a grown up."

"We did! We told Niko and he snitched." Cove turns to glare at her big brother. "And we told Sage."

All eyes dart to Sage who up to this point has remained quiet, seated next to Chef.

"You *knew?*" Blanche growls at her older daughter.

"Yeah. We needed her help when we thought Elio accidentally killed him with his potion," Cove blabs even more.

"Jesus. H. Christ." Marx mumbles under his breath and I'm certain I hear a snort escape him.

"Wait, what kind of potion were you working with, kiddo?" Pops asks, squatting down in front of Elio, Chewy beside him.

Remy looks fit to burst, Wire doesn't look any better. My sister is deathly quiet and Tav seems calm. A little too calm.

"Kids, I think it would be best for you all to go to the nursery. There will be no tablets, no TV, no movies, nothing. You are to go up there right now, no messing about or disturbing the babies or Kaia and the twins. You are going to think about your actions."

"Aw, but Mama Deb -"

"No. Once you've given it some thought you are going to each write a letter explaining why it was dangerous for you to do what you did and why you need to tell an adult."

"But we di-"

"Your brother and sister don't count!" Blanche growls.

"Holy shit, she sounds like the exorcist," Nitro mutters under his breath.

He got home just before the kids were discovered. He's readying the small trailer for Fox's homecoming tomorrow.

"Sage, we will be having a conversation young lady." Sage drops her head and nods, Chef, placing his hand on her shoulder, giving it a supportive squeeze.

I like what those two have growing between them. The mutual trust, little touches here and there. My thoughts wander to Marx's kiss. My blood still feels bubbly, as if carbonated by his lips on mine. It took me by surprise, as did his words. Is it too good to be true, that he wants me? After all his running and pushing me away, am I a fool to think he's changed? Is it guilt that has him behaving this way? I'm still unsure of his motives, but I know that I want to believe his words. I want to live my life to the fullest and if it means that my gamble doesn't pay off and my heart gets a little bruised then so be it. I've survived far worse and I know I can survive again.

A snort has me glancing at Nitro, then at the three little kids lined up in the front of the large room we've started calling Church.

"I swear to all that's holy if you roll your eyes at me *one more time* Cove Marie Landry I will remove one of them with a rusty spoon," Blanche growls in an even lower voice. So scary that Tav takes a big step away from her.

I stare at Cove, looking for fear, instead a smile spreads across her chubby little face. "Yessss! I'll get an eye patch!"

"Get upstairs! Right now and do as Mama Debs told you!" Blanche goes from a low man growl to a screech.

"Holy shit, I think they broke Blanche," Savage whispers in awe.

The three kids run out of the room and once the sound of their footsteps on the stairs hits my ears I start to snort. Nitro catches my eye and he chuckles before the dam breaks and the whole of the club and the Landrys burst into laughter.

"Holy shit! I can't believe those kids did what we couldn't do," Dex chuckles.

"And they almost fucking killed him!" Rider roars.

Marx sidles up next to me, bumping me with his incredibly large and delicious looking bicep. I never noticed biceps until I met Marx. Now they and his forearms are the things I stare at most when we're in a room together.

"We better keep Bee away from that lot. I don't want to have to lose my shit like Blanche did." He smirks down at me and my stomach flips.

He's talking like it's forever. Or at the very least, long term. Holy moley. What is happening? Before I can spiral Marx bangs twice on the wall, calling everyone to attention.

"We have all six of the fuckers who attacked us. I say we go take care of business." He turns to look at everyone, not just his men, but us women and the Landrys. "We're a team. Landrys and the Girl Gang, if you want to join, you are more than welcome."

"How kind of him, considering we were the ones who caught them in the first place," Ana says under her breath, rolling her eyes.

"And he has to deal with the sheriff before the kids get to him again," Pops mutters back before cackling.

Marx circles his finger in the air and it's almost like a stampede, everyone rushing to get to Pops' office. I've not had the pleasure of visiting yet, and I know it makes me sound like a crazy person, but I'm looking forward to seeing the set up.

"Lovely, would you do me the honor of riding in the ATV with me?" Marx asks, holding his elbow out to me.

I avert my gaze, this gentlemanly side of Marx making me feel all shy. I peek up at him and then nod, tentatively placing my hand in the crook of his elbow. The smile he gifts me transforms his face from grumpy to handsome in an instant.

Leading me outside I jolt slightly when I notice that there is a passenger in the back.

"Is that a minions pillowcase over his head?" I ask, squinting into the dim evening light to get a better look at the man hog tied into the back of the ATV.

"Yes, yes it is," Marx answers.

A snort escapes me and Marx helps me into my seat. It's not something I couldn't do myself, but Marx has been incredibly attentive. I can see that he's trying to make up for all of his past behaviours, and it's endearing. It doesn't mean I'm going to forget the things he said, but I have forgiven him. People may think that makes me weak, but I think life is too short to hold someone's forgiveness in your hands and not grant it.

"Thank you," he whispers, brushing a kiss to the top of my head and then moving to his side of the vehicle.

"For what? I haven't done anything?"

"For giving me a chance, Lovely."

"Everyone deserves a chance, Marx." A muffled groan comes from behind me. "Well, most people deserve a chance."

Marx gives me a crooked grin and we ride in comfortable silence, each of us in our thoughts. We pull in next to all the DRMC SUVs and bikes and other forms of transport, all parked outside Pops' office. Office is an understatement. The place is a full sized barn. Excitement fizzes up in my tummy and I rush to get out of the ATV.

"Slow down, I promise you won't miss out on anything." Marx shakes his head, a smile on his lips at my excitement.

He throws the sheriff over his shoulder, then with a hand on my lower back he guides me to the door of the office. I open it as Marx has his hands full and we step inside.

"Dammit Chewy! I thought I told you to stay away!"

Marx

I should have known she had been playing it too cool. The last time I was in here was when I had to talk Sniper down from killing his brother there and then. Instead, he gave him a hell of a beating and we agreed the only people in and out would be TumTum, Chef and Niko, to keep everyone fed and watered. As per usual Chewy has done what Chewy likes to do.

"What? I was keeping them comfortable."

That's debatable. All five of the men are hanging from the ceiling, with just enough chain to have their toes touch the ground. All of them seem to be trying to get themselves higher, and I understand why. In front of each man, sitting on stools at crotch height are jars filled with Chewy's favorite fish. If that isn't pants pissingly scary enough, the Landrys have their gator, Gretchen, with them.

"Aww, did she lose another toe?" Lovely asks, spinning to look at Vic, Chris and Dom.

"Yeah, poor old girl. She's been having trouble healing, that's why we brought her with us," Vic answers.

"Well, that, and disposal."

"I dunno guys, flash freezing and meat grinding them seems to be pretty efficient," Chewy says, moving around the room with the ease of someone who grew up in this space.

"No reason we can't do both," Rhodie says, snagging his Ol Lady and dropping a kiss to her upturned lips. I can't wait to be able to do that with Lovely. She's given me a chance, and there's no way I'm gonna fuck up again.

The sheriff on my shoulder squirms and I dump his ass on

the ground. It's a long way down for someone who can't break his own fall, so he lands with a long groan, rolling in pain.

"Tsk tsk, should have been a good boy, huh Sheriff?" Chewy asks, whipping the cheery yellow pillowcase from his head.

Kelson's eyes dart around the room, eyes growing wider and wider until it looks like it hurts. I run my gaze around the room, taking it in just like Kelson. The outside is rustic, the typical red barn you'd see on any patch of land in rural America. But that's where the rustic ends. The inside of Pops' office is lined in stainless steel. We are standing in the main room, but there are at least 5 other smaller rooms on one side of the barn. There is also a bathroom and one of those shower things you see on pandemic films where they go in there to decontaminate. Why Pops and Chewy would need this shit is beyond me, but after seeing what the kids had set up in their own clubhouse, I'm sure they'll appreciate this space in the future.

"Babe, untie him and move him to the hot seat, please," Chewy says in a perky voice. Doing this type of work is the only time her voice has animation to it.

The brothers and I line ourselves against the walls. There is a small seating area, but that's been taken by the Girl Gang and Pops. I know Chewy has a plan. She always does. She deftly ties the sheriff to the chair, and then runs her hands over his body, my brother growling when she gets to Kelson's junk.

"Where are his weapons?" Chewy asks, looking puzzled.

"He didn't have any on him," Niko answers. He's the one who hog tied him and threw him in the ATV, so he'd know.

"You don't think it's weird the sheriff, who tried taking us out, who is in bed with two cartels, is unarmed?" Chewy says frowning.

"Those damn kids!" Blanche growls. Niko must know his

152

mother is about to lose it because he yells that he'll check the kids clubhouse and is gone in moments.

"Anyone else thinking we should just send the kids to take care of the cartel? They're dangerous as fuck and really the only thing holding them back is their early as shit bedtimes." Blanche glares at Rider and he grins back at her. One day all the shit he gives people is gonna come back at him and it'll be fucking glorious.

"Babe! Music me. I feel in the mood for something, hmm, something perky," Chewy demands.

Rhodie fucks about with this phone, then the opening vocals of "Bye Bye Bye" blast out through the surround sound system.

"Oh I know the dance to this one," Rider brags. Sniper gives him the death glare and he just flips the bird back. Shit, maybe Rider is right. Those little kids are more grown up than these fuckers.

"Right, let's get this show on the road!" Chewy straightens, stares Kelson in the eye and rips the tape from his mouth. He yells and pisses his pants at the same time.

"Eeeek! My favorite show is on!" Mira claps.

Chewy shakes her head in disappointment at the Sheriff, before patting him on the shoulder. "Pleasure to meet you, Sheriff. Welcome to the office. It's nice to have you here. As you can see your cartel buddies are all a little too busy to help you." Kelson's eyes dart around the room before they pinch shut.

"Uh, uh, uh," Pops sing songs. Within seconds he has those weird eyeball things in Kelson's eyes. The ones that hold his eyelids open. "You wanna see every little thing that happens, my friend." Pops pats him on the back comfortingly.

Chewy waves me to start and I don't move from my position.

153

I just bark questions at the man while Pops holds his head in whichever direction Chewy is. So far, she's gloved up and checking the other guests' penises for candiru fish.

"Got one!"

Kelson whimpers so I ask him again. "Who exactly ordered the hit?"

"I-I was just meant to make sure the police stay away. I didn't mean this to happen!"

"You mean you didn't mean to get caught on our cameras with your arm out the window firing bullets at people?" Chewy says, tugging on something hanging out of one guy's dick. "Sorry buddy, I can't get it out. We'll have to amputate." In the blink of an eye the guy's dick is severed and his scream bounces off the walls.

Kelson's bladder lets go again, and he vomits when Chewy throws the appendage into the waiting mouth of Gretchen.

"Dammit, he has a weak stomach. That is not what I was hoping for," Chewy mutters. She and Pops confer over something before a grin appears. "Perfect solution!"

She gestures to the guy with Lovely's dick on his chest, and some other lacky. Rhodie gets both the men down, both look grateful when their tiny dicks leave the jars of dick fish. Pops moves fluidly toward Rhodie, pushing a what looks to be a fucking sex chair in his direction.

"What the fuck are they gonna do with *that?*" Tank asks, eyes wide. Mira is scribbling as fast as she can, noting everything down for her next bestseller.

They strap dick chest guy to the chair, wrists cuffed to his ankles, body angled over the top, his asshole winking at us. I avert my eyes, not wanting to look, because who the hell in their right mind would? My gaze catches on the women, the lovely women we've brought into our club and it's clear they're the type of people who want to look. Each has their eyes focussed on the dude with his ass in the air.

"He threatened Pops with a gun! Do your worst, Chewy!" The girls cheer her on and I try to hide my chuckle. Shit, even Lovely is right up there, egging her on.

Chewy gestures to have the other one attached to the St Andrews cross that Pops just happens to have handy. I would ask what the hell is wrong with these people, but I doubt anyone really knows.

"Kelson, you will answer Marx's questions. For every non-answer, your buddies will take the hit. Got it?" Kelson hesitates and Chewy shrugs, stepping up to the one on the cross. With the flick of her wrist she has his eyeball out of his socket and sailing across the room to Pops who snatches it out of midair and promptly shoves it in the other guys waiting asshole.

Both men scream. Kelson sobs, snot going everywhere as he begs her to stop. Clearly he doesn't know Chewy. "Do you understand how the game is played now?" Chewy asks in a sweet as pie voice.

"Yes, Yes, anything you want to know. I'll tell you.," he splutters.

Huh. It's interesting that Chewy decided to play it this way. I figured she'd cut Kelson up into little pieces, but instead she's playing on what conscience and care for the public he must have had when he started out as a rookie wanting to make a difference in the world. Just because he's a piece of shit criminal now, doesn't mean he always was.

"Who's pulling the strings, Kelson?" I growl at the man, making him jump.

"There's two of them. Serpiente is one, but he has a partner. I don't know who they are. That's all I know." He stares nervously at Chewy but she keeps her word. She doesn't slice off any more body parts, but she does use her knife to paint a pretty picture on the now one eyed man.

"Who's heading up the cartels? I need names."

His eyes dart to Sniper's brother and I know this isn't going to be good. "I don't know who heads up Cartel de Silencio, but Joseph is head of La Sombre Roja. He's the one who called the hit."

"You motherfucker!" Sniper roars and flies across the room, fists hitting Joseph's already bruised and burned flesh. "You motherfucker! You saw what it did to Maria, to Mama, you fucker!" Sniper roars and his voice breaks.

Stepping up behind him I wrap him in a bear hug, gripping him so tight he has no option but to drop his arms. His weight leans into mine and I know there's no way I can let him finish off Joseph, no matter how much he wants it. The fresh scent of Lovely and the soft touch of her hand on my back has any tension I was holding for Sniper, leaching from my body. Her delicate touch grounds me as she moves around my bulk, to then lay a hand on Sniper. She stands on her toes and whispers in his ear. His body slumps when she pulls back and lays a hand on his chest, giving him a nod and a tight, sad, smile.

"I'm done, Pres. As far as I'm concerned, I have no brother," Sniper whispers, voice broken.

I release him from my arms, and instead of letting him leave the office alone, brother after MC brother steps up to grip his shoulder, pulling him into their bodies as he passes.

Judge catches my eye and dips his chin, a steady presence at Sniper's back as they move to the door.

"What did you say to him?" I murmur to Lovely, standing so close I could reach out and wrap her in my arms.

She turns to look at me, her face tipped back, looking more beautiful than I've ever seen her. "I told him that his family will take care of Joseph. We'd make him beg for death, but it won't come quickly. We'll make him suffer prolonged torture the same way his family suffered waiting for their little girl to come home. He'll feel all the hurt they did until Sniper wishes to put an end to it." A slow grin spreads across her face and fuck if my cock doesn't thicken.

"Ah, love birds, can we get back to business?" Switch asks, clearing his throat.

I wave a hand in Chewy's direction and she indicates to Rhodie to line up another victim.

"So, who wants to see how many of these dudes' body parts we can fit in this guy's ass?"

Chapter 14

Lovely

Well, it's official. Chewy can fit a heck of a lot more in an anus than I ever thought possible.

"I never knew a prison pocket was so roomy," Ana says, voice full of wonder.

"What did you just say?" Dex squints at her.

"His prison pocket," Ana points in the direction of the dead man, still splayed out on the chair, with a foot hanging out of his rear.

Dex blinks at her before he bursts into laughter, as does everyone else. It seems odd, to be laughing at a time like this, surrounded by blood and vomit and who knows what else, but that's kinda how we roll I guess.

"You people are fucking loco!" Joseph yells, violently bucking in his chains.

The man has had a front row seat to all of Chewy's techniques tonight. Slicing, dicing, chemical burning, injectables, feeding bits to Gretchen and Chomper. He's stayed stoic this whole time, only just losing it now. Silence descends over the room as we all, as a collective stare at the man that called the hit on us. On my baby. Marx turns to look at us, all scattered around the room. His hard gaze making contact with everyone, then he tips his chin. He moves across the room to the mechanism that will lower Joseph closer to the floor. Rhodie unhooks his hands and then sharing a look with his brother, marches Joseph toward the St Andrews cross. It seems to be an integral part of Chewy and Pops' repertoire. Using one hand to hold Joseph by the scruff of his neck, Rhodie uses the other hand to release the corpse still attached. He lets the body fall to the floor, then forces Joseph to stand on the body of his cartel brother. Rhodie roughly attaches Joseph to the cross, making sure the restraints are tight enough to hurt.

Marx takes measured steps toward Joseph, until a blonde blur rushes past. "You threatened my *daughter*," Remy seethes, her arm moving in a wild arc. She leans back and spits into Joseph's face. He sneers at her as her saliva rolls down his bruised cheek, mingling into the blood welling from the cut on his neck. "For Sniper," she whispers, stepping back into Wire's arms.

Rider moves next, "For Sniper," he too swipes at Joseph, this time blood seeping through a cut on the man's thigh.

One by one we step up, repeating the same mantra, cutting him anywhere and everywhere. The inside of his groin, his penis, his nipples, chest, stomach, anywhere we can reach while reminding him that while he turned his back on family, we didn't. Chewy and Pops are singing and dancing around to the playlist on mix. Lady Gaga is singing how we're all on the edge of glory, and I can't help the snicker that escapes my lips. Marx raises a thick dark brown brow at me, and I grin back.

The scene is just so fitting. Joseph is pinned to the St Andrews cross sans skin, Lady Gaga is playing and Chewy and Pops are filling a tub with vinegar.

"Oh oh, let's make it a tub of *piss* and vinegar!" Rider says with glee, unbuttoning his jeans and taking a pee right in front of us all.

I quickly avert my eyes, staring anywhere but in the direction of jeans being unbuttoned and unzipped.

"This really is good stuff," Mira mutters, her little pen really getting a workout tonight.

"Babe, let's get him in the tub," Chewy calls out, Rhodie eager to do her bidding. So eager in fact he stops to make out with her for a long moment before doing as she asked.

"Lovely." Turning toward Marx's rough voice I'm surprised by the tenderness in his eyes. He gathers me in his arms, my face to his chest., "Close your eyes, babe." His large hands, one on either side of my face, move to cup my ears, pressing me further into his chest as a blood curdling scream reverberates off the stainless steel walls and through my body causing me to shiver.

The gut wrenching sound stops abruptly, Switch moving in fast to take Joseph's vitals. His broad shoulders slump a little. "He's all good, just passed out."

"Grab the smelling salts. I want this fucker to feel every moment of his pain," Marx growls, the vibrations in his chest soothing against my chest.

I curl in deeper to his chest and all those big words I spoke - dating, getting over this man, finding someone new, they all fly out the window. Perhaps I was always meant to be in this place, right here. Maybe I needed to hear those words to make myself stronger, to push myself to do more than just be a mother, and maybe a wife. Or maybe Marx was just being a jerk because what I've learned recently is that men can sometimes be idiots, their own worst enemies, really. I've sat by and watched some of the DRMC men find their women, and then almost lose them, and then find them again. Maybe this is just part of the story.

Joseph jerks awake on a gasp, then groans, his body shuddering violently in the vinegar bath.

"I don't think he'll take much more tonight, Pres," Switch booms, close enough to make the prisoner flinch.

"Chewy, can you keep him on ice until tomorrow?"

"Even better. We can just roll him, tub and all, into the light room." I turn to look at Pops. "Dark is good for torture cos it makes a man lose hope. But constant bright light fucks with your internal body clock. Your body doesn't know when to sleep or when to wake. Fucker will lose his mind before he loses his life," Pops grins maniacally, Chewy leaning in to high five him.

"Get it done. I'm taking Lovely home." With that Marx turns us toward the door, arm still around me.

We make our way to the ATV, Marx helping me in like a true gentleman, then he gets in his side, taking the winding trip back to my little cabin. I should really head to the nursery, to check in on Bee and make sure my girl is OK, but after the excitement of today not only am I physically tired, but I'm emotionally wrung out, too. I know that rage and fury at those men fuelled me through a lot of what we did tonight, but now, in the quiet darkness, my soul aches a little.

A large, warm hand lands on mine, squeezing gently. "You alright?"

I clear my throat., "Yeah. Just never want to see another bumhole for as long as I live."

Marx's laugh booms out in the quiet evening, the sheer mirth makes me smile. "Where the hell does she get these ideas?" he sputters out.

"I'm not sure, but I'm glad she's on our side."

We pull up to the cabin, and before I can even move out of my seat, Marx has me in his arms, carrying me up the porch steps and into my home. As per usual it's dimly lit, the warm light coming from the lamps dotted around the living area. I have no idea how Tav did it, but they're all set to come on with a gentle glow at a certain time of the day. It's very clever.

"You get cleaned up, and I'll be back in a little bit." Marx walks through my home, gently depositing me in the bathroom before turning on the shower to heat. "Will you be OK?"

I'm exhausted, but I also know there is no way I'm getting into bed with blood and who knows what else still on me. Instead of answering I nod, and then watch as Marx's lips quirk up as he backs out of the bathroom, pulling the door closed behind him.

Shucking off my clothes I step into the hot water, letting it sluice down my back, washing away the night. The hot water beats down against my back, easing any aches and pains I have lingering from my injury. I run my soapy hand over the wound, Switch having let me know that it's OK to start gently washing the area now. It's amazing how something so small can so fundamentally change your life. A week or so ago I swore off Marx and vowed I'd find my own happiness. Now I'm standing here after being showered by words and affection from the very same man.

Shaking my head I turn off the water, stepping out and wrapping myself in my soft, snuggly towel. It was one of the first things I bought with my first paycheck. Homewares, new towels and sheets and pretty things that Bee and I could enjoy. I dry myself, then pull on my pajamas. In the Keep we wore plain cotton nightgowns that tied at the neck and were floor length. Now I wear Marvel superhero pajamas that Chewy gifted me.

Leaving the bathroom I walk into my bedroom and stop in my tracks. There, lying on my bed, hair damp from the shower is Marx. Shirtless, with low slung sweatpants. And lying on his chest is my heart, my little Bee with a huge smile on her face as his large hand rubs her back.

"Hey, I, ah, figured you'd want Bee to be close tonight. Mama Debs said she was being a little stinker and not wanting to sleep." As if on cue Bee pops up and squeals, clapping her hands and bouncing her little butt on Marx's abs.

Jeez Louise, I'm going to need another shower at this rate. I'm hot and bothered and not once have I felt a feeling this intense when looking at a man in my bed. In the past seeing Royal in bed would cause me to break out in a sweat. Seeing Marx is also making me sweat, for a completely different reason.

His gaze runs over me like a caress, but his face changes when he reaches my eyes. He looks sheepish, almost a little embarrassed.

"Shit, sorry Lovely. I didn't mean to just invite myself in and lounge everywhere, I should have asked, I just thought you'd want Bee to be here and-"

I rush over to him, placing my hand over his mouth, stopping the verbal diarrhea. "It's OK. It's a surprise, but a nice one. I love how thoughtful you were."

I don't give him a chance to say anything else. Instead, I climb into the other side of the bed and let Bee launch herself between the two of us. "Marx, would you like to stay the night?"

The smile he gives me makes my heart flutter.

"I'd love to."

Marx

I quietly extricate Bee's foot from my face and roll to sit up on the side of the bed. Glancing behind me I take in the peaceful faces of the woman and little girl who have stolen my heart. Who knew that as soon as I stopped being an asshole my life would feel happier, more settled even with a fucking war on my hands? Not me, obviously.

Scrubbing my hands down my face I decide I may as well start the day. It's still early out so I decide to take a jog around the perimeter, to get my head in the game. We learned a lot of good shit last night, shit that will help us when it comes to hitting the cartels, but it still doesn't feel like enough. I quietly move through the house, stopping by the door to shove my feet in my boots. Yeah I should be jogging in wanky running shoes, but I don't own any so my trusty boots will do. I mean, in the Marines all we had were our boots and we did just fine. It's not like they gave us the luxury of ergonomic footwear. Sneaking out the door I pull it gently behind me.

"Whatdya know, kid?"

"Fucks sake, Pops!" I hiss at the old man perched on the swing seat just outside Lovely's door.

"Yeah yeah. Does she like explosives or not?"

Taking a deep breath I let it out slowly. "I'm not exactly sure on that one, but she keeps surprising me, so she could."

Pops rolls his eyes, following me down the steps. "Do you know *anything* that might help your cause?"

I start to gain speed before breaking out into a slow jog. Not one to be beaten, Pops starts up the ATV, pulling in next to me, matching my speed.

"Fine. I learned that she loves to draw and she's fucking good at it. She used to tattoo at the Keep and I think she might take Mad Dog up on his offer,"

"No fucking way? That's awesome. I'll get my tools out, check them over," my dad's voice comes from out of nowhere and I almost trip as a second ATV pulls up on the other side of me.

"Fucks sake you two! Don't you have anything better to do?" I growl, speeding up a little more.

"Not really," Pops and Mad Dog reply in god damn unison.

"Shouldn't you be off checking up on everyone or helping with breakfast or something?"

"Listen son, there's nothing more important to me than your happiness," Mad Dog says, flicking me sincere glances while trying not to crash into anything.

Flicking my eyes to Pops, he shrugs. "I'm not too interested in your happiness, but I am interested in Lovely's. For some reason, I think her happiness lies with you, so I need to make sure you're doing all the shit you're meant to be doing."

"Well, she's talking to me, and she asked me to sleep over."

"You've been sleeping there for days, kid. That ain't a big breakthrough." Pops rolls his eyes.

I let out a huff. "In her *bed*. With her and Bee. Last night was a big night for her. As furious as she was, it's not her natural setting to wish ill on people." The old men remain silent in their agreement, but I know they think I'm right.

Pops' mouth works as he chews on his lip. "And she said that? She asked you to stay and just...sleep?"

I nod, whilst keeping pace. It feels fucking good to get my blood pumping in a way that isn't jacking off in the shower.

Mad Dog lets out a low whistle, leaning forward in his seat to look across me at Pops, who nods back at him.

"What?"

"Do you know how big that is? Her letting you lie next to her?" Pops asks quietly.

Slowing to a stop I rest my hands on my knees, catching my breath a little. I look around at where I am on the property and find I'm standing not far from Pops' office. We really need to call it the Rev Room II because the office just isn't as catchy.

Pops and my father circle their ATV's around until they're parked right in front of me.

"Did you know when Lovely first arrived she had nightmares?"

"What? She was at the clubhouse when she first arrived, for months. I don't ever recall hearing anything about nightmares." I run a hand down my beard, trying to think back to that time. I definitely would remember that.

"You were probably busy worrying about running away from that tiny little lady," Pops snorts. "Besides, you wouldn't have noticed because Blanche spent most nights sleeping on the floor next to her. Lovely couldn't even have her sister in the bed next to her." I stare at Pops in shock. He lets out a sigh. "Do you know, kid, that one of the most intimate things you can do with another human, is to let yourself relax and just sleep? Think about the amount of trust someone needs to have to be able to do that. Now think of where Lovely came from. How she could never trust that her husband or the council wouldn't do something fucking evil to her when she least expected it."

Thinking back to Lovely's face, her expression was peaceful, her plump lips relaxed in sleep, dead to the world. She trusted me with not only her heart last night, but also with the one person who means everything to her.

"Ah, now he's getting it," Mad Dog smiles.

"She trusts you enough to sleep next to you. You're doing alright, kid, but you could always do better."

I swallow the lump in my throat. "What do you suggest?"

"How the fuck should I know? She's your woman. Think about shit she's been deprived of, and then give it to her." Pops revs the ATV and takes off toward his office, probably to check on Joseph or the massive fucking incinerator he showed us last night as he and Chewy calmly threw in body parts.

Think of something Lovely missed out on. Fucking easy for Pops to say, that woman missed out on a whole bunch of shit. I start the trek to the farmhouse, wondering what Lovely has always wanted to do and never got the chance to. I think back to when my men met their women. Rhodie came to me in my office to ask where he should take Chewy on a date. That's fucking it! Lovely would have never been on a date before, maybe I could organise a date night for us? Feeling buoyed by my idea I realize that I'll never be able to get her off the farm and on a date with the fucking cartels hanging over our heads. According to Roman's intel, they'll be making drop offs of their product in four days. That gives me today and tomorrow to plan, and then split my club and send my men out. It doesn't really sit well with me, but it's the best plan we've got.

I wave to Nitro and Fox sitting outside their trailer, Fox's

167

eyes closed as he basks in the morning sun.

"How you feeling, brother?"

Fox cracks an eyelid. "A fuck ton better than the guys you had in the barn last night," he smirks.

"Heard about that, huh?"

"Fucking heard it in surround sound when Judge and Sniper walked through the door. If I were you I'd get the Girl Gang to have a word with the new woman, she was on the fucking war path this morning."

Shit. I'm going to have to get Judge to rein her in. Or maybe I'll ask Debs to chat to her. If I send the whole Girl Gang the fucking thing could go sideways before we know it.

"Will do, brother. You just get better." I squeeze his shoulder, and turn to walk the rest of the way to the farmhouse.

I may want to take Lovely on a date, but first things first. Shower, breakfast and then tighten up plans to take down two fucking cartels. Child's play.

Chapter 15

Lovely

By the time Bee and I wake, Marx's side of the bed is cold. I feel a slight pinch in my chest until I check my watch and realize that it's well past ten in the morning. Bee makes grumbling noises and I know she must be starving, but this little girl has never been an early-to-rise type of kid.

"Come on, little Bee, let's get you some brunch," I smile down at her, running my hand over her thick, dark hair. Every now and then I'm amazed at how much she looks like Blanche's kids, but then I remember that they all have the same father, even if Sage, Cove and Elio's mothers are different. The Landry genes are damn strong. I suppose at some stage we should be worried about them having issues, given they're all related in more than one way. Maybe I'll ask Chewy about it. She would know. Heck, Elio probably does too.

"Mark?" Bee asks, pointing to where Marx slept last night.

"He's gone to work, and we should too. Come on lazy bones!"

I let Bee bounce around on the bed as I get dressed. Usually

I'm in one of my brothers' oversized flannel shirts and jeans, but today I decide to put on a pretty purple tank top I bought when I went shopping with the Girl Gang one time. I have lots of prettier things than what I normally wear, it's just that I never felt the need to wear anything different. Now though, I think it is time to try something new. It's warm out but not warm enough to only wear a tank with jeans, so I throw the flannel over it and leave it unbuttoned. I've seen Nat wear the same type of thing and it makes her look effortlessly cool.

Staring at myself in the mirror, I decide to try and do a messy bun look. Normally I leave my hair long, or in a single braid, but not today! Today is a good day. I slept all night with a man and I didn't wake up in a cold sweat. In fact, it's the first time I'd ever just *slept* with a man. I feel triumphant and strong and I want to celebrate with a new look.

"Mommy pretty!" Bee coos from the bed.

I rush toward her with tickle fingers, attacking her sides before I scoop her up carefully with my good arm, and my heart flutters when she throws her head back, messy hair and all and lets out a loud squeal. She really is the cutest little girl and the light of my life. Although I guess there are lots of little lights around my life now.

I set her in her little booster at the island and prepare her favorite breakfast - oats and strawberries. It's a good nutritious breakfast and something I ate everyday as a child. Not all the memories I have of the Keep are terrible. In fact, up until I was a teenager my life was pretty idyllic. Kids at the Keep got to have childhoods, playing outside, entertaining themselves, good food that was grown by the men and women of the Keep. We were healthy and thriving. It's just as you got older and pulled back the curtain you realized things weren't all as they appeared.

A quiet knock pulls me away from watching Bee demolish her breakfast, so I check to make sure she's all secure before moving the short distance to my front door and opening it to find Kaia on the other side.

"Good morning! How are you?" I ask her, turning back to Bee and gesturing that she follow me.

"Um, I'm good." She stands awkwardly at the edge of the counter, before she drops her wringing hands and clenches them. "Actually, no, I'm not."

I hesitate for a moment, not sure what to say, but thankfully, Kaia carries on her train of thought.

"Look, I'm not an idiot, I know that what the DRMC gets up to isn't always above board. I've done my research, and I know that while you guys do good stuff, charity and things, you also do bad stuff to keep people in Rose Grove safe." I nod my head. I don't interject because she seems to be talking through whatever it is that's upset her. "The twins and I, we heard a snippet of the bad last night. I was looking out the window and saw Leo, um, Judge leaving that barn out the back, and the scream, I could hear it from the trailer."

I reach out and lay my hand on hers. "Kaia, sometime-"

"It made me mad."

"Huh?"

She flicks her blue gaze to mine, "It pissed me off. Everyone got to go down there and beat on the men that threatened us. He had bullets with *my* babies names on them. I wanted to be there with you and I felt, I felt, like an outsider." She raises her eyes to look at me and all I can see is doubt and sadness. She swipes a tear away, "It's OK, I mean I'm used to it, it's just -"

"You've been alone with the twins for a long time, haven't

171

you?"

Kaia drops her head, nodding, letting out a huff. "After we left town it was just me and my dad. Then the twins came along and it was just the four of us. I had a boyfriend, well, a failed relationship, and ugh, I never wanted to be put in that position ever again." She looks wistfully out the window, where I can see the twins are hovering just outside my cabin.

She doesn't say it in as many words, but I know that this woman has been through the wringer.

"Kaia, the DRMC is a family. I know this situation isn't the best way for Judge to get to know the twins, but trust me, those kids belong to Judge, and they and you, belong to DRMC now. No matter what happens. Last night was something that doesn't happen a lot," I try to hide my smirk, "and you're new at this. So, give it time."

She nods, sniffing, "OK, I was just really pissed and wanted to get a few licks in, you know?" she peeks at me and I can't help but laugh.

"Oh, you're gonna fit in perfectly! Hey, come back tonight after dinner. I'll get all the girls together and we'll watch a movie. What do you say?"

She makes out like she's thinking for a moment. "I'll see you then."

Marx

"So, we're in agreement?" I raise my brow, looking around the table at my MC.

The women have sat this Church out, preferring to get together for a movie. It seems after dealing with the men in Pops' Office, they're quite happy to leave the cartel up to us. I was surprised, and any other time I'd be suspicious of their motives, but at this point they haven't given me any reason to doubt what they're up to. Still, I'll have Mad Dog keep an eye on them. And Pops as well, seeing as he's with the women somewhere.

My men and the Landrys nod. Roman sits smirking in the corner but I'm choosing to ignore him. He's offered to help provide backup and all clean up services, so as long as he keeps his word and doesn't get in the way, then I'll leave him to it. The quicker we can get this business over and done with, the better as far as I'm concerned.

"Our second piece of business I wanted to discuss involves the Landrys. They've come to us to ask to start a chapter of the DRMC in Louisiana." My men all trade glances. Some are nodding, others like Rider and Flack have smiles on their faces.

"What about prospecting?" Dex asks, "Those of us who patched over from Death Riders never prospected. The Landrys, as with the Tombs, have had our back through a lot of shit."

Everyone makes noises in agreement, only stopping when I thump the wall. "I don't disagree. However, prospecting is an integral part of joining an MC."

"What about an expedited prospect phase? Instead of a full year, they do, say six months for the Landrys, less for the Tombs. They've been here since before the Death Riders," Tank offers.

173

Brothers are nodding, chatting amongst themselves and I'm feeling a little overwhelmed. My club is about to grow by six if we all vote to have the Landrys and the two Tombs who aren't already members. On one hand it's fucking great, having that sheer number of men all wanting to band together to keep people safe. On the other hand, that's another six men for me to worry about. The pros outweigh the cons and I'm sure with Lovely by my side I can handle fucking anything life throws at me, including an almost 20 strong club.

"All those in favor?" The vote amongst patched members is unanimous and like they stated to me, the Landrys make it known that Chris and Dom will prospect here first, then they'll swap out for Vic once patched.

I close Church and take a seat on the porch swing outside, my boot pushing off the wooden deck, rocking me gently.

"Fucking hell brother, who would have thought when dad and his cronies set up the DRMC it'd grow this big? A Louisiana chapter? Fucking wild," Rhodie snorts, shaking his head as he leans against the railing, facing me.

"Fuck I know brother. I mean, who would have thought we'd also be torturing fucking cartel members in our spare time as well?"

Rhodie barks out a laugh. "If it makes you feel better, *we* don't do any torturing."

"You're right. We leave that up to your woman and her elderly grandfather," I snort.

"No two better people to do it," he grins, his teeth white in the dimming light. "You feeling OK about what we're about to do?"

"As usual Chewy's plan is foolproof. Fuck, why am I even the Pres? We should just give it to Chewy and be done with it."

My brother chuckles at the thought. "Look, Chewy is fucking good at all sorts of shit, but you're the Pres because it's more than just leading us into shit. Or getting us out of shit. Don't think I don't see how much you counsel the brothers. How many nights you've spent helping us sort through our bullshit. Fuck, half the men here were broken when they joined. You're the one that gave them something to aim for. Can you fucking imagine Chewy having to talk through someone's feelings?"

"Shit, Rhodie, I'd pay to see that," I laugh. It feels good to laugh, to blow away the fucking doom and gloom of what we're about to do.

"So, brother," Rhodie pauses.

"Yes, brother?"

"You know that in two days' time we could be riding to our fucking deaths, right? We may not all make it back in one piece."

I scrub a hand down my face, "Yeah."

"Have you thought about what that would do to Lovely?"

My jaw ticks, because I have thought about it. I've thought a fucking lot about it. On one hand I should leave her alone until all of this is done. On the other hand, for selfish reasons, I want to spend an evening with her just being together. We don't even need to kiss or touch, I just want to be in her orbit, soaking up the goodness one last time, just in case.

"Word from the wise?"

"Is that you?" I joke, trying to lighten the mood.

"Don't wait, brother. If you want to take her on a date or something like that, then do it. Nothing in this life is guaranteed. You have to grab the sweet moments whenever you can, cos you never know when it'll turn sour."

With that he slaps me on the shoulder, giving it a squeeze

175

before sauntering off. He's right, I know he is. There's also some part of me that thinks if I take all I can with Lovely before I go, then I'll fight harder to come home to her and Bee.

"So, we putting together a date?"

"Where the fuck did you come from?"

"Eh, its my house," Pops shrugs. "I can be wherever the fuck I want to be."

I stare at him for a moment, before letting him win this one. "Yes. We're going to put together a date. Is there a nice place around here where we can picnic or something? I don't want to take her to town just yet, it's too fucking dangerous."

"Let me ask the kids."

Before I can ask what the hell that means he takes off like his ass is on fire, back to Lovely's cabin and the Girl Gang.

"What the fuck have I gotten myself into?" I mutter to myself.

I kick at the floorboards again, getting the sway going, thinking about all the shit that needs to happen, and in what order so we can all get home safe. I'm not willing to risk anyone. I almost fucking lost Fox and Lovely, I can't have anyone else on my conscience.

Chapter 16

Lovely

"**L**et's get this party started!" Ana whoops, Jr on her hip. "Mama needs a drink."

She pushes past me in the doorway and heads straight for the counter. Nat gives me an apologetic smile and all my ladies file in through the door. Vi with Juno, Chewy with Laney, Blanche with Tess, Nat with Rosie, Remy, Mira, Kaia, Mama Debs and Pops. Pops is an honorary lady we decided. I mean, it's not the Girl Gang without Pops, is it?

"Knock knock, do you have space for two more?" An accented voice drifts through the open doorway.

"Yes! Come in, come in," I wave both hands at Sasha and Dima and we all make room for them in my cabin.

"And one more hanger on?" Mad Dog's voice drifts through the door as he enters with a cheeky smile.

"Yes, and you too." I roll my eyes, closing the door behind him.

It's not the largest space, so it's definitely filled to the brim tonight, and I wouldn't trade it for the world. I love having guests, making them feel at home. For some reason it feels different here than it did at the Keep. There it was an obligation. Here it's a pleasure.

"What film are we watching?" I call out, bringing bowls of chips, dips and a whole charcuterie board I learned to make from the internet.

Vi lets out a low whistle, "Well, well well, look at little Miss Domesticated here." I roll my eyes at her and flick her with the dish cloth.

"Let's put a kids film on in the background and then while they're busy watching all the colors and sounds, we can catch up on gossip."

"Yeah, good plan. I don't feel like we know enough about the new girl yet," Nat winks at Kaia.

The other woman doesn't flinch. From what I know of her she's one tough cookie. We talked for around an hour today before she thought she better see what her twins were up to. I really like her and I think if she gives us, and Judge a chance, it'll be the best thing that ever happened to her little family.

Dima very helpfully finds some kids show to put on, and the toddlers all make their way to the colorful rug in front of the TV.

"Should we be worried? They're all staring at the thing like we don't exist," Remy mutters.

"Nah, I'm sure they'll be fine. We'll counteract it with some classical music or something, right Chewy?" Vi asks.

"I can come up with an easy to follow brain growth routine if you all would like one?"

"So, Lovely, how is Marx?" Pops butts in, saving us from having to decline Chewy's very generous offer.

I wait for my friends to stop making "ooohing" noises before I say anything. Well, that and I have to get my thoughts straight. "Marx is fine. He said he wants to try to, I guess, date me? He wants a relationship, so, whatever that looks like."

"And he's treating you well? No saying shitty things?" Ana asks, eyes narrowed. "Cos if he is, I can get Sasha or Roman to kick his arse for you."

"As nice as that sentiment sounds, he is treating me well. I mean, we've had rocky patches, but I get it. The pressure on him is immense at times. Look how many of us look to him for guidance, or to keep us safe."

Nat bobs her head from side to side, and Mira shrugs. Remy looks thoughtful and I know she is more like me personality-wise. She spends time watching people.

"I don't care what he's got going on. As long as he's treating you right," Pops grumbles.

I can't help the smile that blooms on my face. "He's treating me like Wes does Buttercup."

Everyone swoons, well, most everyone. Chewy nods and Dima sits stiffly next to his swooning brother.

"Has he asked you on a date yet? Oh my gosh, what will you wear?" Mira asks, then gets all excited at the prospect even though no date asking has happened. "Ugh, it's going to be soooo sweet, I can already feel my teeth getting cavities. It's kinda like a second chance romance. Big alpha dude puts his foot in his mouth-"

"Over and over," Pops butts in.

"-and then he sees the light! Realizes he's been a dick and needs to win back the woman's heart." She sighs. "He's got it pretty easy really. We all know the way to your heart is Bee.

All the man needs to do is treat her right, and woo you Wesley-style and BAM! Lovely is the first lady and all is right in the world."

I smile gently at her. Mira sees things the same way she sees her romance stories. Probably in more ways than one seeing as her romance stories do seem to have an awful lot of murder in them.

"Do you think it's worth giving him a second chance? Is anyone worth a second chance if they've proven they were idiots the first time?" Kaia asks, brows furrowed.

I'm not sure it works for everyone, but I'm willing to try. I open my mouth to say as much but Nat beats me to it.

"When Savage and I were a new couple, he made a series of really dumb decisions. Late to dates because he was drinking with the boys, he missed a romantic home cooked meal because he was out with the boys. He thought he could have all the fun in the world, and I would wait for him whenever he was ready. So I dumped the romantic dinner over his head and dumped his ass. Took him two months of wooing for me to give him a second chance. I'm glad I did because he's the love of my life."

"I freaked out and ran away up a mountain. Gus, who hates the great outdoors, hiked 8 hours to find me," Ana adds.

"Jules fucked me and then hit me with a stone cold line about it meaning nothing. I gave him shit about it until he panic attacked himself into being the best damn boyfriend that ever lived."

"I ran away to infiltrate a human trafficking ring without telling Rhodie. I've gotten myself kidnapped a couple of times and he still lets me peg him because he loves me," Chewy beams.

"Ah," Mad Dog clears his throat, clearly not expecting that

revelation from Chewy. "I think what they're trying to tell you, sweetheart, is that people do dumb shit. But it's up to you if you think they deserve a second chance."

I walk over and drop a kiss on Mad Dog's cheek. He beams up at me and I turn to drop one on Pops' too, seeing as both these men hold a piece of my heart. They're always there for pep talks and counseling.

"Ah, where's Pops?"

"He mentioned something about going to the big house to get ice or something," Mama Debs says, gazing out the window with a smile on her face. She loves that man to distraction.

We settle into relative ease with each other, Ana growing more and more tipsy as the night goes on. Remy shows us some sweet self defense moves and Kaia tells us a little more about her life with the twins. By the time everyone's Ol Men arrive to take them home, I am officially filled to the brim with joy at spending an evening with my friends. Even more so when Dima leaves us with a mysterious "The time is near ladies. I'll be in touch," as he walks out the door with Sasha.

"I'm guessing your night went well?" Marx's deep voice rolls over me as I stand in the kitchen putting leftovers into little containers. "We could hear the laughter from the farmhouse."

I whirl around to face him, cheeks immediately heating. "What did you hear?"

He looks thoughtful, brows pinched, "A whole lot of squealing, giggling and someone, I think it was Vi, yelling 'We all need replicas of our men's dicks!'"

I snort, but don't confirm or deny anything. "I had a wonderful evening. They really are the best group of women I could ever wish to meet." I meet his gaze with my own. "I'm really glad I'm here."

"I'm really glad you are too." He smiles softly, moving close enough to run a thick finger down my cheek. "Um, Lovely," he clears his throat, suddenly looking nervous, "Would you do me the honor of accompanying me on a date tomorrow? We can make it early, before Bee's bedtime because I know you like putting her down yourself."

My stomach flutters and my mind immediately flicks to my wardrobe and what the heck I'm going to wear. I don't even realize I haven't answered him until he clears his throat again, looking a little constipated.

"Oh, I'd love to, Marx, I would love that very much." I smile, "But, we're on lockdown?"

"Leave it all to me," he winks.

Marx

"And you're sure this will work?"

"Sure. I mean, what's the worst that could happen?" Pops says with a little shrug.

I look toward Mad Dog, Rhodie, and damn near every man in my club, including the new bastards who all stand there grinning. They know as well as I do that this could go fucking amazing, or turn to shit.

"We're *sure* that Elio has this shit covered?" I check again. I want to be sure. And I also want to settle my nerves. This shit needs to be perfect.

Pops rolls his eyes and I catch Elio behind his back pulling the same move. I'd growl at the little shit, but I kinda need his expertise. He must sense that I'm apprehensive because he walks up to me, places his small hand on my forearm and with a serious face he says, "Trust me Pres."

I nod, because what the fuck else are you meant to do when a seven year old asks you to trust them?

"It'll be fine. Besides, you should be more worried about you messing up than us," Cove loudly points out. Now her? Her I know I shouldn't trust. Luckily her best friend Jovie gives me two thumbs up and makes me feel a little better.

"OK, good, this is good. And everything else is set up?" I flick my eyes to Rider.

After Pops' big song and dance to Mama Debs, I knew that I needed to call him in if I wanted some type of musical director. Actually, scrap that, I wanted a band to give Lovely the kind of date I'd take her on if we weren't on lockdown. You know, dinner, dancing, that sort of thing. Instead I've got Rider going rogue on the music and dancing part.

"Pres, we got this. Just chill, everything will be fine," he assures me. I narrow my eyes at him and his grin grows wider, not making me feel at ease at all.

"If this turns to shit," I address everyone circled around me in the middle of the main room of the farmhouse, "You're all to blame. I'll seek each and every one of you out and nut punch you. Not you kids," I add when Jovie gasps.

"I'd like to see you try," Cove mutters under her breath. If she wasn't so scary I'd pick her to lead the next generation of DRMC.

"OK. Good. Now fuck off so I can get ready."

My men all rib me, some slap me too hard on the back and

183

they all file out of the room. Everyone but Rhodie who sits on the couch, spread out like a fucking king, with a shit eating grin on his face.

"Stop looking at me like that."

"No."

I growl at him but it does nothing. Being my little brother means he was born to give me shit. "Go on, ask."

"Ask what?"

"Ask me how to date so hard that you get the girl. I mean, I got Chewy to go on a date with me and bam! She's my Ol Lady. I know how this shit works big brother. If you want advice, ask now or forever hold your piece."

My eyes narrow. "I remember some fucker coming into my office shitting his pants because he'd never been on a date before. I also remember giving that same fucker the idea on where the hell to take his date."

"You sure about that, big brother?"

I lunge toward him and he shoots up and out the door, giggling like a little girl. Shaking my head I move to the same bathroom I showered in when I first got back from the hospital. The day I learned Pops owned a massive incinerator. I really should add one of those to the new clubhouse build. I can't risk Chewy having more damned tanks of liquid nitrogen turn up. Where the hell does she even get half of that stuff from anyway?

Shrugging I rush through my shower, mindful that I want to trim my beard and shit and that takes time. One time I rushed it and cut it all crooked, then to fix it I had to keep trimming and trimming until in the end I had to shave the whole lot off. I'm not an ugly mug, but a full grizzly beard demands more respect than a baby smooth face. Besides, after Lovely and I kissed

I could smell her scent on my beard for long moments after we'd parted. I want my facial hair to catch all of Lovely's scents. There is one particular scent I'm very interested in capturing, but only when the time is right and she's comfortable with me. So I really need to nail this damn date.

"Yo kid! You almost ready? You'll be fucking late to your own date if you don't quit lollygagging!" Pops bangs on the door with the ferocity of a hopped up deputy, but he's not wrong.

I have five minutes before I need to be on Lovely's doorstep. Taking one last look at myself in the mirror, I decide that's as good as it's gonna get, so I interrupt Pops' incessant banging by opening the door mid-bang and dodging his fist coming my way.

He makes a low whistling sound, "Well, it looks like you can sprinkle glitter on a turd and dress him up." I give him a death glare but the mad old coot just laughs in my face. "Here, give her these. You picked wildflowers behind my office. The land is quite fertile over that way." He gives me a pantomime wink. "Oh, and these. You baked them this morning with Mama Debs."

At the sound of her name Mama Debs peeks around the corner and gives me two thumbs up.

"Right, remember to ask her questions about herself, but in a natural way, not like an interrogation. Whatever shit lights her up is the stuff you should ask questions about. Also, remember those conversations and then after the date note them down in your phone. That's good stuff that'll serve you well in the future when you wanna buy gifts and be romantic and shit. Also remember that she came from that wacko cult with that mean as a snake mother fucking husband, so you need to not only be better than him, but the best fucking version of yourself

185

that you can be for her. If you ain't that got in ya, then tap out now."

I stare at Pops. A little in awe and maybe a little in fear. I know we all give him shit and write him off as being a crazy old man, but the advice he's giving is convincing me he really is the damned Love Pres. Being with Lovely is more than the fact she makes my dick hard. Somehow, she makes me want to be a better person. I had the most gut trouble I've ever fucking had those times I had talked shit to her. It's like my goddamn soul knew it and the guilt would eat me alive til it gave me an ulcer. Thankfully I'm very good friends with a man who should own shares in Tums.

I clear my throat, weighing my words. "I don't want to be a better man for Lovely-" Pops growls like a rabid dog. "I *need* to be a better man for her and Bee. I got this Pops. I'm not giving up, no matter how many mistakes I make or how much I need to get on my knees and beg Lovely for another chance. I got this."

He glares at me for a moment before a sly smile blooms on his face, "Shit, you better get outta here then and win that woman." He slaps me so hard on the back that I almost topple over. My initial instinct is to deck him, but I hold back. He knows it too if the shit eating grin on his face is anything to go by.

I pull open the door only to be met with my men, flanking both sides of the porch steps, ready to slap me on the back as I walk through them all. It's the only time I'll let them get away with this shit, and that's just because I have Lovely's front door in my gaze like tunnel vision.

In six long strides I'm on her porch, knocking on her door. I look down, checking myself quickly. I cup my hand over my mouth and breathe out, making sure my breath is as fresh as it was when I brushed my teeth about five minutes ago. My head snaps up when the door slowly opens and my gut clenches when I'm met with the sight of six Ol Ladies and the woman Judge probably hopes will be his ol lady.

"Ladies."

"Pres."

Seven sets of eyes glare at me before Blanche steps up into my space, a little too close. "If you even *think* of hurting my little sister's feelings with your bullshittery and dumb words I swear what we did to Joseph would look like child's play. Got it?"

"Go Blanche," Mira whispers, then grunts when Vi elbows her in the ribs.

"I promise that I only want good things for your sister, and your friend," I add, looking all the women in the eye one by one. "I don't deserve her, but I'm willing to try my fucking hardest to earn her."

"Good enough for me. Let's go, we got stuff to plan." I raise a brow at Chewy. She gives me that wide-eyed stare she does when she's trying to be charming and throw us off the scent. "Girl stuff to plan. There's eight fertile aged women in the club and our bodies will synchronize. That's eight menstrual cycles. The average cycle expels 3 ounces of blood. Times that by eight and, well, you can do the math." She stares at me while I stare speechlessly back at her.

"You've broken him nice and good now Chewy." Remy pats Chewy on the back.

"Lovely! We're leaving now. Wait five seconds and then get your beautiful behind out here!" Mira yells.

"Yeah, you have a jackass waiting for you!" Ana adds on,

snorting.

The women all file past, mean mugging me on the way out. I'd be intimidated if more of them were taller than 5'5". Mira is around 5'8", but she walks past with a huge smile and a wink. That woman loves love too much to stand in my way.

As soon as the door closes behind the last Ol Lady, I take a deep breath, close my eyes and count to five. As soon as the number five leaves my lips I open my eyes slowly, to be met with the vision in front of me.

"Holy fucking shitballs."

Chapter 17

Lovely

"Holy fucking shitballs." Marx stares at me, wide-eyed and mouth gaping.

I glance down at my body, checking to make sure everything is where it should be. I don't usually wear things like this, but when the Girl Gang all arrived with around eight wardrobes' worth of belongings, I knew this would be the perfect time to try something new. I've never been on a date before, but I knew from watching the movies Tav recommended that the best way to make an impression is to pretty much dress not like yourself. Which is a little opposite to the advice the women gave me, which was to be myself, but dress in a way that would make Marx swallow his tongue. I have a feeling that the red and white polka dot, sweetheart neckline dress that flares out above the knee and shows a decent amount of cleavage is doing the trick.

Marx remains silent so I take him in, his neatly trimmed beard, his tousled longer length hair at the top and short sides, his button up and dark jeans without rips or stains. He still has biker boots and his cut on, and much like me, he looks like him, the him I know and I'm pretty sure I love, but a much more refined version. One that I hope to see again, but not all the time. The Pres needs to be thinking of what's important to the wellbeing of the club, not what his beard is doing.

"You look very handsome, Marx," I say, my voice barely above a whisper.

His heated gaze snaps to mine, as if he forgot we should be talking to each other. "Fuck, Lovely," he gulps, then takes a deep breath in, letting it out slowly. "You look absolutely breathtaking. If I thought you were stunning before, I was mistaken." He steps up to me, gently brushing his thumb across my cheek, then presses a gentle kiss to the corner of my mouth, so gentle that it almost feels as though I imagined it. "These are for you," he holds a small bouquet of wildflowers up, along with a small container of something. "Pops said to tell you I picked them and baked the cookies, but that would be a lie, and I'm not starting this date on a lie."

I huff out a laugh, taking the flowers from Marx's large hand. Our fingers brush and it sends a flutter from my belly to lower down, heat pooling below. I turn to move toward the kitchen, needing a vase for the flowers. "I'm glad you came clean. I already knew it was Pops. I saw him when Bee and I went for a walk earlier."

Marx grins, shaking his head. "Oh, and Lovely? Call me Johnny."

Placing the flowers in the vase, and moving them to the center of the island, I raise my brows, "Are you sure?"

"Yes," he clears his throat. "Yeah, I want to hear my name from your lips, my real name."

A little smile plays on my lips. "As you wish."

Marx, I mean, Johnny, gives me a mock frown, "That's my line!" he growls, causing a giggle to escape me. "Now, if the sweet lady would please accompany me to our ride for the evening?"

He holds out his elbow and I slip my hand through, resting it on his forearm. Johnny's other hand comes to a rest on top of mine, grounding me from floating away on a cloud of fizzy happiness. My very first date with a man that I've had feelings for for some time. Sure we had a couple of blips there, but don't all relationships? I move in sync with Johnny, laughing when I come face to face with Pops in the driver's seat of the ATV, the back decked out with cushions and flowers and twinkly lights.

"He insisted on being our chauffeur to dinner. We're on our own after that." Johnny's lips brush my ear as his warm breath sends shivers through me.

As a woman who was married for ten years, this feeling, these feelings, are all brand new to me. Not the arousal, I've had that and have become quite adept at pleasuring myself since I escaped. It was one of the first things Blanche gifted me. She told me that now that I was free I needed to love myself, in all the ways. One of those ways was to spend time with romance novels and the Satisfier Pro. I would get Bee to bed nice and early and relax with a nice book and my new toy. Being able to pleasure myself was a huge moment for me. To feel what I should feel when with a man was shocking. Never once when I was with Royal did it feel anywhere near what it felt like with my hand or my toy. Now, here with Johnny, his scent, his touch; it's igniting something in me that I thought only existed in books. The heat in me swirls and builds, pooling in the space between my thighs. I feel needy, empty and yet as much as I would like to feel Johnny's weight on me, hands and mouth on me, I also feel a terror that it will be like all those other times, the times it hurt and felt dirty and shameful.

"You OK, babe?" Johnny's hand cups my face, the thumb under my chin tipping it up until all I can see is him.

"Yeah," comes out on a harsh whisper. "Sorry, away with the fairies."

His smile is one of understanding. "We don't have to do anything you're uncomfortable with. Tonight is a night to just be ourselves, no pressure, no end goal other than for you to be you and me to be me and there's nowhere and nothing we need to be other than together."

I rest my forehead on his hard chest and take a deep breath before looking up into his ridiculously dark brown eyes. "I'm ready."

"Your chariot awaits," Pops says, elbowing Johnny out of the way and making a big scene about getting me settled into the back.

I share a look with Johnny who rolls his eyes but still tips Pops. It possibly wasn't enough because Pops looks at it with disgust but still pockets it anyway.

We sit in comfortable silence as Pops drives us through the farmland he owns. There are no animals here, but a lot of trees and random plantings here and there. I can only imagine what the little outcrops are meant to be hiding. Before long we pull up to what looks to be a hedge.

"Just wait for it," Johnny whispers in my ear, causing those darn shivers and a flutter deep in my core.

Pops hops out of the ATV with the agility and energy of a man decades younger. I'm shocked when he performs some type of elaborate knock on what I thought was a hedge but seems to hide a solid wall. The door opens outward and I get a glimpse of more twinkly lights. Delicious smells waft out of whatever this place is and I have to tear my attention away when Johnny moves to stand, offering me a hand to help me out of the back of the ATV. Holding hands we step inside and I'm in awe. We're standing in a large room with fairy lights hanging from the ceiling and the walls are decorated with kid-sized crossbows, swords and all manner of things. There are tables set up, complete with white table cloths and candles. Fox and Nitro are sitting at one, dressed nicely and sharing what looks to be sparkling water. With Fox still recovering I'm sure Nitro would have a conniption if the man tried to have a beer. Blanche and Tav are here, hands entwined on the table, and I give a little wave to Kaia who is frowning at Judge on the other side of the room. At another table Pops takes a seat where Mama Debs was waiting for him.

"Shit the old boy moves fast," Johnny says under his breath, making me giggle.

"Ahem, do you have a reservation?" Dex stands behind a podium of sorts, an open book in front of him.

Johnny growls beside me, and then growls more when Dex smirks at him. "Just show us to our table, jackass," Johnny grumbles as Dex throws his dark head back and laughs.

"Please, follow me." With a flourish, he shows us to a table near the back of the room.

It's a little more private than the other tables and I appreciate that. I also appreciate how somehow Johnny and the club have managed to make this feel like a date at a real restaurant. I'm having trouble trying to keep the fizzy feeling inside me and not gushing out everywhere. It's just, never in my wildest dreams did I think that someone would want to take me on a date, and put this much effort in. It's overwhelming and my heart is full to the brim.

"Sir, madam, would you like to start with a drink?" Niko stands dressed in a black shirt and trousers, a white napkin draped over his forearm, holding a bottle of wine.

Johnny raises a brow and I nod eagerly. I finished the last of my pain pills and antibiotics yesterday so I should be fine to have one glass. No more than that because I've heard the other women's stories and I don't want my vagina to turn into a hussy. Just yet.

Niko lets out a small grunt and then with the most concentration I've ever seen etched into his face, he pours two glasses of wine before nodding once and bustling away to the other tables.

"To the first of many dates," Johnny says, holding his glass toward me.

I giggle and clink mine against his, feeling all sorts of giddy. I take a sip, the sweet bubbles make my nose tingle.

"So, Lovely, have you thought more about Mad Dog's offer?" Johnny asks, staring at me over the table, his face illuminated by the lit candle.

My mouth twists as I try to find the words. "I have and I haven't. It carried such terrible memories for me, but when we had Candice in the Rev Room I picked up the gun and it just felt... natural. I mean, it was a poor job, the girl gang wanted to make her look hideous, but it still didn't feel as bad as my memories feel. Does that make sense?" I worry my lip, before looking at the man across the table.

He reaches over and gently tugs my lip from my teeth. "I know what you mean. I've seen your drawings. I'm sure having a pencil or paintbrush or tattoo gun in your hand feels natural.

It's your gift, Lovely, and whether the memories are good or bad, you'll always be drawn to making art."

I nod, as usual the Pres of the DRMC hits the nail on the head. "I like the thought that I could help the women Mad Dog can't. Maybe doing good could help wipe away the bad."

Johnny smiles gently. "I think you would be perfect to help Dad, and all those women, make a fresh start."

We grin at each other, the candle light flickering, making me forget we are surrounded by couples, friends and family until Cove walks straight up to the table, dressed in her black halloween dress.

"The food is ready. Are you ready to eat?" she yells, causing both Johnny and I to jump in our seats.

"Yes, thank you Cove," Johnny answers, a smirk playing on his lips.

"Thank you Cove, you're doing a great job,"

"I know!"

She bustles off, hurrying up the other big little kids as they ask the other couples if they too, are ready to eat. We all share smirks amongst ourselves while Pops looks proud as punch, obviously having something to do with the organisation.

"OK, so I've seen this done on a movie, can we do a quick round to get to know each other?" I ask Johnny, peeking up at him. He grins so I take that as a green flag. "OK, favorite childhood memory, a food you hate, and if you could choose any super power, what would it be."

He leans back in his seat, his large, blunt fingers tap on the table as his brow furrows, thinking deeply. I know he's the type of guy who would put thought into my question.

"My favourite memory would be when Rhodie was born. There's five years between us. My mom was trash, an ex club girl that tried to trap Mad Dog. When that didn't work out she would leave me on my own for hours on end, out scoring drugs. She disappeared and I got to live with my dad. Rhodie's mom came along not long after. She was the type of mom I wished I had. Gentle, kind," his eyes flick to mine, some type of awareness shining through, " a lot like you actually," he chuckles. "Then she was pregnant and I remember thinking that she would have her own baby and love them more than me. I was bad and that's why my mom was bad. Molly was good, and her baby would be good." I reach across and place my hand over his, squeezing, "Anyway, the day she had the baby, Mad Dog came to take me to the hospital to meet my little brother. I was nervous they wouldn't love me anymore."

He pauses for so long that I decide to coax him. "What happened?"

A smile plays on his lips. "Rhodie was in his crib beside her, and she held her arms open for me. Dad put me on the bed and told me to be careful. I was a big kid so I made sure to be extra gentle. She didn't care, she pulled me in, wrapped me tight in her arms and told me that she knew I was going to be the best big brother in the whole world and that she loved me so much. She made dad lift Rhodie out of the crib and I held him, with my Mom's help. I have a photo of that moment on my desk."

This man, this gruff, grumpy man just turned my heart to mush. The harsh words he directed at me weren't in anger or dismissal, but as he said, out of fear. The thoughts and feelings of a little Johnny reveal more than his words ever could. This is a man who feels deep and is afraid of never being enough. For his men, for his family, for me. Well, no more. I'm going to show him that he deserves everything and more.

Marx

Most people outside of my own family don't know anything about my shit egg donor. The older members of the MC before they retired and became snowbirds, or died of old age, they knew. But my men and their ol ladies don't know that Rhodie and I are half brothers. As far as I'm concerned we're not. I clear my throat and shake off the sadness that always lingers when I talk about my mom, the one who raised me. Molly, my mom, was the first woman I ever loved, and I know for a fact, with the way I burn for her, Lovely will be the last woman I will ever love.

"OK, um, the food I hate most in the world is corn, and my superpower would be mind control." I smile at Lovely, trying to lighten the mood.

She beams in the candlelight and I still can't believe I'm the lucky son of a bitch that gets to date this woman. Even if I don't fully trust what the kids and Rider have planned.

"Your turn, Buttercup." Her cheeks blush at the nickname and I make a note to call her that more often.

"Well, my favourite childhood memory would have to be any time I spend with my mom. So, my mom was Blanche's mom's sister, way younger than her though. She went to the Keep to find her and ended up married to my dad. Anyway, the Keep was always a busy place. With so many people everyone had to work together to get things done. My mom worked in the laundry, but every Sunday, after Church, we had a rest day. Those days were always my favourite. One time, just me and her, we went for a walk along the border of the Keep and found this amazing meadow full of beautiful flowers. My mom showed me how to make a daisy chain. I made one for me and one for her and we wore them like crowns and danced in the meadow. I remember lying on my back and pointing out the different shapes in the clouds. My mom pulled me into her arms and kissed my head, and gave me a gift, wrapped up in brown paper with a little bow. At the Keep we didn't celebrate birthdays, but my mom would sneak me a gift every year. That year it was a little set of coloring pencils and a pad. I did my first drawings that day." She beams at me, the happiness radiating off her. I make a note to make sure to not only find out her date of birth, but to throw her the biggest fucking birthday party ever. She never had birthdays at the Keep? Well, for the rest of our lives we will be celebrating the day Lovely Landry graced this earth.

"Your meals are served!" Cove booms, clapping to get our attention, as if her fog horn voice wasn't enough.

Jovie places two plates of spaghetti bolognese in front of us. Lovely claps her hands and wriggles in her seat. "I love spaghetti bolognese! It's my favourite," she sing songs.

My eyes meet Pops over Lovely's shoulder and he flicks me a wink. Well played old man, well played. Lovely dances in her seat out of pure joy and I commit this to memory. The whole thing is perfect. Absolutely perfect. We eat our meal in companionable silence, murmuring things here and there, little snippets of conversation, then returning to the flavors bursting across our tongues.

"That concludes our service for tonight. There is no dessert because grown ups don't need it." Cove announces, and like a well oiled machine the kids come bustling out to clear the tables.

I'm surprised to see Judge and Kaia's twins, Jackson and Annie-Bella helping out, although I have a feeling it's so Jackson can keep an eye on Judge. I'll have to have a word with the brother to see how he's doing in the near future. I'll table that for after the hit.

Lovely thanks the kids and I notice she has a spot of sauce sitting on that fucking glorious cleavage that's on show. I want to lick it off her pale skin. Fuck, I want to lick more than the sauce from her cleavage. I want to suck the cream straight from her pussy. Fuck it! I need to calm down. My zipper is digging into my cock and if I dont get him under control he'll have a permanent zipper print on him. Although, would that heighten Lovely's pleasure maybe?

"Ladies and gentleman, allow me to introduce Baaaad - wait, what's the name again?" Cove semi whispers the last part to someone hiding behind the curtain that is blocking the kitchen from the main area. "Really? That's the name you chose? I mean it's not bad, but it's not great either. You sure that's the name you want to go with?" Cove loudly whisper argues with who I can only guess is Rider.

"Baaad Bikers Club!" Rider yells from behind the curtain before throwing an arm out and flinging back the curtain. Savage, Tank and Flack step out in front of our tables, all holding instruments.

"Oh, fuck me," I murmur under my breath. I try to ignore Lovely's giggling and clapping and enthusiasm, but I'm not sure I can.

"Hey daters! Let's dance off that spaghetti!" Rider announces, before sitting down at a drum kit that has materialized out of nowhere.

He lays down a couple of slightly out of rhythm beats, while

199

Savage and Flack play their guitars. They're trying to keep beat with Rider, and they find it momentarily before Tank starts singing. Or at least tries to. I have no idea why Tank got the gig, especially when we have fucking Chef who has the voice of a goddamn angel. Rider mean mugs Tank, almost drumming harder to drown him out, but that doesn't seem to do anything to dissuade him. He's right in the throes of singing "I wanna dance with somebody," which is a sight to behold in itself. Tank, the big, blonde bastard is singing and dancing like his life depended on it. Knowing how Rider rode the brothers in the run up to Pops' Christmas surprise, it probably does.

"Would you do me the honor of allowing me this dance?" I ask Lovely, standing in a fluid movement, holding my hand out.

She blushes beautifully before taking my hand and letting me lead her to the makeshift dance area. The band, Bad Whatever the Hell they called themselves, change up the tempo, playing something a little slower. The kids rush out from wherever the hell they're hiding, shoving tables and chairs out of the way to make more room for everyone else.

"What *is* this place?" Lovely asks, eyes wide at the commotion.

"Would you believe it's the kids' secret clubhouse?"

She stares up at me like I've lost my mind, before blinking twice. "Pops?"

"Who the fuck else?"

She opens her mouth to say more but she's drowned out by Rider's drum solo. The fucker is playing like he's on a god damn spiritual journey, eyes closed, head swaying from side to side. What started out as vaguely sounding like "I can't help falling in love" now sounds like three campfire songs got into a fight. Tank, the poor bastard is doing his best trying to keep a semblance of rhythm, but they're failing miserably.

"I, ah, requested this version. It's their experimental phase," I say, trying to cover for them.

Lovely throws her head back and laughs, the movement mashing her glorious tits to my chest. I can feel her hard nipples poking me through the thin cotton of her dress and my shirt. Her head snaps up and she stares at me in shock, before pressing her pelvis forward a little more, trapping my hard cock between our bodies.

"Is that-"

"Ignore him. He's like this every time you're near."

She mouths the word "wow", her plump pink lips hanging open in a silent "O". Because I'm fucking horny and now embarassed, I misstep. To stop both of us from stumbling I plant my boot down heavily...on Lovely's foot. She sucks in a sharp breath and when I lean forward to look down I smash the top of my nose into the top of her head.

"Ah shit!" We jump apart, both of us feeling it. "Fuck are you OK?" I check Lovely's delicate foot before feeling her head for bumps.

She's standing stock still, not saying a word, and when I'm finally satisfied that nothing is broken I chance a glance at her face. She's beaming at me, joy shooting out of her like fucking rainbows and butterflies. Her soft, small hands cup my face and next moment her lips are on mine, pressing, sipping, kissing me. For the first time, Lovely has initiated physical contact with me and I think I'm going to blow my load right here and now. Her tongue softly licks across the seam of my lips and I allow her entry. Our tongues gently explore, taste, tangle with each other. Gripping her face gently in my hands

I angle her head just right, allowing me to deepen the kiss. I need more, just a little more. One moment more, two moments more and then we break apart, breathless.

"Take me home, Johnny. I would like to -" She stares at me, wide eyes full of excitement, a hint of fear, and a lot of determination. "I want to try, with you," she whispers.

Nodding, I take her hand, leading her toward the door and away from the claps and hooting and hollering. I scoop her up, bridal style, and stalking to the ATV I set her down in the passenger seat gently. A loud as fuck boom explodes out from behind us and I throw myself over Lovely, protecting her with my body.

"Shit!" the kids all yell in unison.

"Sorry everyone, just a misfire!" Pops shouts.

I whirl around on him but before I can summon the words another loud boom pierces the evening air and glitter comes flying out at us from a trash can. Lovely lets out a loud whoop, staring up at the sky, where clearly, against the twilight the words "M4L 4 Eva" is written in fireworks. I admire them with Lovely as they fizz and drip out of the sky. Looking toward my family they all grin, offering thumbs up and whistles and words of encouragement. Lovely's hand finds mine, entwining our fingers as my gaze finds Elio, the corner of his lips tipping in as close to a smile I've ever seen on him. I give him a nod of thanks and then help Lovely back into the passenger seat, taking my place in the driver's side and peel away from the madness.

"Best. Date. Ever," Lovely whispers, her hand on top of mine which is resting on her thick thigh.

A snort escapes me, but as we pull up to our cabin, I can't help but agree.

Chapter 18

Lovely

I 'm riding a high and I'm pretty certain it isn't from that small glass of bubbly wine I had at dinner. No, it's because of the man beside me and the family we left behind cheering at us. I've never felt so many good feelings all at one time. My skin feels too tight, but in the very best way, as if it's just too small to fit all the big wonderful feelings whirring around inside me.

Johnny pulls the ATV up outside my cabin, and the feverish hunger we shared earlier seems to have simmered down to a shimmer just below the surface.

"I would like to escort you inside, and I would love to sleep next to you tonight, Lovely. But I do not expect anything else from you. We have all the time in the world, OK?"

I suck in a breath, then nod. I'll let my actions speak louder than my words. Stepping out from the ATV I walk to the top of my stairs, stopping at my door to wait for my date. My Pres. My Johnny. He sucks in a breath, and then grins at me, moving so fast I'm almost shocked that a man of his size can move like that. In the blink of an eye he's beside me, walking through my door. I kick off my low heels and Johnny removes his boots, using his foot to straighten them next to my door. I take two deep breaths, then entwine my fingers with his much larger ones, leading him to my bedroom. I know that he's nervous, probably because I am too, but I am ready for this. I know Johnny, I know that he would never hurt me physically. More importantly, I trust him. But that doesn't mean this will be smooth sailing. Blanche took me aside before my date and shared a little about her first few times after Royal. Thanks to Blanche I feel fully prepared for things to maybe not go well or go a little sideways. I know that trauma can rear its ugly head at the worst time, but I also feel prepared enough that if it is not going well, I am confident enough to use my voice to tell Johnny what I'm feeling. Blanche put my mind at ease by telling me that men seem to like a vocal woman, and someone who knows their worth. I have all these things buzzing around my mind and yet when Johnny leans forward to press a gentle kiss to my lips, all of the buzzing ceases, flying straight out of my mind, leaving it deliciously blank.

He pulls away, a gentle smile on his lips. "You looked like you were thinking too hard," he whispers, nipping at my mouth once before dropping a kiss just beneath my ear, sucking on the skin.

My head tips to the side, giving him better access. A low groan is pulled out of me and my hands have a mind of their own, untucking his button up shirt, allowing me to run my hands up his muscular back, and around to his firm stomach. Coarse hair tickles my palms and with his warm breath and sinful lips grazing my chest, my body feels like an exposed nerve, zipping and zinging. His hands run up my soft torso, his thumbs brushing under my breasts and my body jolts at the pleasure. Taking that as a sign to continue, Johnny's hands wander up over the swell of my breasts, rough fingertips brushing the bare skin of my cleavage before hooking my top down, allowing my breasts to spill free. I don't even have any brain cells left to think about covering them, not when one is covered by Johnny's palm, the other by his hot, wet mouth. My knees buckle as a throaty groan is ripped from me, Johnny catches my weight, pressing me to him, every inch of my front plastered to the front of his.

"L-Let me take my dress off." I whisper hoarsely. "A-and can you take your clothes off? I want to see you."

Gaining control of my wayward body I untangle from Johnny's arms, stepping back once, then twice for good measure. If I stand too close his sinful mouth will attack me and I don't want to ruin Mira's dress with any bodily fluids if you know what I mean. I take a deep breath, moving my hands to the back zipper of the dress and then yank it down swiftly. My stomach is full of butterflies and my knees tremble, knowing that for the first time ever, I will willingly be naked in front of a man. But not any man, the gorgeous, rugged man that is sitting on the edge of the bed, naked save for a pair of tight black boxer briefs that the books speak of. His manhood is so hard that the purple crown is poking out past the waistband. I know that he is holding himself back, making sure I'm comfortable with everything we are hopefully about to do, but he needn't worry. For the very first time, sharing my body will be my decision. A sense of power comes over me, and it fills my chest with pride. It compels me to use my voice, to communicate with this man about what I want.

"Johnny, I want to see you, all of you. Can you please take off your boxers?"

His gaze finds mine, eyes boring into mine as if to make sure I'm confident in my request. He must find what he's looking for as he stands to his full height, hooking his thumbs into the waistband, and shoving them down his legs. His large cock points directly at me and I have no idea how or why, but my mouth waters at the sight.

"Touch yourself," comes out in a hoarse whisper, but Johnny doesn't hesitate. Taking his length in his hand he tugs roughly, moisture beading at the tip before dripping down the large vein that runs along the side of his cock.

My body clenches and I feel too hot, my dress suffocating me. I slide my arms out of the sleeves and then shove it to the ground, standing in just a bra with my breasts hanging over the cups, and a small pair of pink panties.

"Fuck me, you are absofuckinglutely breath taking," Johnny groans out, stumbling back onto the bed, his hand shuttling faster and faster at the sight of my naked body.

The body that was always too fat, too pale. Breasts too big, vagina too dry, too frigid. But it's not what it feels like here, at this moment. My body feels on fire, beautiful under Johnny's gaze, perfect. More importantly, I *feel* beautiful. And powerful.

He groans when I move to my knees in front of him. I've been in this position before, but not of my own volition. While I don't think I can do what I've been made to do in the past, I have the burning desire to taste him on my tongue.

"Shit, baby, you don't need to do that," he pants out, chest heaving, hand gripping his length tighter.

"I want to taste you, I want to watch you lose all control."

His dark eyes bore into mine, his hand slowing, "One taste

is all I'll allow, and then I need you off your knees, sweetheart. Never on your knees for me, got it?"

I can feel the smile blooming on my face, the power somehow shifting fluidly between us. Johnny holds the base of his large cock, pressing it forward in offering to me. Licking my lips I ignore his groan as I lean forward and swipe my tongue over the plump mushroom head. I lap at the precum leaking from him like a faucet before tracing my tongue down along the vein to his balls, then back up again.

Johnny angles his hips away from my greedy tongue, lightly gripping my chin. "You need to stop babe, I refuse to come on your beautiful face." His heavy lidded eyes stare at me as if I'm the best thing that ever happened to him.

Leaning forward he captures my lips, devouring my mouth. In one swift move I'm somehow on the bed, Johnny looming over me in the very best way.

"I'm going to taste you, every inch of you, and when you've come shaking and screaming on my face I'm going to gift you my body. Whatever you want to do with me, I'll be at your mercy."

All I can do is nod, my mouth dry at the prospect that Johnny's face will be between my legs, his hands running over my breasts, my belly, wherever they choose to roam.

"Need your words sweetheart, tell me what I want to hear."

I swallow thickly, a carousel of words and scenes from books I've read and wondered how true to their words they are. I want Johnny to make love to me. I want him to fuck me. I want him to taste and touch and please me in all the ways. But first I want him to give me something no one other than my own hand has given me.

"Please, Johnny, please make me come undone with your

tongue and fingers."

The grin he gives me is pure sin before lowering himself between my legs, his fingers petting me lightly. "As you wish, Buttercup."

Marx

I gently tug her panties down her thick thighs, the triangle of her dark hair neatly trimmed, as if an arrow pointing to the ultimate prize. I remove first one foot, dropping a kiss to her ankle, and then the next, flinging her panties somewhere behind me. I slowly spread her thighs and almost lose my load. Her scent intoxicates me as I lay on my stomach, ready to devour her. As soon as my tongue touches the inside of her thigh her body bucks like it's been hit with an electrical current. Fuck, if she's this sensitive with me only at her inner thighs, I can't wait to see her when I edge closer to the fucking heaven between her legs.

Using my fingers I spread the plump lips of her pussy, shocked to see how ready she is. Her pink folds glisten in the low light, I can see her muscles clenching under my inspection and I have to take a few breaths to not fucking blow my load on the bed. With her open to me I move my hands up her sides, caressing everywhere I can reach, her ribs, the sensitive spot under her large tits, her plum colored nipples that pucker under the attention my fingers give her. I touch and tease her, wanting her to feel even half as crazy as I felt with her eyes on me, her soft voice demanding my clothes off. Shit, when she pulled her shoulders back and full of confidence told me to touch myself, well, I almost came there and then. I love how Lovely wants to take charge. After the shit she's been through she deserves it. I'm not going to be another fucker who takes from her without giving back twofold.

Lovely's breathy moans echo in the air, her hips gyrate, as if looking for relief, looking for me. Leaning forward I swipe my tongue across her pussy, from her little puckered asshole to the top of her clit, pausing to suck the nub gently into my mouth. My woman lets out a squeal and then a low, animalistic moan leaves her and it's the fucking most erotic thing I've ever heard in my life. No theatrical screams and panting, no, Lovely is raw in her pleasure. I double down, fucking sucking the soul from her body, lapping at her thick lips, fucking her with my tongue, sucking every part of her. There is no technique in what I'm doing, I'm feasting on her like a starving man, wringing the cream from her body. I want more, more, more and then she gifts me with everything she has, her back bows off the bed, her hands grip my face as she rides her pleasure, her pussy gripping my tongue, juices running down my chin onto the bed. I drink up as much as I can before her shaking legs clamp closed, her hands scrambling to push my face away from the pussy I'll never have my fill of.

I slowly climb up over her body, dropping gentle kisses here and there. One on her hip, on her ribs, a gentle suck of her nipple, all as she twitches on the bed, her gaze hazy. She has the energy to cup my face tenderly, pulling me into her. She tips her face up, and the fact she wants to kiss me with her release on my face makes my cock even harder. I devour her mouth much like I did her pussy, her groan into my mouth as she tastes herself on my tongue has my cock spurting a little cum onto her leg. I don't know how much more I can take.

"Am I in charge now?" she whispers, nibbling at my lips.

I grin, and in a fluid movement I roll to my back, bringing her with me. "I'm all yours, baby."

She kneels beside me, taking me in. I'm a big bastard, tall and wide but at this moment, she has all the power. All the strength. "Put your hands behind your head. No touching until I tell you, OK?"

I grin as I place my hands behind my head and then gasp when her soft hands run down my chest, over my abs. She skips past my cock and moves to my thighs, then down my calves. Her touch is feather light, but not tickly. Not that I would give a shit. Just having this woman's hands on me is nirvana. One hand trails up my thigh, gently cupping my balls as she leans forward and nibbles my left nipple, soothing the bite with a swipe of her tongue. I feel my cock kick and another spurt lands on the base of my stomach, my patch of hair thick and sticky with my precum. Without missing a beat Lovely leans forward and swipes it up with her tongue, moaning at my taste.

"Fuck baby, I'm not going to last much longer." I'm panting hard, and no matter how many times I picture the shit I've seen in the Rev Room, my cock is just not going down.

Lovely gives me a shit eating grin, rising up, then swinging a leg over me. She hovers just above me, the curtain of her hair hanging down, covering us so it's only me and her in the world.

"You can use your hands now," she whispers. "I want you to guide your cock, I need you inside me." Her sweet voice breaks at the end with her desperation and I've never felt anything as monumental as this moment.

Lining myself up with her, the head of my cock kisses her hot flesh. She inhales sharply before she slowly, painfully fucking slowly, lowers the tightest pussy I've ever felt down over me, swallowing my body with hers. I know I'm home. My hands rest in the dip of her waist and I hold on for dear fucking life. I'm not going to do anything until she says. She rocks slightly, clamping down on me and moaning that low, guttural groan I can't get enough of.

"Please, Johnny, please make love to me?" she whines, her hips moving the whole time.

"As you wish, my Lovely."

Wrapping my arms around her I pull her into me, holding her tight as I rock up into her. Her hips meet mine thrust for thrust and I whisper sweet nothings in her ear, how I feel about her, how thankful I am that she is giving me this moment, how I want to fill her for the rest of our lives with cock and babies and my love. She responds with her own promises and when she leans back, hands on either side of my face, looking deep into my eyes I see everyday of my fucking future. My cock kicks at the same time Lovely's body clamps down and I come seeing fucking stars. Gripping the back of her head my tongue delves into her mouth, almost stealing the air from her lungs as I try and prolong the moment between us for a moment more. Then I remember that Lovely Landry is mine.

"You're crying," Lovely's gentle voice breaks the obsessive thoughts running through my mind.

She gently wipes her thumbs across my stubble and I notice the same tracks marring her own flushed cheeks. "So are you, baby. Fuck, I didn't hurt you, did I? I'm such a fucking waste of sp-"

211

A soft hand clamps over my mouth, effectively stopping anything else I had to say. "Stop, Johnny. Just stop. You didn't hurt me. You gave me something that I've never had."

I raise a brow, trying to figure out what that might be.

"I've never been made love to. I've never trusted a man like I trust you. I've never had an orgasm with anything other than my own hand," she whispers the end and buries her face in my shoulder.

"Oh, I am definitely going to ask to see that one day." I chuckle when she sits up looking thoroughly scandalized. "Baby steps, Buttercup."

I wrap my arms around her, pulling her back to my chest. Where she belongs. "One more cuddle and then I'll clean you up."

"And we can go for round two?"

I angle my head down to look at her, her adorable face looking hopeful. "I've created a monster."

The giggle that erupts from her means the world to me. I have her, and I'm never fucking letting her go.

Chapter 19

Lovely

I wake to a possessive hand on my hip and an ache in my core. My eyelids flutter open and I'm met with Johnny, head propped on his hand, watching me.

"Hey there, Buttercup, thought you'd never wake up."

I stretch from the top of my fingers to the tips of my pointed toes, working all the kinks out of my body from the three times we made love in the night. Not all as successful as the first, but we're learning each other's bodies, and I'm learning where my hard lines are. Over a decade with Royal has tainted some positions and activities for me, and I know one part there Johnny needed to go punch something, but that made my heart crack open even more for the man. No one, in all my life has felt that strongly on my behalf to want to fight my demons than the beautiful man lying beside me.

I reach over to cup his bearded cheek and I marvel that I can touch him. In fact he likes it when I do. He presses his cheek further into my palm before turning to drop a kiss to it. He inhales deeply and his shoulders sag slightly.

"I know you have to go. Today is a big day for you and the club. Just, come back safe?"

He caresses my cheek with his hand, dropping his forehead to mine. "I've only just gotten you, I'm not going to put what we have at risk. I'll come home to you and Bee. I," he swallows, his throat working to find the words, "I love you, Lovely. I know I was an ass for far too long, so I need at least another fifty years to make it up to you."

Tears prick the back of my eyes, and I grin up at the most handsome man I've ever laid eyes on, "Make it sixty years and you've got a deal."

He lets out a low rumble then presses a soft kiss to my lips. Then another, and another until we're gripping each other, hands fighting with the covers, trying to get closer, clawing into each other's skin like it's the last time we'll ever be in each other's arms. His weight presses me into the mattress, rough chest hair abrading my tight nipples as a low moan is ripped from the depths of me. His cock notches at his home, my entrance ready and waiting to welcome him even after the times we made love through the night. I know what the other couples mean now, the insatiable hunger to be with their person, their other half. I never knew that being with Johnny would fill in all my cracks until I was complete, unbroken and yet here I am. He drives his pelvis forward in one brutal movement and I feel my arousal build to almost fever pitch. The chemistry between us is undeniable. My legs wrap around his hips, heels digging into his firm ass as he powers in and out of me, long strokes designed to drive me mad.

"That's it, baby. Let me in as deep as I can go, I want you to feel every inch of me while I'm away. I want your pretty little pussy to ache for me, wanting her man back where he belongs."

"Yes, yes," I pant, words useless as my brain is so addled by Johnny. His scent, his touch, his filthy words breathed in my ear.

"Take it all, baby, take it all, everything I have to give you."

The words are barely out when my back bows, legs clenching as I convulse in a way that makes it feel as if my soul has left my body to join as one with the man I love. A low growl rips from Johnny and he arches back, the veins on his neck standing in stark relief as his head rolls back, planting his seed deep inside me. His head tips forward and he stares at me with awe, love, and a joy I've not seen in him before.

"I love you, Johnny, Marx, Pres."

His lips quirk up slightly, "I'm all those things, but to you, I'm just your man."

He slides out of me, our combined release leaking onto the sheets and yet I couldn't care less. Gathering him in my arms I hold him to me, his head pressed to my chest, my hands in his hair. I want to remember this, immortalize it in my memory for years to come.

After long moments Johnny helps me into the shower, the hot water beating down on us. My thighs ache, I'm sure I'll be walking bow legged today and I can't wipe the smile off my face. We steal kisses in the privacy of our room, our little bubble about to be burst at any moment.

We move to our bedroom and I side eye Johnny, watching him get dressed. They way the muscles in his back flex and move as he pulls his shirt over his head, the flex of his biceps, his long, thick fingers as they tie his boots. By the time he slips his cut over his shoulders I know that I'm now with Marx, the

Pres. Not the sweet man who took me on my first date and made my body sing.

I smile up at him as I straighten his cut, as if I'm sending him off to war. In some ways, I am. We are at war with the cartels, and Serpiente, and only one of us can win.

He clasps my hand in his as we walk to the farmhouse together, him to meet his men, me to collect little Bee and sit with my best friends as we wave our men off. With a kiss to my forehead and whispered words of promise and love, he goes his way, and I make mine to the nursery.

Every step I take away from him feels heavy, and I'm waiting for my legs to carry me to the main room, where I want to put up a fight and stop him from going. But that's not my role today. My role isn't to fret and cry and beg. My role is to stand by Marx's decision and make sure everything here runs smoothly.

"Knock, knock," I sing as I walk through the nursery doors.

"Mama!" Bee hollers as she comes running headfirst into my legs.

Scooping her up I breathe in her little girl scent. "Thank you so much for keeping her last night, Mama Debs."

"Psh," Mama Debs waves a hand at me. "When Marx suggested an early date so you could still put Bee down I decided to meddle. I mean, you're a mum, you don't have too many opportunities to get your world rocked, so you needed a fairy godmother to whisk this little stinker away." Mama Debs tickles Bee in my arms and I grin as my little girl throws her head back and lets out a belly laugh.

"It's about time you got here. We need all the dirty details," Vi says, waggling her eyebrows at me while Juno scowls from her hip.

I grin at Juno and her scowl softens, turning more into a frown.

"I have never seen such a grumpy baby. You could make a meme out of that grumpy little face and make a killing," Kaia says, from her place in one of the rocking chairs.

"Holy moley, yes!" Mira jabs a finger her way, eyes wide. "We could make a mint! Like that grumpy cat! Sponsorship deals, modeling, all sorts."

"You're not selling my beautiful little girl's grumpy face!" Vi hisses, cradling an even grumpier looking Juno to her chest.

"Yeah, not selling that baby's face even though she'd make us millions," Chewy agrees. "Besides, she's boring. I want gossip. I think. I don't actually know because I don't really care, but everyone else wants it so I guess I should too." She gives me a puzzled look. "Anyway, did you manage to do the deed and not freak out? I know trauma is a thing."

I smile softly at Chewy, "It was wonderful, but not without some struggles."

"Ooooh, was it the massive wang? I bet it was the massive wang," Mira whispers, pulling her notebook out of her cleavage.

Kaia stares at her for a moment. "Why does she do that?"

"You mean you don't know?" Remy asks, looking shocked at Kaia shaking her head. "Mira isn't just Mira. She's *the* Melody Baldwin."

Kaia's eyes grow wide as she stares at Mira, "No. Way! Licence to Thrill and Swoon?" Mira sits back, a huge grin on her face. "Well, shit! As you were!" Kaia waves at her and Mira poises her pencil, looking at me expectantly.

In fact, all the Ol Ladies are looking at me expectantly. "OK, yes, he's big all over and so caring and gentle and, and I never knew it could be like that!" My lip trembles and my eyes burn as a sob is pulled from me.

In seconds I'm surrounded by warmth, embraced by my girls, well, most of them. Chewy is sitting in a bean bag with Laney and Chomper on her lap.

"Who the fuck made my woman cry?" Marx's deadly tone rings out but instead of jumping back and claiming innocence, my Girl Gang all snort. As a collective.

"Settle down caveman, she was telling us what a wonderful night she had," Blanche rolls her eyes.

A rough grunt near my ear has me turning into a broad chest. "We're heading out now. Walk with me?" he murmurs in my ear.

Taking a deep breath I clasp the hand he holds out to me, moving down the hall with the rest of the women at my back, on their way to see off their ol men. Even Kaia, as much as she complains about Judge, I know that she is just as concerned as the rest of us.

There is an electricity in the air as the men ready their weapons, and whatever else they need to take with them. Jules and Gus have the Tombs' SUVs wired to within an inch of their lives, and Tav has Chewy's kidnapper van. The brothers riding out start their engines, the low rumble rolling through me, almost comforting. Stepping up to Marx I stand between his spread legs as he leans against the side of his girl, his eyes intense as they stare into my soul.

"I've been a dumb fuck for a long time, but I'm not that dumb that I'll get myself killed and not make it home to you."

"I know," I whisper, pressing my forehead to his full lips, his beard rough on my skin. "Just don't get hurt."

"As you wish, Buttercup. I love you, my Lovely."

"I love you, my Johnny."

He gives me the sweetest kiss, a gentle brush of his lips and I step back, pulling my shoulders back, head held high. He doesn't need to see me in pieces, he needs me to be the strength at his back as he leads our family.

Looking around me, the other women do the same. Not a tear is shed as they all stand beside me, heads held high, the gripping of each others' hands the only sign that we are holding our emotions, tamping them down inside to show a united front for our men. This is what being a family is about. In good times and bad we stand together, and we overcome, no matter what happens.

We stand there until long after the last pipe can be heard in the distance, when a dark car comes rolling up the drive.

"Who the fuck is this?" Mad Dog mumbles under his breath, stepping in front of us, Chef, TumTum and Pops at his side.

The car slows to a stop, and I can't help the sly grin that grows on my face when I see who exits the car.

"Ladies. I have information for you."

Marx

Having to leave Lovely's bed this morning almost fucking killed me. Actually, being *in* her bed almost killed me. Seeing her in all her glory for the first time, pale skin on display, soft curves, those delicious, fat tits, the fucking sight of her almost gave me a heart attack. I don't think she gave me enough credit

219

for not coming all over myself and the bedsheets. Then to have the pleasure of discovering her, making love to the woman who has driven me crazy all this time, I felt like the luckiest bastard to ever walk the earth.

Sure, we had a moment there where that bastard Royal reared his ugly fucking head, ruining the moment, but with clear communication we worked through it. Well, that and I left the room to go punch some shit outside. I would kill that fucker all over again if it meant I could slay Lovely's demons.

The stomping of boots pulls me from thoughts of my woman, reminding me that today is the day we've been counting down to. Today we put a stop to the shit that rained down on us, almost taking some of the most important people in our family away. Casting my eyes around the living room I hold the gaze of each of my men, both original members and new.

"We got shit to do and I don't have to explain to you what is hanging in the balance. The most important thing is we get in, destroy the fuckers, and get out unscathed. I'm not coming home without each and every one of you riding beside me, got it?"

"Yes, Pres," the words are all said emphatically, brothers slapping hands on each other's backs, the mood jovial despite what we need to do.

"Mad Dog, Chef, TumTum, Fox, Niko and Flack, I need you on the women, children and Pops."

"Ah, shit, are you sure we can't come with?" Flack grumbles, a small smirk playing on his lips.

"I'm trusting you with the most important job."

Flack straightens, dipping his chin once.

"Landrys, you know Louisiana better than any of us. I'm sending Dex, Sniper, Tav, Rider, Switch and Judge with you.

Roman has men on standby for both backup and clean up. Any questions?"

"We have our own backup as well. A small number of men who work at the Keep with us. They have good links into the railroad system we use to rehome women and children. If we come across any in our raid we'll get them out of there and to safety," Vic says, looking around the room.

Running a hand down my beard, my shoulders lose some of the tension I've been holding. Knowing that I can trust these men to not only follow instructions, but to also have plans for the aftermath, takes a lot of weight off me.

"Good, that's good. Rhodie, Tank, Nitro, Savage, Wire, the Tombs and myself are taking care of the Cartel de Silencio. As with Louisiana, Roman will also have men there. Remember that they may have your back, but they work for the bratva, so keep your heads about you. Roman is after their drug trades so, as long as he gets that, everything will remain as it stands now."

"An uncomfortable partnership?" Rhodie, the bastard, smirks.

"Something like that," I deadpan. "Wire will be working surveillance with us, Tav for those in Louisiana. Chewy and Remy will be coordinating here. We need to hit at the exact same time. All it would take is for one team to be off by 30 seconds and that gives them time to make a call and flip the script on us." My men all nod. They know what's at stake.

If we can't shut this shit down then we'll never be able to go back to our lives. There is no way to thrive when you're constantly looking over your shoulder, and I owe it to Lovely to see her and Bee thrive. I owe it to all the kids and the brothers and Ol Ladies. It's time that we put this shit to bed.

"OK men, let's get ready to roll out."

Whoops and hollers and bangs assault my senses as my men rev themselves up to an almost fever pitch. I know I have my shit pretty much ready, so I make my way to the nursery, taking the stairs two at a time to reach the door in time to see Lovely burst into tears.

"Who the fuck made my woman cry?" I growl, mean mugging all the women in the room.

Instead of shrinking back in fear, they all snort simultaneously. "Calm down, caveman," Blanche says, rolling her eyes.

I ignore her as I bring my woman into my arms, feeling everything in me settle down as soon as she's there. She clings to me as we make our way downstairs, to our sleds. Leaning against my bike, Lovely steps between my legs, my arms wrap around her, pulling her close, committing her scent to my memory. It seems like mere seconds and whispered declarations and I'm straddling my girl, Lovely in the rear view.

She stands like a fucking queen, head held high, shoulders back, a look of determination on her face. She's joined by her Girl Gang, each woman looking like the warriors they are. I circle my hand in the air, leading my men out to the road before Judge takes over as Road Captain. The rumbling beneath me soothes my nerves as we ride as one to the outskirts of town. It doesn't come naturally to me to split my club; in fact, it feels downright fucking wrong, but if we want to have any chance to end this, we have to hit them hard, and without mercy.

"Feeling OK, brother?" Rhodie's voice crackles through the bluetooth.

"Gut tells me this is right."

"But your head is screaming power in numbers?"

222

"Something like that."

He grunts. "Need I remind you that you've been into enemy fucking territory with less men?"

I inhale, then let it out. "I had eyes on everyone. Splitting the club feels like a missing limb but I know it's the only way to shut this shit down."

It's quiet, and we resume the ride in silence, alone with our thoughts until the team heading east peels off, Tav following the bikes in Truck Norris. My crew raise our fists in solidarity with our brothers. We have a planned Zoom meeting or some shit later, to go over intel, then I won't hear from them again until after both hits are complete. Who the hell would have thought that an MC from sleepy Rose Grove would be having online meetings to take care of two cartels? I snort, shaking my head. Damn Mad Dog and his OG cronies would be giving us hell if they knew this is how we deal with shit. Actually, they would have given us shit before now, especially with Chewy being the damned club icer.

The road soothes me, giving me the time to think through all our plans and contingencies. The only time we stop is to receive updates from Chewy and Remy. They seem sporadic, both Cartel De Silencio and La Sombre Roja laying low so as not to draw any attention to themselves before handover. Makes sense as they're both bringing shipments of drugs and girls over the border. The girls will be taken by whatever small time shitty gangs they're working with to transport them to that Renae Sullivan woman. We'll be taking care of those fuckers while the Tombs' contacts in Texas will take care of the girls here, and the Landrys' contact will take care of them in Louisiana. After that, the only loose end we'll have is Renae and let's face it, we'll be leaving her up to the women.

My comms beep and I accept the incoming from Chewy. "Word is two groups have crossed the border, one heading your way, one headed toward the other team." With that she hangs up, no pleasantries, nothing.

"Rhodie, have you spoken to your Ol Lady?"

"Yeah, why?" Rhodie's voice says over bluetooth.

"I dunno, just a weird feeling."

He's silent for a beat. "Do we need to call Dad?"

Chewy is with eight other women, Mad Dog, Chef, TumTum, Fox, Flack and the only prospect we have. Surely they can't get into any trouble with that many people around.

"Pops is with them, brother." Fuck. Yeah he is.

Hanging up from my brother I direct dial Pops. If shit is going down he'll be right in the middle of it so I'll know whether I need to chew out someone's ass or not.

"What?"

"Hello to you too, Pops."

A grunt comes over the bluetooth, "We're all here, the house is still standing, no one is doing anything and no one has turned up. Is that what you want to know?"

Judging by the noise in the background I can tell he's in the kitchen with Mama Debs. I can hear some of the men and women we left behind and all the gurgling I could feel in my gut dissipates pretty much immediately.

"Yeah, this is what I wanted to know. We're just pulling into our target location. We'll send messages back to our Ol Ladies once we're set up. Give us half an hour."

"Huh. The way you worded that is like you have an Ol Lady." Cheeky fucker.

"You know damn well I do," I growl down the line.

"Dunno 'bout that, son. I don't see a property cut on her. I know buttery leather would look good on those shoulders of hers."

"As soon as this shit is put to bed, you can guarantee to see one on Lovely." I smile as I say the words, because I can't think of anything better.

"Fair enough. Don't die." With that the old bastard hangs up.

Rhodie flicks me a side eye as he pulls up even with me, his brow raised in question. I give him the thumbs up. Our women are safe and sound, and we're well on our way to where we need to be.

Chapter 20

Lovely

"They can tell something is up," Vi whispers, eyeing up the men standing on the other side of the room from us.

"Well, duh, they were all there for the big reveal," Mira says, doodling something in her book.

Chewy has been suspiciously quiet for the past hour, choosing to sit in a rocking chair with Chomper on her lap. Laney is messing around on the floor with her blocks while the other toddlers cruise around the room, asking for cuddles and being picked up and doted on by no less than twenty people.

"We know she's on her way here whether we like it or not. The question is: is she in town to scare us, or something else?" Nat asks.

"I'm going with 'something else'. I mean, she has the backing of two cartels, some low level gangs and that fricker, Serpiente. If they know where we are, they'll come for us."

"Ana's right. If what Dima sees is correct, then they're on

their way with force."

"Remy, how many men do both cartels have in total? Also, cross reference against their contacts here," Chewy murmurs, petting Chomper.

Remy starts tapping away on her laptop as I turn to peek at the men in charge of our safety, all of them leaning against the wall, eyes on us.

"Quick, give them a smile and a wave so they don't think we're up to something," Mira says through a fake smile.

"She's really good at that," Kaia mumbles before doing exactly as she was told.

"The way I see it there are almost as many of them, as there are of us," Chewy states, staring at our bodyguards. "If Renae turned up here they wouldn't be able to stop us from fighting. I mean, look at them. One of them is injured and two are old." Chewy waves at them.

She's not wrong in her assessment, but I still think even with years on their side, Mad Dog and Flack could definitely take us.

"So, what's the plan, girlies?" Pops says in his loudest voice, plopping down on the couch next to Nat.

"What makes you think there's a plan?"

Pops raises an unimpressed brow at Blanche before she cackles.

"Both cartels, and their little gang banger cronies have a total of fifty men, give or take. Twenty won't make it across the border due to criminal charges. They're already smuggling drugs and women, they won't risk bringing those men with them and blowing the whole operation," Remy interrupts.

"Thirty men. So we can say around half should be at the handover points, both here and in Louisiana and our men will take care of them."

227

Pops lets out a whistle. "That leaves at least fifteen for us. That's a lot of killing."

"I'm not sure, that's less than one each," Mira so helpfully points out.

Chewy strokes her imaginary moustache, with a glint in her eye. "How far out did Dima say Renae is?"

"Around two hours."

"Good. Gives us time to set up."

Pops nods once, a smile growing from a small grin, into something more maniacal. "I've been planning for this day."

Kaia looks from Chewy to Pops. "Anyone wanna tell the new girl what's happening?"

"We're gonna let them come to us," Chewy shrugs.

"Let them? Them and all their weapons with my kids names on them? Those guys? The bad guys that kidnap kids? Those ones?" Kaia's eyes bug out the more she says until she reaches a pitch high enough for dogs to hear.

"Yep, those ones."

"Trust us, girl, we got this," Pops says, waggling his brows.

Kaia fixes Pops with a stare before reluctantly nodding.

"OK. We have an hour and a half to get this place locked down and ready for war. Pops, I'll need two nests up on the roof."

"Aye aye, Dayz."

"Ladies, when the time comes we'll need half of you in the bunker with the kids. Decide amongst yourselves who that will be. I'm going to talk to the men," Chewy says and we all look at each other.

No one is saying anything so I decide to take the reins. "Hands up who wants to fight?"

Every feminine hand shoots up in the air. Mira giggles when she looks around, before shrugging at me.

"Well, that's not going to work." I say, blowing out a breath. "Kaia, Mira, Nat and Ana, you're in the bunker. Vi, are you good to be on hand for medical emergencies?" Vi nods her head emphatically, "Remy, you'll be good to offer tech support," Remy nods at my instruction, "Blanche and Chewy you'll be the blunt instruments, so to speak." Once I've finished bossing everyone around, I'm breathless and I can feel my cheeks heating.

"Well, well, well. Go Lovely, running ops. I *like* it," Nat says, throwing me an impressed look.

"That's First Lady material right there!" The Girl Gang all whoop and holler for me, the toddlers joining in what they think is a dance party.

"Right let's split up and get this place locked down ready for war." Chewy claps her hands and makes her way over to the men.

"You sure about this, *kotiro*?"

"We don't really have a choice, Mama Debs. They're coming for us whether we like it or not. We either hide or we get ready to fight back. We need to get rid of them otherwise we'll never be safe."

Mama Debs stares at me, assessing me with her keen gaze. "Can I tell you a secret?"

My brows furrow as I nod. "Of course. I won't say a word."

She leans closer, her comforting scent dampening the butterflies in my stomach. "I kinda wish I was up here fighting with you ladies," She gives me a cheeky smile and I can't help but pull her into my arms.

"Next time."

"*Ae.* Next time." She holds my gaze. "I'll protect the kids, don't you worry." She cups my face and I press my cheek

229

further into her warmth. I know if anything happens that she will protect her *moko*, her grandchildren, with her life. But I know it won't come to that. We'll take them out first.

"I've briefed my kids. They'll help entertain the others," Kaia murmurs, stepping up beside me.

"You're OK with this?"

"I don't have much of a choice." She turns to hold my gaze. "Being here with the MC was meant to keep my kids safe. Now the fight is coming to us and our men are out on the road fighting their fight. If I need to step up I will. No one touches my babies."

I don't miss the way she says "our men" as I nod in understanding. Our worlds were tipped upside down, and now we're all fighting to set it back to rights. If that means breaking some rules and maybe unaliving some people, then so be it. We're not bad people. We're good people who do bad things to make the world a safer place for our kids.

Patting both her and Mama Debs on the shoulder I scoop up little Bee, giving her kisses on her chubby cheeks. I notice Blanche is doing the same with Tess, and Chewy with Laney and Chomper now that the men have stopped yelling. I think they know deep down that what Dima says is true. Renae and God knows who else is coming this way. We can either choose to bury our heads in the sand, or strap in and give them one hell of a fight.

Everyone starts to disperse, Chewy has barked orders at everyone, going ahead with my initial plan. It feels good to contribute in such a way, but I'm still worried that we won't have nearly enough power behind us.

"Yo, I heard you needed a little law and order?" Moss grins at his terrible joke, wandering into the dining room.

"What? One single cop?" Pops spits out in disgust.

"One is all you need to legally be able to put down as many people as you like without Rose Grove PD investigating and landing your old ass in prison."

"Fair enough," Pops says, before turning to Mad Dog, "Hey! Old Man, are you gonna help me with this shit or not?" Pops indicates two duffel bags at his feet that Moss and I both clocked as soon as Pops gestured at them.

"Tell me that's not full of illegal weapons."

Pops stares at him the way Chewy does when she's trying not to get into trouble. He silently picks up a bag, Mad Dog gripping the other in his large hand and they scuttle out of the room like their butts are on fire.

Moss lets out a long sigh. "Let's get this show on the road. Flora has bingo later and I need to be back for the twins."

We share a smile and move to complete our tasks. We have a storm coming and we need to be prepared.

Marx

"Anything?"

"All quiet. *Pres*," Gus smirks at me with a side eye.

"Don't you start. I've just had Jules mocking me too."

"I've never had a *Pres* before."

"Quit it before I kick you out of my MC," I grumble, trying to hide the twitching of my lips.

"What can I say? It's a gift. We get it from our grandpa."

I roll my eyes and let him get back to his surveillance. Cartel de Silencio has been quiet as hell, and yes, I do get that it's in the name. But still, with a huge shipment coming through I would have assumed that they'd be getting shit in order. Moving existing shit, coming and going a lot more. Instead, they're tucked into their ally's gang house having the lamest looking party I've ever seen. Pizzas were delivered, there is no trace of music playing and there are no women on site either. It all feels off somehow.

"Something feels weird," Rhodie grits out.

"You're getting that too, huh?"

"Just an itchy feeling."

"Gus, get Tav on the phone, I want to know what they're seeing there," I bark.

Crossing my arms I tense my thighs, then release, then tense again trying to work some of the jitters out of my body.

"Yo, bro, what's up?" Tav's face fills Gus's screen and instead of waiting for Gus to speak, I lean over his shoulder.

"What are you seeing there?"

"Sweet fuck all, Pres. Some slick suit guys turned up around half an hour ago, at least six of them. They went inside and it's been a docile get together. Pizza arrived ten minutes ago. If they're partying they're doing it in silence because there's no music or anything."

Rhodie and I share a look. "Tav, wrap it up. Pack it in and head home. Something isn't fucking right."

"What's happening Pres?" Tank asks from where he stands next to Wire.

"What are the chances that two cartels, in two different places, with trucks of illegal merchandise coming in would have the exact same behavior at the exact same time? Pizza

232

delivery, no one in or out, a party yet no music?"

"Shit."

Tucking my lower lip I let out an ear piercing whistle. "Pack up your shit we head out ASAP."

"Ah, Pres, I got Dima on the line," Wire says while his fingers fly over the keys of his laptop.

"Put him on speaker." Clenching my fists I wait for whatever weird shit is going to come our way.

"Marx, thank you for taking my call," Dima's accented voice says through the speaker. "You and your men are needed at home."

"Do I need to ask why?" I grit my teeth, waiting for what is probably going to be some mystical shit.

"You'll know why soon enough. It's the reason you had to split the club." With that he hangs up.

"Does that guy creep any else out, or just me?" Nitro grumbles looking around the room.

"I don't mind him being creepy," Wire replies. "I'd just like him to be more thorough with the information he shares. The guy is super light on the details."

Dima may not be the best at sharing information, but he never seems to be wrong. If he's telling us we need to head home, then so be it.

"Wire, hit the dark web, see if you can find anything out. Gus, call Ana, ask her to check in with Roman, he may have fresh intel. Rhodie, call Chewy."

His brow raises at my barked instructions. "Why don't you call her?"

Closing my eyes, I let out a sigh, "She never picks up my calls. Waits 'til I hang up then asks me to text."

Nitro snorts and then spins to look at the wall when I shoot a glare his way.

Rhodie chuckles and calls his ol lady who unsurprisingly picks up on the second ring.

"Hey babe."

"Hey ba– Chewy, are you in a vehicle?"

"Noooooo."

There's some rustling over the line, a couple of grunts and then what I imagine a wind tunnel would sound like. There's also a male voice I can't quite put my finger on, and feminine voices. One I know very fucking well because she was screaming my name this morning.

"Chewy, who's with you?"

"Oh, you know, just Lovely and Blanche. We're having a nice time. We're, ah, making cookies for the kids."

"Lovely I can believe, but I've never once seen Blanche bake anything. And Chewy refuses," Gus whispers with narrowed eyes.

"Chewy, where the fuck are you? Tell me right now before I hunt you down and tan that plump little ass of yours."

"Whoa hey!" Jules growls.

"Oh kinky," she purrs over the line. There's more rummaging and the male voice again.

"That's fucking Moss Davies!" Tank says, pointing to Rhodie's phone lying face up with the speaker on.

"Oh! That's the timer, gotta go byeeeee." She hangs up and we sit in silence staring at the blank screen.

We wait a beat, then two, then the room erupts in movement. "Pack it in boys, we're heading home!"

Chapter 21

Lovely

We sit in wait as the clock ticks over another minute. "I'd almost prefer they just surprise us at this point. Watching that clock is driving me crazy," Blanche whines.

"Could be worse. We could be perched up on the roof in the afternoon sun." Mira shrugs.

I think of Pops on one roof and TumTum on the other. Texas sun isn't known for going easy on a man, so we should have really sent someone less pale than TumTum up there. The poor kid will be burnt to a crisp.

"I hope TumTum has sunscreen on," Ana says, echoing my thoughts.

Mama Debs is still bustling around the kitchen, finalizing the last of the food she has panic baked for the kids. As far as they're concerned they're going to have a bunker party and sleepover. Kaia's kids and Sage know what's happening, and are more than happy to help Mama Debs, Nat, Ana, Mira and

Kaia out.

"I'm ready, *kotiro*. Let's get these kids downstairs, yeah?" Mama Debs says, arms loaded with food, the older kids trailing behind, with babies in their arms.

The Girl Gang is splitting up and I can't help but feel a little emotional. What if something happens? What if this is the last time we see each other? I grip each woman, one at a time, and hug her tight to me. These women have helped me through some of the worst times of my life, and have been there for some of the happiest. I'm blessed to have such amazing friends that I can call family.

"You sure you want to do this? You could come with us?" Nat whispers in my ear.

I'm shaking my head before she finishes her sentence. "No, I have to do this. If only to rein Chewy in, if need be."

She nods and gives me a little smile. "Good thinking, her and Blanche need someone level headed like you, otherwise they'll go on a rampage."

We share a smile and she gives me a little wave as she heads to the stairs leading to the basement.

"Give them hell."

Those of us staying wave to our friends and babies. I blow kisses to Bee as her smiling face descends down the stairs in Annie-Bella's arms.

"You all good?" Mad Dog asks, his large body near mine giving me comfort I didn't know I needed at this point.

"Yeah. Just want this to be over with."

"It will be. I've seen some of the shit Pops has set up. This place is like the fucking Home Alone house."

I snort at the description because that was one of the first movie's Tav made me watch. If that's what Chewy and Pops have set up, then I can't wait to see Renae and whoever she's bringing with her step onto our land.

"We got blacked out SUVs rolling through town heading this way," Remy's voice comes through the comms we're all wearing, keeping us updated.

"Everyone in position," Chewy barks.

"Pops and TumTum, don't fire until I say the word."

"Ten-four."

Mad Dog, Vi and myself are off to the side in the kitchen. The butcher block island has been tipped on its side, and we're all sitting behind it. Chef is in the front hall, Fox is further back in the house with Niko and Chewy, Blanche and Moss are in the dining room with Flack hidden away on the other side of the room. Mira is convinced that no killing will be done until after Renae has monologued about her evil plan, and I hope that's true, because at this point my sister is a sitting duck in that room.

"SUVs, two minutes out." Remy's voice rings out. She's in the kids hideout watching the footage from the twelve cameras we set up. Everything is being sent to Roman and his team who are waiting offsite somewhere.

"Eyes on," Pops' voice cuts in, and I can hear his excitement.

I try to stifle my smile, but at his age Pops should want a quiet retirement, not to be planning an ambush on the cartel. Doors slam, Mad Dog's holding up fingers for every door he hears. One, two, three, four, then at least four more in quick succession. Doing the math and that perhaps three men were in the back of each vehicle, we could be looking at least ten people. Counting up those of us not in the bunker, it's an even match. Although as Chewy pointed out, we have three older guys, and an injured man.

"Knock, knock!" a sweet voice with a cold edge calls out. "I'm looking for the Devil's Rose MC, I heard I could find them all hereeeee." High heels tap on the wood floors, then come to an abrupt stop. "Huh, I thought this was an MC and I'm looking at two women, and what are you? A cop of some type?"

"Something like that," Moss's deep voice says, sounding bored.

Silence rings out, and I'm not sure what's happening, not until a loud, grating feminine laugh hits my ears. I shuffle to the side a little, managing to peek around the butcher block I'm stationed behind. From this angle I have a clear view of Chewy through the doorway into the dining room. Renae Sullivan comes into view every now and then, and so does a tall, gaunt looking Latino man. I'm guessing this is the infamous Serpiente.

"Oh, you must be Tuesday. I've heard all about you, you know." High heels start click clacking on the floorboards again, this time as if she's circling someone or something. "I heard you 'saved' my little girl." Chewy's face stays neutral, however I don't miss her eyes snapping to Renae. "Don't you think she has Tito's eyes?" How Chewy keeps her bored expression I have no idea. The only way I can tell Renae's words have affected her is by the tapping of her fingers, a more staccato beat than she uses when she's plotting. "Don't worry, me and Tito don't want her back." Chewy's fingers stop abruptly, her hands curling into fists. "We just want what's owed to us. When you took her it annoyed so many people, especially the sheik that paid for her. So, you can see our dilemma I'm sure." Silence echoes through the room, Chewy's gaze set on the wall behind Renae's left shoulder. "If you reimburse us, with interest, we *promise* we won't hurt you, right baby?"

238

Renae says, looking at Serpiente with doe eyes.

Mad Dog and I share a look. In the words of Johnny, holy shit! Not only is Laney Renae and Serpiente's child, but he's here, with her in the house. Energy zings through my veins, if we can take them both out, we can put this whole thing to bed. We can be free of the cartels and all of it.

"That's a generous offer," Chewy says, "but I'll have to decline. Oh, and I also *promise* that I'll hurt you so good you will be begging for death." Even without seeing what's happening I know that Chewy is smiling. "*Inaianei*," Chewy says quietly.

Bullets ring out from outside in a flurry and I'm certain I hear engines and screeching tires before it all goes silent.

That hideous laughter rings out again, chilling me to the bone. "You're going to regret that," Renae hisses before all hell breaks loose.

Marx

I push my sled as far as she could safely go, the road disappearing under my tires as I push harder and harder to get home. I may not like the Russians, but they've never steered me wrong since we've had our understanding. They leave us alone, we leave them alone and every now and then we have a delicately balanced relationship where we all work together like good little boys. I mean, Roman is hardly going to turn on us when we do his dirty work, is he? That is why when Dima calls, I answer. If he's ordered us home, then that's where we need to be. That's where my heart is, and if I find a hair on her head has been touched, there will be hell to pay.

My bluetooth beeps and I connect immediately when I see the caller ID. "Remy? What's going on?"

"The farm has been ambushed by Serpiente. Renae Sullivan is with him, and more men than we calculated," Remy rushes out.

"How many men?"

"Fifty, at least. We're surrounded and are managing to hold them off, but we need backup!"

"What about the bratva?"

"We have as many as Roman could spare, the rest of his men were split between your team and the Landry team. We killed a few but there's a crap ton more we need to get rid of."

The bite in Remy's voice surprises me. I know that she is as badass as every other woman, but it's rare that you see it.

"We're ten minutes out."

A low growl comes over the line, "Tav and the others are twenty out. We need you here now Pres!"

The line goes dead and I push even harder, my men recognising the urgency and following my lead. We speed through town and I doubt anyone is going to stop us. Hell, if they haven't been called out to a fucking farm house under siege, they ain't pulling us over, goddamn pussy police force. I need to have a word with Moss. If the state ain't willing to give us a good force, then I will.

By the time we hit the road leading to the farm house we've cut almost five minutes off our usual ride time. I know our sleds won't be liking it but shit, it is what it is. We roar in, guns drawn picking out any men we see that we don't recognise. Most of them are low level scumbags, baggy jeans, oversized hoodies, and rent-a-goons. I'm guessing these are the guys we were meant to be focussing on in the first place. Instead, they waited until we were lying in wait in their territory, and ambushed our women and children like the cowards they are. I let out a roar at how dumb we were to be splitting up, even though it was the right thing to do with the intel we had. But the intel was wrong and now we're joining a battle where we are completely outnumbered, caught with our pants down. I don't even know what the damage is yet.

My brothers and I take out as many men as we can before I get to the porch, throwing myself off my bike. The firefight has slowed down out here, but there are still gunshots and screams coming from inside the house. Pops' house that he was so damn generous to provide for us. I hesitate at the bottom of the steps until some bastard I was unaware was coming at me, goes flying backward, my head snapping to the roof where TumTum salutes me.

"We've got you covered, go, go!" he screams before turning back to his site.

Looking at the roof space across from his I spy Pops' nest, the old man perched up there like he's king of all he sees. Stomping up the steps, I'm shoved out of the way by some guy running past, screaming as the hair on his head is covered in flames, encompassing his face, licking toward his throat.

"What the hell-" Savage is cut off by another guy, this one fully on fire.

"Well, that's two down," I mutter under my breath.

I glance at my brothers before stepping inside, wary now that I've seen two men screaming out of here on fire.

"Is that-" Rhodie tips his head to the side, eyes on the blow torch attached to the door jamb of the kitchen.

"Yup."

"That's Home Alone shit right there," Tank whispers, looking around, bewildered.

Grunting from the dining room draws my attention pulling me in that direction. Before I can say anything my men fan out, guns drawn. At Remy's last call there were fifty men swarming the place. There are at least twenty bodies lying out front, so anyone else will be out back or inside, and that's a lot of men to put down. If Remy's correct we are severely outnumbered, at least until the others get here.

Stepping inside the room I come to a dead stop at what I see. Blanche is covered in blood, Chewy has bruises and a shitty look on her face, and Lovely, *my* Lovely, is in the arms of that bastard Serpiente. Some dark-haired bitch, I'm guessing Renae Sullivan, holds court, standing in the middle of the room, high heels, pencil skirt and silk blouse. Her face goes from docile to predatory when she sees me notice her.

"Oh, yes, he'll do nicely I think."

"You don't touch him, you bitch!" Lovely spits out with such venom it shocks me.

"I'll do whatever. I. Want," Renae says, punctuating each with a step closer to me.

Lovely struggles to get out of Serpiente's arms, fighting until the arm banded around her chest comes up, his hand gripping her throat, squeezing hard enough to cut off her air supply.

"You'll do well to let go of her. Right. This. Fucking. Instant." I aim my gun at his head, the bastard grinning at me, pulling back enough that I can't get a clean shot without risking my woman.

"Uh, uh, uh," Renae sings, her voice grating on my last fucking nerve. "That's not how to play nice, is it?"

My head is yanked back roughly by a hand in my hair, and cool metal pierces my throat, just a little, to warn me not to move. I don't dare take my gaze off my woman. Lovely's eyes are wide as saucers, filled with tears and yet she doesn't let them fall. She's terrified, but I know it's for me, as the fear in her eyes wasn't there until I was threatened.

"You gonna be a good boy?" That bitch Renae runs a hand over my chest, down my stomach and over my flaccid cock. Gripping and rubbing trying to get him to work, but he'll never rise for anyone other than Lovely Landry.

I stare at my woman, the one who makes me want to be a better man. I will her to fight, but I can already see the blood vessels in her eyes have burst. If that motherfucker doesn't take his hands off her soon, I'll lose her, the best thing that ever happened to me. My men's voices drift down from upstairs, each calling out "clear!" as they work through the warren of rooms up there. It seems our lesser numbers have somehow overcome the men who are here to destroy us.

Moving my weight ever so slightly to the balls of my feet I take a deep breath, ready to launch at the dead man with his hands around Lovely's delicate throat. Distant motorcycle pipes echo through the air and I know the exact moment the power changes hands, panic registering on the face of the bitch who dared lay her hands on me.

Blanche catches my eye, flicking her gaze over my shoulder before staring hard at me. Giving her the smallest chin tilt I launch forward, knocking Renae off her heels with my bulk, slamming her to the ground as I lunge for Serpiente, pure rage fuelling me. I don't see anything other than this man. His face, his hands, his goddamn evil touching the purest human to ever walk the earth. I don't know where she is or what is happening in the room, all I see, hear, smell, and feel is him. I hit, pummel, kick, bite, claw, anything and everything. I want to tear him apart, blood whooshing in my head, making it pound with every hit I land.

In one moment I'm deaf and blind, the next, screeching has my attention on Renae, phone in hand, "I need them all, all of you, he's killing him!" Her eyes are wild and her laugh maniacal as screeching tires and gunfire fill the air outside.

Blanche looks up from Lovely, the man who once held a knife to my throat dead on the floor beside them. "Make her stop, she's giving me a damned headache!"

Chewy moves like lightning, knocking Renae out cold. "I'm taking her to Pops' office. Meet you there later."

Lovely's big dark eyes find mine, the burst vessels causing fury to rise again, but I tamp it down. Serpiente isn't going anywhere soon, and my woman needs me.

"I'm here baby, I'm here."

She crawls into my lap, curled up, so tiny and fragile, her face pressed to my throat. I hold her tight to me, breathing her in, whispering that everything is going to be OK. I have her, and my men have our backs.

She tips her head back, looking me in the eye, "Destroy them, Marx. Destroy them for me and Bee and everyone else who needs them gone to feel safe." Her voice is rough, barely a whisper but I hear the order.

Looking at Blanche she holds my gaze, then gives me a nod. "You heard the first lady, destroy them."

I drop a kiss to Lovely's plump lips, gently move her to the arms of her big sister, then move to stand. Stepping over Serpiente's broken body, I know he'll keep until I can get someone to move him to Pops' office. I'm not quite finished with him yet.

I move like death himself, past another sorry bastard with his head in flames, a guy missing an arm from below the elbow, and a body on the floor, limbs at an impossible angle. Looking up, my brother smirks down at me before shrugging. A laugh builds deep in the pit of my stomach, building up until I'm on the porch, gun in hand, laughing like a mad man. Fuck, I love the DRMC.

Chapter 22

Judge

My head pounds as I look around at the carnage. It was only by sheer luck that we arrived just after twelve SUVs, filled to the brim with gang bangers and cartel members. I'm not sure what the hell is going on, but I'm damn glad we got the call to turn around when we did.

We don't even wait for orders, pulling our guns and taking out anyone that doesn't look friendly. Some of my brothers head around the back, in case the house is surrounded, but I concentrate on the front and the front only. My gaze is fixed on the front door and I hope like hell that Kaia and the kids are in the bunker, safe and sound. The problem is, I know Kaia better than I know anyone, even with us being separated all these years. That woman is stubborn as all get out, and the fear I have coursing through my veins that she is actually not tucked away safe, is killing me.

I ride toward men, firing at will, watching with satisfaction as they drop, one by one. Some drop by my hand, others by the snipers sitting on the main roof and one of the cabins to my left. For some reason there are men screaming out the front door on fire, and I'm not sure how or why that's happening but I bet it has something to do with Pops. Or shit, even Elio. I don't know what they've done to the house, but there seems to be walking injured everywhere. The men who made it to the house seem to be running screaming from it in matters of moments. Noticing a gang banger scaling a side wall I head that way, gun raised to stop him from entering through the window to the dining room. My finger twitches on the trigger when he goes flying back into the bushes, screaming. Aiming my bike for him I notice blood the closer I get. I skid to an idle, staring down the barrel of my gun at a man who is full of nails and other shrapnel. His eyes are clenched shut, blood pouring from them, and it's a shame that he doesn't see my bullet coming. Revving my engine I blow dust over his body as I head around the side, eager to cut off any more brave fuckers who think to infiltrate the house my woman and kids are in. And that's what they are. *Mine.* I just have to convince them.

Lovely

It's complete and utter chaos. Men in suits or jeans and baggy hoodies seem to be coming out of the woodwork. I may have been almost choked to unconsciousness, but that doesn't mean I can't still put up a fight. It's ironic, I guess, that as much as the Keep taught us girls to be meek little housewives, it also bred a protective instinct within the women for their children. There is no way that Bee will suffer at the hands of anyone, not on my watch. If I have to die to protect her, then so be it, but you best believe that I will take as many of these men down with me as I can.

"You need to get to the bunker," Blanche whispers, our guns trained on the doorway, picking men off one by one as they make the mistake of walking past.

"I'm not leaving you," I grit out, not looking in her direction. "You saved me, Patience. You and our brothers saved me and got rid of the monsters. I will not leave your side." I glare at her and her busted lip curls at the edges, her bruised and swollen face lighting up.

"Well then, little sister, let's see how many more evil doers we can kill."

We move slowly through the room, eyes on the doors and windows in case another unfortunate soul dares to walk past. Serpiente is still lying where Marx left him, his breathing shallow, likely due to how mangled his face is. Although I'm sure Marx broke ribs so perhaps the guy was unlucky and one punctured a lung. Either way, I don't care too much. He deserves everything he gets.

Peeking out the window next to me I watch my wild man in the front yard, stomping and slashing through men intent on harming us. I know later tonight, in the dark and quiet of our room Johnny will tell me that he's evil, dark and dirty and doesn't deserve someone like me. I know he will. What he doesn't understand is that he deserves someone better than me. Someone who can give him the world. Does that mean I'll give him up? No way. All it means is two people who think they are undeserving of the other, will spend the rest of their lives proving we are worthy until we inherently believe it. Because we *are* worthy of each other's love.

A groaning, scraping snatches my attention, drawing it to the broken man clawing his way to the doorway. He's coughing up blood and trying to wheeze out for help. I watch him with pity, before bringing my switchblade down on his calf, pinning him to the floorboards below.

"Gunfire and screaming seems to be settling down," Blanche murmurs, peeking out the door, gun drawn and ready to fire.

I nod, not that she's looking in my direction. I sneak a peek out the window again, this time seeing the men standing with hands on hips, looking at the carnage around them. Mad Dog stomps through the fallen, aiming his weapon at their heads, pulling the trigger once before moving on to the next. It's been a massacre. One that should have taken place in two different states, however it came to us instead, almost destroying our home.

"Shit, Mom! Are you OK? Holy fuck, Aunt Lovely, are *you* OK?" Niko looks stricken as his gaze flicks between the two of us, both of us looking worse for wear.

Blanche's face took two punches from Serpiente. She has dried blood around her nose and mouth, a split lip and a black eye. I was choked out and I know from experience that I can look forward to burst blood vessels and bruising around my neck. My throat is hoarse, my voice barely above a whisper.

"We're fine, baby," Blanche answers for us.

The look on Niko's face is filled with disbelief and shock and I can't help the giggle that bubbles up inside me. I burst into peals of laughter and even though it hurts I can't stop.

"Ah Mom, do you think she's in shock?"

"I'd say that's a pretty good guess, kiddo," Vi says, walking in from who knows where.

She has blood on her jeans, and some of her shirt is missing along the bottom hem. She must catch me staring because she shrugs, her dark hair bouncing, "tore some off to stop a flesh wound."

"Please tell me Rider was shot in the ass again?" Blanche begs.

"Worse," Vi answers, her lips twitching, she lets out a snort, "I have no idea how it happened, what with him wearing his cut, but somehow the bullet grazed his nipple."

"Wait, first the ass then the nipple? Jesus, the guy can't catch a break," Niko mutters.

"I dunno, could have hit his junk," Vi replies.

"Leave my nipples out of this!" Rider yells, stomping into the dining room. He jabs a finger in Serpiente's direction, "He's to blame! I'm taking his ass to the Office. I'm going to carve said ass til it's scarred like mine. Do you know how beautiful my ass was before one of his men shot at it? And now I'll have a fucked up nipple too!" he lets out a low growl before lunging toward Serpiente.

He grips him under the arms, yanking him to move him. "What the hell-" he yanks once more, pulling him so hard that my switchblade moves through more of his flesh. Serpiente wakes screaming, giving Rider a fright who throws him down on the ground. "Look what you made me do!" He yells in Serpiente's face. He kicks his injured leg, then pulls out my switchblade handing it to me.

Without a word he throws the gurgling, moaning man over his shoulder, stomping out of the room bitching about nipples and asses. We stare after him and I can't help the huge smile I have on my face. As ridiculous and gruff and grumpy and hilarious the DRMC is, they really are the very best of men.

"Roman's here," Niko says, gazing out the window.

We watch as the slick town car slowly moves up the long drive, bobbing as it runs over anything and anyone in its way. Marx stands to attention, the hard line of his body held so tight I feel like he'll snap at any minute. It's a guarantee. I don't think as I let my feet carry me out of the room, down the hall littered with broken and battered bodies, out onto the porch. My man is right there, like a coiled snake ready to attack. Even the comfort of his men, standing shoulder to shoulder with him isn't working to calm the rage inside him.

Moving down the steps I pick my way through bullet casings and more broken bodies, coming to a stop behind Marx, my hand resting in the center of his back. Slowly, so very slowly the tension begins to drain, his muscles relaxing under my touch, until he reaches behind him, grasping my hand and tugging me around into his side. His warm arm heavy on my shoulders as he draws me near.

Sasha moves silently as he exits the car, moving to the back passenger side, opening the door for his husband. Roman's shiny black shoe steps out of the car, the puddle of blood he's standing in oozing onto his shoe. He ducks out of the car, looking around, but with dark glasses over his eyes it's hard to read his expression.

He claps slowly, whistling low, as if impressed by the carnage. "Well, I must say, you have been busy,"

"Quit the smart ass remarks, Roman. Care to tell me why the fuck our ambush turned to shit and instead of taking out two cartels on the home turf of their allies, they ambush our women and children instead?" Marx seethes, voice low.

"President, the plan was sound," Roman placates, hands

open in the air as if to appease my big, pissed off man."There was no indication that the trade wouldn't go ahead. In fact, the men I had posted reported that two trucks, smaller than we expected, did in fact make the exchange. But rest easy, my men handed the women over to authorities, and in the case of Louisiana, they handed the women over to the Landry contacts."

"What condition were they in?"

"Comatose. The women were all hooked up to machines, pregnant."

"What the fuck!?" the men explode.

The thought that innocent women are all kept comatose while they grow babies is horrific. I start to shake, out of anger or shock I'm unsure. Marx pulls me closer to him.

"Breathe, my Lovely," he whispers into my hair.

I follow his lead, taking a deep breath, then letting it out. My ear is on his chest, the steady rhythm of his heart soothing me more than breathing ever could.

"I don't appreciate being sent on wild goose chases, Roman. If not for Dima our women and children could have been killed," Marx spits out.

"The women and children, they are safe? You got here in time?" Dima asks, nerves in his voice.

"I have men checking on them, but so far, yes, I believe they are safe."

Dima deflates, shoulders slumping under the weight that his gift makes him carry. It must be hard to constantly see people who need to be saved, and never know if you got there in time.

"Dima is a good man, and I think you know me well enough to know that I would never double cross you or send you to your death," Roman says, his voice steady, but his eyes hard.

"Sometimes I don't believe I know you at all," Marx mutters.

"It wouldn't do to underestimate me," Roman says, pointing a gun directly at Marx.

"No! No, what are you doing?" I croak out in shock and horror, scrambling to move in front of Marx. The MC brothers all move, seemingly at once but in slow motion.

What is happening? This isn't the man who has sat and eaten meals with us. This isn't Ana's best friend that she brags about having a good heart. A whooshing sound pounds in my head, heart fluttering as my stomach drops.

"Looks like you give me no choice." Roman shrugs.

He squeezes the trigger, the gentle "pop" hitting its target, a cartel member standing directly behind Marx. My knees buckle at the realization, shouts from our family calling Roman a fucking psycho, as Marx slumps slightly next to me, my smaller body taking his weight.

"You're welcome." Roman says, returning his gun to his holster in the back of his black trousers. "My men are on their way. Clean up will take an hour, they'll be out of your hair as soon as possible."

He turns to walk away, only stopping when Marx barks out his name. Turning to look over his shoulder, he raises a brow, looking in all ways the cold, calculated head of the bratva.

"Thank you. I still don't trust you though," Marx grits out.

Roman smirks, letting out a soft laugh. "We'll overcome that hurdle one day *brat*. Thank you for my new drug business. Until next time."

Sasha moves behind his man, shutting his door securely after Roman climbs in. He rounds the car and instead of moving to the drivers side as per usual, he joins his husband in the backseat, Dima taking his place. He stands staring thoughtfully at us, at Marx's brothers in arms, all lined up like a human shield in front of the house.

"Can I ask why you said we had to split up?" Tank calls out. "On the phone, you said we split up for a reason. What was it?"

Dima tips his head to the side, his eyes glowing almost white before returning to the piercing blue color he shares with his brother.

"It was easier for you to win the fight if you split up."

"Shit," Savage runs a hand down his face. "He's right. The second crew pulled in behind the cartel, effectively ambushing them from behind. If we were together in the house we would have been sitting ducks."

Dima smiles softly before dipping his chin, opening his car door but stops himself from entering. "There is a mole or a tracking device. That's how they knew where you were." with that he folds his large body into the driver's seat slamming the door behind him.

"There's no way we have a fucking mole," Dex growls."No fucking way," the men are all vocal in their agreement.

"We'll get to the bottom of it," Marx grumbles. "Baby," he says gently, rubbing my cheek, "go check on your girls. If they want to join us in the Office they can." He presses a gentle kiss to my forehead, before moving to press his lips to my cheek, then the space between my shoulder and ear. "Love you."

"Love you, too."

Roman

Sasha wraps my hands in his larger ones, holding them tight until they stop shaking. *Blyad'*, that was close.

"When are you going to tell him?"

Glancing up at my husband I try to ignore the disapproving look he gives me.

"He doesn't need to know."

"*Yerunda!* Dima spent six months looking for Marx, you inserted yourself into his life and you still won't tell him? He thinks you're an asshole who is using him and his family for personal gain!"

"It's the only way to keep him close!" I growl back, pulling my hands from Sasha's reach. He doesn't understand. He will never understand.

He lets out a sigh, and I try to ignore the disappointment on his beautiful face. "You can keep him close by telling him the truth."

"What? That our mother loved me for three years before leaving for an MC clubhouse and a quick fuck then abandoning him like she did me? You think he wants to know that?"

"*Moya lyubov'*, he's a good man. He will understand." Sasha grips my hand, pulling it onto his hard thigh, giving me a squeeze of reassurance.

It doesn't work. I'll never tell Marx how or why I've inserted myself into his life and the lives of his family.

"One day, Roman. It will all come to light one day, but today is not the day," Dima says quietly, his eyes clearing, shining bright blue in the rear view mirror.

I relax back into the leather seat. Today is not the day. And neither is tomorrow.

Chapter 23

Marx

"**F**ucking Roman," I mutter as I storm my way to Pops' Office.

I could take one of the ATV's, but at this point the walk would do me good. I ignore the men dressed head to toe in hazmat suits, instead concentrating on the sheer number of men laid out in the backyard of Pops' farmhouse.

"Marx," Moss waves out as he helps bag and tag the men.

"Moss, what the fuck? There was a full on shoot out and yet no one from the public alerted the cops? Law enforcement in this town is a goddamn joke."

He looks unbothered as he moves on to the next man. "No one called because I alerted all the nearest neighbours, and the precinct that I would be running a practice training model out here. What? Would you prefer we swarmed your asses, hauled everyone in and after 48 hours of processing let you all, including the cartel, go due to lack of evidence?"

"When you put it that way," I grumble.

"Look, Johnny, I get it. You've got women and kids out here. I assisted as best I could, but shit, my sister was part of the original attack at the clubhouse. If I had to choose between the law coming in and sorting out Serpiente and his crew, or the DRMC wiping them off the earth so they can't hurt anyone else? I'll choose you guys over mine any day."

I stare at him thoughtfully, "Have you thought about running for office?"

"To be sheriff? Since Kelson left," we share a look, "I've started thinking more and more."

"So, what's the problem?"

"A team I can trust."

I eye him for a moment, an idea forming. "What if I told you I have two men, ex marines, who are also trained law enforcement agents within the military?"

"I'd say give them my damn number yesterday and tell them to call me. We're understaffed and half the men in the office were Kelson cronies. If I run and make it in, I'll be doing a clear out." A smile grows on Moss's face. "I mean, I can't rely on the DRMC to take care of all the bad guys."

"I'll talk to my men."

He gives me a nod, then goes back to bagging and tagging bodies, leaving the really messy ones for Roman's clean up crew. I head toward Pops' office, jogging a little to catch up to Rhodie and Savage.

"What was that all about?"

"I have a plan forming. If it works out, it'll be good for all of us."

Savage's brow raises. "A plan that involves Moss Davies?"

"Exactly."

Walking through the door I'm met with at least half the MC.

Pops and Chewy are already here, and by the looks of Sniper and his brother, he's been here since we pulled in. He walks to one of Pops' handy stainless steel benches, throwing a small metal object down. It rattles and spins before settling on the countertop.

"Is that–?"

"It's a tracker. They've known where he's been the whole time we've had him. It's how they found us." Sniper says through gritted teeth.

Dex lets out a low whistle as he peers at Sniper's handiwork, his brother's arm cut from wrist to shoulder. Moving my gaze from that sack of shit I'm met with Serpiente, who is unconscious on a table, and a snivelling Renae Sullivan, looking not so smug now she has Chewy to contend with.

"Where do we want to start?"

"She's last." Chewy grits out, and there's something bothering her, that I can't quite put my finger on.

She's always some level of unhinged, but here, at this moment, she looks like she's barely hanging on by a thread.

"Can we just get rid of this asshole? I've had enough of him and his shit." Flack says, punching Serpiente's foot, causing a low long groan.

Renae cries louder until Chewy puts a stop to it, shoving a ball gag into her mouth. "Still want your money now, bitch?" she hisses, using her hand to shove Renae's face away from her in disgust.

"Sheesh Chewy, what did she ever do to you?" Rider asks, voice light,

"This," Chewy points, her gaze moving around the room, "piece of shit and her boyfriend over there," she waves toward Serpiente, who is now somewhat lucid, but in a shit ton of pain,

259

"Are Laney's biological egg and sperm donors. They want us to pay for the pleasure of being her parents."

Rhodie is deathly quiet. He stares between Renae and Serpiente, both shrinking under his gaze. He steps up to Renae, tied to a chair with the ball gag in her mouth. He flicks the catch at the back, letting the gag fall into her lap.

"Did you demand my Ol Lady pay you for the daughter you threw away?" he quietly asks in a voice so quiet it sends chills down my spine.

"I-I, no, she misunderstood-"

Rhodie leans closer, his nose squishing her's into her face. She tries to turn away from his gaze but Chewy is there, her fists in Renae's dark hair, holding her steady.

"Are you calling my Ol Lady a liar?"

"N-n-, not at all, um-"

Rhodie steps back and the bitch's shoulders slump.

"So, Serpiente is your husband? Boyfriend?" Rhodie strolls his way and I see the moment Renae realizes that she may have dodged Rhodie's wrath, but her sick fuck man hasn't.

"You leave him alone! Let me go, let me go! Baby, don't tell them shit! Baby, baby, look at me-" she struggles against her restraints, hissing and spitting like a wet cat.

Rhodie yanks him up by the scruff of his neck, pulling him off the table he's been lying on, letting his body fall to the ground with a yelp. He drags him along the floor, Serpiente's broken body at odd angles, his breathing shallow, blood still oozing from his leg. Renae's screams are getting on my nerves, and I'm hoping that Rhodie will put an end to them, and soon.

My little brother pulls Serpiente into an almost standing position, one arm banded around his chest as the two love birds stare at each other.

"I love you, baby," Renae sobs, her shoulders shaking, her cries turning to screams when Rhodie's knife slides through skin, tendon and muscle along Serpiente's throat.

Blood sprays on Renae's face and into her open mouth, effectively gagging her. Rhodie drops the dead man at Renae's feet, before leaning into her, wiping the blood off his knife on her silk blouse.

"My daughter doesn't exist to you. You will never speak of her, you will never think of her for as long as you live." He brings his clean blade down into her thigh, pinning her to the chair.

Her mouth opens on a wail but her eyes roll back and she slumps down in her seat.

"Thank fuck, her voice was giving me a headache," one of my brothers mutters.

"Grab some Tylenol, my girls have arrived and it's time to have a little fun," Chewy grins, her eyes fixed on Renae's slumped body.

The heavy metal door slams behind the Ol Ladies, each one beelining for their men. Lovely smiles wide, seeming in good spirits considering she has to be in pain. She must read my thoughts because she moves to her tiptoes, pressing a gentle kiss to the corner of my mouth.

"It doesn't hurt too bad. Vi gave me a pain reliever and as long as I don't talk or move my neck too much I'm fine." She pats the center of my chest with her hand, and I grasp it in mine, holding it against my heart.

Her eyes turn soft and she leans into me, breathing deeply before turning, allowing me to trap her in the circle of my arms, her dark head leaning back against my chest. I nuzzle into her hair, breathing her scent as I press a kiss to the top of her head, then fix my gaze on Chewy.

"What's the plan?"

"Let me just confer with the girls."

The women make their way to the other side of the room. I'm reluctant to let Lovely go, but she throws me a cheeky grin over her shoulder and mouths "I'll be back" as she sashays that plump ass across the room.

"No ogling until she's patched up," Pops jabs me with his finger while mean mugging me.

"I agree, Son, Lock that woman down, and fast," Mad Dog adds.

Before I know it all my brothers are murmuring their agreement. I rub the center of my chest, feeling damn warm inside knowing my brothers approve of Lovely. I didn't really think I'd give a shit whether they liked my choice of ol lady or not, but to know they not only like her, but approve wholeheartedly means a lot. Having a first lady that the MC loves and respects is not only preferable, but powerful. Her brothers were right, she's the type of person the club will go to war for.

Feminine giggles draw mine and my brother's attention to the other side of the room, the women looking animated, Mira scribbling frantically in her book while the others look like all their Christmases have come at once.

"Should we be afraid of how excited they all look?" Rider asks, tipping his chin in their direction.

"Should I be afraid that Kaia has slipped right into their Girl Gang bullshit?" Judge grumbles, never taking his eyes off Kaia.

I slap him on the back and give him a rueful smile. The brother has always been quiet and collected. The fact that he's set his sights on a woman that I'd be afraid to piss off has my lips tipping up even more.

"Judge, I think you have a lot more to be afraid of than the Girl Gang."

He lets out a sigh, "I know Pres. Kaia is fucking everything wrapped up in this dynamite package. I'm convinced she could rip my balls off at any moment."

I slap him on the shoulder. "So? She may be scary, but can you imagine yourself with anyone else?" He stares at me before shaking his head. "Good luck, brother, it's worth it."

"AND BREAK!" The women all clap their hands like they've been discussing plays in an NFL huddle and make their way back to their ol men.

Chewy frees Chomper and Gretchen from their homey little cages in the corner, leads them to Serpiente's prone body and nudges them closer. "There, babies, have a snack before bedtime," she coos. She prances past Rhodie, stopping to suck face with him, before her and Pops go to the storeroom.

"You girls have a plan?" I whisper to Lovely, as she automatically finds her way back into my arms.

"Sure do," she whispers hoarsely.

"Should we be worried?"

She just grins up at me, a twinkle in her eye.

"Ladies and gentlemen! Before we start the show I need two strong volunteers!"

Lovely

I watch Chewy ham it up and I'm not sure why I'm surprised that her and Pops are both wearing sequined top hats. The lights have been dimmed slightly, and "The Final Countdown" is playing in the background, the beat building suspense. Tank and Judge, some of the largest men we have in the club, step forward. They nod, hands on hips as Chewy gives them instructions. While all this is happening Pops is assembling what looks to be some type of rubber bladder, the kind that goes inside basketballs, but much larger. There's a long thin hose coming out of it and he slaps it down on the stainless steel bench. He slams a pump bottle full of lube beside it and then gently places down three syringes of something or other.

"I know I should be used to this shit by now, but they still make me nervous," my big brother Vic says.

I catch his eye and give him a thumbs up. I'm so excited that my brothers will be patching in. I mean, given the way we were all raised, it shouldn't surprise me that all of us Landry kids have landed here. Communal living with a chosen family? Clearly it's what we're built for.

"Flack, can you wake her ass up?" Chewy asks in a sweet voice, while adding stirrups to the metal table Serpiente had been lying on.

Another clatter on Pops' stainless steel workbench has us all turning.

"What? Just lubing the speculum."

"The what-u-lum?" Nitro asks in a high pitched voice.

"A speculum. In laymen's terms it's a pussy spreader. Goes inside, holds the vagina open so we can check the cervix amongst other things," Switch yells from his place next to Sniper's brother, Joseph.

I have no idea how long the brother is going to keep him

alive, but he doesn't look like he'll last much longer. No use keeping him anyway. His whole cartel has pretty much been destroyed.

"Jesus," Flack says, staring at the contraption Pops is holding.

Judge and Tank, at Chewy's instruction, unshackle Renae from the chair, carrying her limp body to the table, strapping her wrists down in the handcuffs on other side of the table, then strapping her legs wide open on the stirrups Chewy put in place.

There's a certain level of perverse satisfaction that runs through me, knowing that not only will this woman's life be ending tonight, but it'll be done in a way that takes away her dignity, much like she did to the women she kidnapped and forcibly bred. I shudder, remembering what Roman said. She had comatose pregnant women growing babies, like all they were was an incubator. She disgusts me to my soul.

Flack wafts something under her nose and she comes awake with a jolt, screaming blue murder. Before anyone can complain about the noise, Chewy shoves another ball gag, this time a bright pink one, into her open maw.

"You OK there, Renae? I know you're probably wondering what's going to happen next, right?" Chewy asks, gently, in a voice that sounds open and caring. "Well, we're going to give you a little of your own medicine." She pats her head roughly, before holding her hand out to Pops.

He plops the lubed speculum into Chewy's hand, and she grins maniacally as she holds it up for Renae to see. She slices Renae's panties out of her way, not caring when Renae jolts and blood starts to drip down onto the bed.

"Whoops," Chewy says unapologetically as she snaps a

sterile glove on her hand.

She places the speculum where it needs to be, twisting the handle to open up enough space for her to work. I know what's coming and I can feel my vulva trying to crawl its way up into my body for safety. Glancing around, all the girl gang are staring in fascination, as the men are either side eyeing the scene, or looking at the ceiling or floor.

More rummaging between Renae's legs before Chewy stands straight, pulling her glove off with a flourish and pinging it in Rider's direction. The big man squeals then gives every woman here the evil eye when we laugh at his misfortune. I love Rider, don't get me wrong, but that man seems to have the worst luck.

"And now, for my amazing trick! It'll leave you gobsmacked, in awe, and horrified in equal measure!" Chewy flips a switch and the mechanical whirring of the air compressor fills the room.

"What the hell is that?" someone murmurs.

"I dunno, but whatever it's doing, it's going up her pussy."

I snort, then curse internally when it causes my throat to burn a little. Marx leans down to look me in the eye, gently rubbing a thumb along my cheek. I give him a thumbs up and a smile, more interested in seeing if our plan is running smoothly.

"Holy shit, it's working!" Kaia whispers in awe, her wide eyes on Renae's stomach.

I step forward for a closer look, then notice that flanking me are the rest of my Girl Gang. We stare in awe as the air compressor fills the bladder, Renae's stomach inflating slowly, going from a little bloated, to a couple months pregnant in size. Her eyes are screwed shut and she whimpers and whines as

Chewy grins proudly.

"Shit kid, this is working better than I expected!" Pops says with excitement. He leans forward to get a closer look, then takes a big step back. Then another.

"Ah, Chewy, care to explain?" Dex asks nervously.

"Oh yeah. She's kept women against their will, using them as incubators to then sell their babies. I'm giving her a little taste of her own medicine. But instead of nine months, I'm aiming for nine minutes." She waggles her brows, a huge grin on her face. One I'm sure mirrors the rest of us. "Pops, crank it higher, I wanna get back to put *my* baby to bed," Chewy says, making sure she's staring into Renae's eyes as she says it.

The woman whimpers, her thigh muscles tensing as the pain bears down on her. Her stomach is quite distended now, stretching her blouse tight, but there's still more to come. Pops cranks the air machine higher, the noise going from a soft whirr to a buzz.

"Fucking hell, it's so gross and yet I can't look away," one of the brothers mumbles, not sure which one. The rest seem to all be staring in disgusted awe.

"Holy schnikes, look how tight her stomach looks! It's like she's having triplets!" Mira says, clapping her hands and then staring intently as she notes down all the gory details.

I'm sure she'll be dropping a book soon with this type of scene in it. I better put my name down for that one. I've read all her others, that's pretty much where I learned all about gentle lovemaking. The kind that you have with someone who truly loves you, and who you love. Feeling Johnny's gaze on me, I turn and meet his eyes. His full lips tip up in a crooked smile, revealing his straight white teeth. I read his words as he mouths "I love you." My hand raises to my chest, rubbing at the tight feeling as my tummy bursts with butterflies and chickens flapping and all the feelings I resigned myself to never having when I was Royal's wife.

"I love you," I mouth back at him, jerking when warm wet hits me the full length of my back, dripping down my hair.

Looking up I'm met with silence and the wide eyes of the DRCM men, all covered in blood and God knows what else.

"Well, she blew a lot quicker than I expected."

Turning ever so slowly, I gawk at Pops and Chewy, both covered in Renae Sullivan, but looking like the cats that got the cream.

"*Chewy*!"

"OK, show's over folks, thanks for coming and be sure to tip your waitress," Chewy finishes before turning and walking toward the clean room.

Epilogue

Marx

"Mmmm, yes baby, just like that my love, holy fuck, that looks so damn good," my toes curl and my eyes roll back in my head as Lovely rides me reverse, giving me the perfect view of her little pink asshole winking at me while her pussy works my length. Sucking my thumb I gently press it to her back passage, slowly massaging. Her low groans are music to my greedy ears, so I explore her more.

We've come a long way in the few months since we cut a swathe through the cartels, effectively shutting down the bogus adoption agencies while we were at it. The only loose end we have is Sniper's brother. It's cruel that he's still hanging around, but it's Sniper's call and I'm not taking that away from him.

Lovely swivels her hips, and my mind blanks, utterly and completely. The little minx knows what she does to me because she peeks over her shoulder, with a little smirk on her full pink lips. I flex my hips, driving into her deeper, revelling when her eyes roll back and she moans louder still.

"More Johnny, please," she whines, not even riding me so much as leaning on all fours, making shallow little rocking thrusts on me.

"Baby, do you trust me?"

"With my life," she whispers, head rolling forward to rest on the bed.

I tap her ass, sliding out of her to move directly behind her, my hands cradling her hips. My cock finds his way home into her wet sheath, pressing slowly, getting her used to being on her knees with me behind her.

"Is this OK? If it's not let me know and I'll stop immediately, OK sweetheart?"

Lovely doesn't answer, just rocks back, slamming her thick ass against my thighs with a whine, "Please Johnny!"

I hold her still, even though I would love nothing more than to ram deep inside over and over. My woman's needs come first, always. "Need the words baby, need to know you'll be OK."

She looks over her shoulder, holding my gaze with her own, "Yes, Johnny. I trust you and if I freak out I will let you know. Always."

"Good girl," I whisper, running my hands over her smooth pale skin, gripping her ass cheeks and pulling them apart obscenely so I can see where we're connected, my cock covered in her cream.

"Johnny?"

"Yes, Buttercup?"

"Fuck me."

My restraint snaps and I thrust hard and deep, my balls

slapping her clit in this position. She bucks forward, but the moan she lets out tells me I'm on the right track. I pull out and thrust back in, mercilessly pumping into her, gripping her hips hard enough to bruise, covering her back with my body so my hands can pinch those fat nipples I love to have in my mouth.

"More baby, more, give it all to me, I need it, I need you," Lovely pants, and I'm not sure how much more I can give.

The base of my spine starts to tingle and I can feel my balls drawing up but that's not good enough, not for my Lovely. I pull out, flipping her onto her back, hooking her knees in my elbows and hoisting her pussy closer to my mouth. I take one long look at her pulsing hole, wide open from my cock, looking empty and like it needs to be filled. Leaning forward I slide my tongue into her tight little channel, spearing her over and over, fucking her with my tongue as she bucks and writhes, her hands clawing at the bedsheet, balling them up in her small fists. Her thighs start to shake on either side of my face so I double down, sucking her sensitive little nub into my mouth and batting it gently with my tongue coated in her essence.

She explodes, her spend dripping down my beard, onto my chest but I'm not done. Lowering her slightly I shove my cock into her quivering pussy, my name ripped from her lips, screams bouncing off the walls.

"That's it baby, one more, give me one more and I'll fill you with my cum," I pant, feeling my release building, higher, higher as I pump in and out of her.

"Johnny!" she clamps her legs around my waist, back arched, nipples pointed heavenward, her head thrown back, face serene in her ecstasy.

Her sheer beauty has me in awe as my release fills her, over and over, wave after wave of my cum fills her tight pussy and not for the first time since we've been together have I hoped that I've gotten her pregnant. I collapse on top of her, mindful of how large I am compared to her. As is her way she wraps her arms tight around me, running her fingers through my hair, petting me, stroking away all my worries and insecurities.

With Lovely at my side, I'm a man who can do and achieve anything. The clubhouse rebuild is already finished. Probably because once everything was said and done, no one wanted to move away from the farm. It was a unanimous decision to move our compound here. The farmhouse was renovated to be the new clubhouse with a self contained master suite for Pops and Mama Debs, and the houses that we've built for the brothers with Ol Ladies are ready for us to move into. The land the farmhouse sits on is enough space for us to continue to build our community should the single brothers want a home of their own once they're ready. The Tombs farm suited our needs better, tucked away from the road means less drive bys, the kids have their clubhouse, and Pops' Office, now the new Rev Room, has all the space and the facilities that can keep Chewy and Pops happy. We're not sure yet what the old compound will be used for, however its location on the main road into town makes it prime real estate for the business ideas that seem to be coming out of the woodwork, including the tattoo shop that Mad Dog and Lovely want to open.

"Have I told you how happy I am that I landed on your doorstep?" Lovely whispers, dropping a kiss to my sweaty forehead.

"Have I told you how happy I am that you gave me a chance?" I prop myself up, grinning at her before dropping a gentle kiss on her lips. "Thank you, Lovely. You own me. Mind, body and soul."

I gently wipe the tears from her eyes with my thumbs, then press my forehead to hers.

"Johnny? Make love to me again?"

"As you wish, My Lovely, as you wish."

Lovely

I turn away from the pop up bar so Pops can't see my smile. I've been biting my lip ever since Johnny presented me with my property cut and the Landrys, Gus and Jules with their DRMC cuts. Moss got a small patch that he can wear wherever he likes as he has MC affiliations, but isn't a patched member so to speak. Everyone is walking around with soft leather over their shoulders, and Pops is looking more and more like thunder, the scowl permanently etched into his face. The rest of the MC circulate around the gazebo we set up in the farmhouse yard so we could celebrate now the threats are all gone. The big little kids are break dancing on a makeshift dance floor, the twins are chatting away to Sage and Chef, and the babies are all in what I think might possibly be a petting zoo set up, short fences set up in a large square

"May I have this dance?" Johnny's deep voice washes over me and my hussy vagina clenches at the thought of being in his arms.

I'm always starved for his touch, even though we were together in the pantry not an hour ago.

"Of course my ol man can have this dance," I beam up at him as he leads me in a two step, moving us around the dancefloor, bumping us into the other couples.

We all share knowing smiles and I feel the need to bottle up all this happiness, to keep it close forever. When I ran from the Keep, rescued by my sister and older brothers, I never could have imagined finding a place that not only accepted me, but helped me grow and morph into a woman I know my daughter will be proud of.

"When are you going to put Pops out of his misery?" I ask quietly, trying to hide my smile in Johnny's chest.

"Dunno. Do you think he's stewed long enough?" Johnny raises a thick brow at me when I tip my head back to look at him.

"I think if you wait any longer, all hell is going to break loose. He'll probably blow something up."

Johnny snorts, presses a kiss to my head and gives me a wink, leaving me on the dance floor as he strides to the microphone on the makeshift stage. He lets out his famous whistle, the music cuts off and everyone falls silent.

"I have one more announcement, but I've been waiting for the right time." He looks over the crowd, holding my gaze for a long moment. "When I think of family and leadership, there is no one here that encompasses that more than Pops. Pops? Can you come up there please?"

Pops' brows are in his hairline for a quick moment, before they pull down in confusion. "What the fuck did I do now?" he grumbles, making his way to the stage.

"Ever since Chewy landed at my MC you have been there. Pushing, pulling, being a wayward pain in the ass, but always there. Standing shoulder to shoulder with us, or at our backs.

Not only did we gain Chewy that night she broke into my compound, we gained three brothers, and a grandfather figure that would do anything for every single one of our dumb asses." We all laugh, Johnny using Pops' own words. "When we needed you, you were there. When we needed advice, you were there. When we needed shelter, again, you were there. Sidney Tombs, there is no one I would want to have my back more than your scary old ass. Do you accept this Devil's Rose MC cut, as a sign of brotherhood and family?" Marx holds up the patch, the DRMC rocker on the back, and his name patch, "Pops," fixed on the front.

"Of course I fucking will! What a dumb fucking question!" Pops says, looking disgusted.

It's all a show and I'm not the only one who sees the tears in Pops' eyes as he pulls Johnny in for a man hug, slapping my man so hard that I can hear him grunting from where I stand.

"*Now* let's get this party started!" Pops calls out, hands in the air, cut resting on his shoulders.

Johnny walks toward me grinning, scooping me up and twirling me around. "Fucking love you."

"I fucking love you, too," Johnny throws his head back, laughing at my curse.

Holding me close we cuddle on the dancefloor until Mama Debs brings little Bee. I place her on my hip and Johnny wraps his arms around us both, swaying us gently. Overwhelming love, I feel it radiating out of me, glowing, covering Johnny and Bee and my whole entire family. In Bee and Johnny's arms I'm safe, loved, perfect. But here, surrounded by my family, I'm home.

Epilogue II

Kaia

"**W**hat are you doing all the way out here?"

I spin, startled by the gruff voice. I take a look around, not actually sure where "here" is until I spot the barn-like structure that we call the Rev Room now.

"Oh, just needed a little space. So I took a walk." I shrug, looking into the dimming light at Sniper.

I've been around the brothers long enough to know them all now. Some, like Rider and Flack and Tav are very easy to get along with. Others, like Sniper, are a little quieter, preferring their own company. Or in his case, the company of the brother he's been keeping alive.

"What are you doing all the way out here?" I return the question.

"I don't actually know," he answers quietly.

I blink once, then twice. I'm not sure if that's an invitation for me to ask what's bugging him, or for me to leave the man alone.

"You ever just wish you could let things go? Just get over it?"

"Oh, I'm the wrong person to be asking, buddy. Have you not seen me hold a mean grudge at Judge this whole time?" I smirk.

He stares at me, as if staring right through me. "That's not a real grudge. I know you want to be close to him. You'll forgive him, you know? You're already there. I, on the other hand, I can't forgive."

I swallow, not wanting to concentrate on my feelings for Leo. Judge. "Can you forget maybe?"

"Not while he's still alive," His gaze moves to the office, as if able to stare right through the walls to his brother.

"Have you thought about ending it for him?" I inch closer, wanting to see his face when he answers.

"I don't think I'm strong enough." His shoulders slump and he stares at the ground. He takes a deep breath and then shakes his shoulders out. "We should get back, care to walk together?"

"Nah," I swallow, "You go on. I think I'll walk and think a little more."

He tips his head at me, ambling back toward the party, DJ Rider playing Shaboozy. I turn to look at the building behind me, Sniper's words ringing in my ears. He's a good man. Hell, the whole MC seems to be filled with good men. Well, kinda. I mean, they seem to kill people pretty well, but I don't think it counts if you're only killing bad guys. Probably.

My curiosity gets the better of me and I slip inside, the LED overhead lights flickering on. My gaze roams the large open room, settling on the man in the corner. I thought he looked terrible the first time I saw him, but now, he looks barely alive. He's covered in cuts and bruises, congealed blood. Aside from looking beaten to within an inch of his life, he seems to have all his body parts, so amputation wasn't one of the torture methods used on him. Although I can't imagine Sniper to be that kind of guy. I know a little about his background, Judge told me and I can see why he wants his brother to suffer like his sister did, however I also know that Sniper can't take this man's life.

Moving closer to him I spy the syringe on the stainless steel table. I've seen how Pops used it on Renae, giving her just enough to relax her before we essentially blew her up. There is more liquid in this syringe than the one he gave her, so I know this will work. My steady footsteps creep closer to the man, lying curled into a ball, whining like a pitiful animal. Removing the cap I hold it up so he can see it, and I'm surprised when his gaze fills with relief instead of fear.

"You know what happened to your sister, and instead of stopping it, you did it to other people's sisters, wives, girlfriends. You deserve everything your brother has done to you and more, but your existence is hurting him. That's why I'm doing this. Not out of kindness to you, but to your brother. Burn in hell." I stab the needle into his neck, his main artery stark against the skin thanks to the lack of food he's been given during his time here.

I watch as his body slumps, his breathing slowing until there are no more breaths to take. Removing the syringe I replace the cap, throwing it in the sharps bin on my way out of the building, stopping when I come face to face with the man who has the same eyes as my children.

"You've done that before, haven't you?" Leo's bright green eyes stare into mine, searching for a lie.

"Yes, I have." I stare back, daring him to ask, daring him to just damn well ask what I've been through these past years.

We stand staring at each other for what feels like an eternity. His face doesn't give anything away. I expect him to walk away in disgust but instead he bands his arms around me, pulling me into his chest. "Kaia, baby, you talk, I'll listen."

Thank you for reading!

Phew! I know, it was a LOT!

Please don't forget to drop a review, reviews for authors are like virtual hugs!

If you want to follow me then please drop into any of my groups or social media, I''d love to hear from you!

Friend me on Facebook

Join my group Cleo Browne's Babes

Follow me on Instagram

What the heck did they say?

Kotiro – Girl/Girls
Inaianei – Now
Brat – Brother
Blyad' – Shit, Fuck
Moya lyubov' – My Love
Oh, entonces sois unas chicas duras – Oh, so you're tough girls?

Cleo Browne Books

Rhodie – Devil's Rose MC Book One

August – A Tombs Security + Devil's Rose MC Crossover

Wire – Devil's Rose MC Book Two

Tav Devil's Rose MC Book Three
DRMC – Devil's Rose Merry Christmas

Tank – Devil's Rose MC Book Four

Jules – A Tombs Security + Devil's Rose MC Crossover

Tuesday – Devil's Rose MC Book Five (novella)

Marx – Devil's Rose MC Book Six

Judge – Devil's Rose MC Book Seven
In progress

Acknowledgements

First off, I'd like to thank all the wonderful readers who took a chance on a kooky little autistic woman and read my first offering, Rhodie. Without you all reading it and loving it, this book would never have happened. I would have just faded away into obscurity, never to be seen or heard from again. So, thank you. I appreciate you all.

Second, I'd like to thank my book besties who all have a hand in helping me get these stories to you guys, the readers. Thanks to Shaye Torrel for the Book Bitch meet ups, Courtney Clarke Michaels for the speed talk meet ups, Gabi Brocklesby for the proof reading because holy crap, without you these books would be a hard read, and Sally Howells for the AMAZING alpha advice and chapter breakdowns and for always knowing where my weird brain is going to go at any moment. Thank you all from the bottom of my weird little heart.

Thanks to my partner PN. Without his constant words of encouragement, "I really didn't think MC books were a thing," I would never have finished this book. Thanks also go to my boys. Ronnie, for being completely disinterested, and Louis for your two hour long phone calls that would eat into my writing time. Love you guys.

www.ingramcontent.com/pod-product-compliance
Lightning Source LLC
Chambersburg PA
CBHW020910130726
47904CB00006BA/1798